Embellished Deception

Cold Case Files - Book 1

Netta Newbound

Junction UK

To Paul—the love of my life.

Prologue

STANDING IN THE BUSHES, the man kept a steady gaze on the cottage, his position masked by the shadows of the tree line. He glanced at his watch—8:27 am. It wouldn't be long now. The air was damp with morning dew, and he shifted his weight to stop the wet ground from soaking into his boots.

At that moment, the front door opened. Catherine stepped out, her eight-year-old daughter trailing behind. She called something back into the house, her voice sharp but unintelligible from his vantage point. She unlocked the red Honda, her hands moving with practised efficiency. The little girl scrambled into the passenger seat, her backpack swaying as she climbed in.

Moments later, her teenage son emerged, slamming the door behind him with a force that made the man's teeth clench.

The boy frowned when he saw the front seat occupied, then shouted something. He pounded his fist against the car door.

Catherine's voice cut through the morning air, firm but tired.

The boy hesitated, then grudgingly slid into the back seat, muttering under his breath.

The Honda pulled out of the driveway, its tyres crunching against the gravel. The man didn't move immediately. He waited, counting the seconds in his head, watching until the car disappeared down the road.

He stepped from the cover of the bushes, his boots scraping against the underbrush. He glanced left and right. The cottage was isolated, surrounded by a smattering of trees. There were no neighbours to speak of. No prying eyes. Still, he kept to the shadows as he circled to the back door.

As he reached for the handle, he paused. A small, satisfied smile tugged at his lips when the door opened easily. Unlocked. He shook his head, a flicker of amusement crossing his face. How careless could she be? A single twist of the knob, and the door had opened without resistance. No deadbolt, no security chain—just an open invitation for someone like him to enter. It amazed him how people could be so lax, so trusting. Did Catherine think living in an isolated cottage made her immune to danger?

Or was she simply naive?

He couldn't fathom it. In a world filled with headlines about break-ins, violence, and worse, she hadn't even bothered to turn a key. It was almost insulting. As if she didn't believe anyone could breach her little bubble of comfort.

It made his job easier, of course. But a part of him—a dark and twisted part—wanted her to realise the error of her ways. To see how a simple act of negligence could unravel everything.

Inside, the house was warm. The air had a faint smell of coffee and lavender. A radio played softly in the kitchen, filling the otherwise empty home with an illusion of life.

He moved, his steps deliberate and measured as he took in the space. A stack of breakfast dishes sat in the sink. On the counter, a crumpled five-pound note, and several coins rested on top of a school consent form, signed but not packed away. That detail gave him pause. Would

Catherine realise she'd left it behind and return for it? He'd have to move fast, just in case.

The black cat perched on the windowsill turned its head lazily toward him, its green eyes narrowing. When he stepped closer, it let out a low, disapproving meow.

"Piss off," he muttered, waving his hand. The cat bolted from the room, claws scratching against the wooden floor.

The rest of the house bore the marks of a busy family. Shoes were kicked off by the front door, an overturned laundry basket in the hallway, and papers scattered across the dining table. Yet the living room was pristine, untouched. It felt like a stage, a place for show rather than comfort.

He ascended the staircase with caution, his ears straining for any sound beyond the faint hum of the radio. The three upstairs bedrooms were just as he had expected. He lingered in the master bedroom, drawn to the personal details that felt like an intrusion even to him. Clothes lay in a careless heap on the floor. He crouched, lifting a lacy red G-string with a deliberate flick of his finger. A grin crept onto his face before he dropped it back onto the pile.

The bedside table held a paperback novel—The Lady Killers—and beneath the pillow, the edge of another book peeked out. He pulled it free. A diary. Flicking through the pages, he chuckled at the tidy handwriting and mundane entries. "Why would anyone write this shit down?" he muttered, shaking his head before sliding it back under the pillow.

His heart leapt at the sound of a car engine in the driveway. The Honda.

Catherine was back.

He moved fast, retreating to the daughter's bedroom. The floral wallpaper and stuffed animals felt surreal against the pounding in his chest. He positioned himself behind the door, pulling the balaclava down over his face. The fabric was coarse and uncomfortable, pressing against his skin. His breath was loud in his ears, each exhale dampening the inside of the mask.

He didn't have to wait long. The front door slammed, followed by the sound of her humming—a light, carefree tune that sent a thrill through him.

She jogged up the stairs.

He peeked through the crack in the door, catching a glimpse of her crossing the hallway moments later, wrapped in a towel, she headed into the bathroom.

Once she was in the shower, he moved back to the master bedroom to lie in wait. His pulse quickened, a steady thrum in his ears as he slipped into the shadows.

Since she'd been in there, she had drawn the heavy curtains just enough to cast the room in a dusky light. He stood against the side of the wardrobe, behind the door, his gloved hands brushing against the cool wood as he braced himself. The faint sound of running water echoed from the bathroom down the hall, muffled by the walls but unmistakable.

Every detail of the moment felt magnified—the damp, earthy smell lingering on his clothes from his time in the bushes, the scratchy fabric of the balaclava clinging to his skin, the slight creak of a floorboard beneath his weight. His chest rose and fell with controlled breaths, but the excitement buzzing under his skin was harder to suppress.

From this position, things looked different. He glanced around the room, taking in the small personal touches. A framed photograph on the dresser caught his attention—a younger Catherine, smiling warmly as she held a baby on her hip, her son standing awkwardly beside her. The boy wore the same scowl this morning, a perpetual expression of teenage disdain. The man smirked, his fingers itching to pick up the frame, to hold a piece of her life in his hands, but he resisted. No unnecessary movements.

The water stopped.

His breath hitched, and he shifted his position, angling himself just right. A minute passed, then another. The creak of hinges as the bathroom door opened sent a thrill down his spine. He could almost picture her, steam swirling around her as she stepped into the hallway, the towel clinging to her damp skin.

Her light footsteps padded almost hesitant as she approached the bedroom. His anticipation was almost unbearable.

The door to the bedroom opened, and Catherine entered. Her damp hair was tied back in a loose knot, and strands escaped clinging to her face. She wore an oversized T-shirt that hung just past her thighs and nothing else. She looked tired and distracted, as she moved to the dresser and began rummaging through a drawer.

The man didn't move, didn't breathe. He watched her, the way her hands moved, the way her brow furrowed as if she were lost in thought. She was close enough now that he could hear her soft exhale, see the rise and fall of her chest.

Then she froze.

Her head tilted, her body tensing as if she'd sensed something—someone. Her eyes flicked toward the corner of the room where he hid behind the door.

His heart pounded, a primal urge to strike coursing through him, but he held steady. Don't move. Don't make a sound.

Catherine shook her head, muttering something under her breath before turning back to the drawer. She pulled out a pair of leggings and began slipping them on, her movements quick, as though she wanted to shake off whatever uneasy feeling had gripped her.

The moment she turned her back, he stepped out of the shadows.

The gasp that escaped her lips was sharp, a dagger cutting through the air as she spun around, her eyes wide with terror.

"What the—" she began, but her words were swallowed by his gloved hand clamping over her mouth. Her struggle was immediate and frantic, but he was stronger, his grip unyielding as he pushed her back against the dresser.

"Shh," he whispered, his voice low, almost gentle. "Don't scream. You don't want to disturb the neighbours."

It was a lie, of course. There were no neighbours. No one would hear her. And that was how he wanted it.

Chapter One

Geri

THE RAIN PELTED DOWN relentlessly, drenching me to the bone. My soaked clothes clung to my skin, and every step felt like wading through quicksand. Mud squished between my toes. My best sandals—if you could call them that now—oozed with every step, the leather ruined beyond repair.

My car had broken down about a mile outside the village, leaving me stranded on the narrow, rain-slick road. I'd been walking for what felt like an eternity—at least half an hour— the icy wind biting at my cheeks. The weight of the rain-soaked air pressed down on me, matching the heaviness in my chest.

Tears burned in my eyes, but they mingled with the raindrops, making it impossible to tell where one ended and the other began. At least no one could see me cry out here. The storm was my cloak, hiding my misery as I trudged along the winding country lane. My whole body ached, and my thoughts churned with the same fury as the storm clouds above.

My useless phone tinkled weakly in my pocket. I snatched it out, desperate for a signal. But the screen blinked low battery before going black, the ultimate betrayal. Not that it would've helped. Out here, in the middle of nowhere, finding a signal was about as likely as finding Simon waiting for me with open arms and an apology.

The thought of Simon sent a fresh wave of pain crashing over me. I shook it off, forcing myself to focus on the road ahead. The rain eased slightly, revealing the familiar outline of the village. The sight of my parents' cottage chimney, puffing a steady stream of smoke, filled me with a momentary sense of relief. Home. Safety. Surely, everything would make sense again once I stepped inside.

But something was wrong. The village felt off. Deserted. Normally, Major Wainwright would be perched on his porch, his green rocking chair creaking in rhythm with his storytelling, but the chair sat empty. The village green, framed by its perfect oval of stone cottages, was eerily still. Even the pub across from my parents' house, usually buzzing with life regardless of the hour, was silent.

I pushed the unease aside. It was just the weather keeping everyone indoors, I told myself. That's all.

By the time I reached the gate of my childhood home, my fingers were trembling so hard I could barely manage the latch. But I did, and there she was—Mum. She stood in the doorway, drying her hands on a tea towel, her face shadowed by the dim light spilling from the kitchen.

"Oh, Mum," I cried, relief breaking through my exhaustion. I hurried up the path, expecting her to sweep me into her arms like she always did when I came home for a visit.

Instead, she frowned. "What the hell do you want?" she snapped, her tone cold and unfamiliar.

I froze mid-step. The words hit me like a slap, my breath catching in my throat. Mum never spoke to anyone like that—least of all me. Her only child.

"Mum?" My voice came out small, barely audible over the rain.

She turned sharply and disappeared back inside the house without another word. The door creaked as it swung shut, leaving me standing there, drenched and dumbstruck.

I kicked off my ruined sandals and stepped inside, hesitant. The warmth of the house enveloped me, but it felt wrong, like wearing someone else's clothes. The scent of roast beef filled the air, a smell that usually wrapped me in comfort. But not today. Today, everything was upside down.

I found Mum in the kitchen, chopping carrots with a ferocity that made me flinch. Her shoulders were hunched, her every movement clipped and angry.

"Mum, are you okay?" I ventured, my voice trembling.

She didn't look up. "Why wouldn't I be, Geraldine? I'm not the one turning up uninvited, dripping all over my nice clean floor."

I stared at her, my heart racing. She wasn't herself. This wasn't my mother, the woman who'd always been my rock. Something was wrong.

Before I could press further, the front door opened, and Dad's familiar whistle floated down the hall. Relief flooded through me.

"Only me!" he called. "Here's your prescription, Gracie—and—oh!" He stopped short when he saw me, his face breaking into a grin. "Geri! What a lovely surprise!" He dropped his shopping bags and pulled me into a bear hug, his warmth thawing the icy knot in my chest.

"Oh, Dad," I sobbed, clinging to him.

"What's this?" he asked gently. "Come now, lass, let's get you sorted."

But as he comforted me, Mum brushed past us, her lips pressed into a thin line. She muttered something under her breath and vanished upstairs.

"What's going on with her?" I whispered to Dad, my voice shaking.

He sighed, his cheerful demeanour slipping for just a moment. "She's... shall I say, she hasn't been herself lately. Don't take it to heart, Geri. She's got a lot on her mind." He didn't elaborate, and I didn't push. "So, what's happened with you?" he asked, changing the subject.

"Everything has gone wrong. I'll tell you all about it later. But I need to sort out my car—it broke down over by the castle bend."

"Don't you worry, love—I'll sort it out. Where are the keys?"

"Thanks, Dad. I left them in the sun visor."

I left him calling a mechanic and headed upstairs to the bathroom where, to my surprise, a hot bath and a borrowed nightie waited.

"Thanks, Mum," I said, hoping she had thawed. But she shrugged one shoulder and rushed off back down the stairs.

I climbed into the bath, but even as the warmth seeped into my bones and the familiar scent of home surrounded me, the knot in my stomach tightened. Something wasn't right here. Not at all.

And deep down, I had a sinking feeling that coming back here might have been a huge mistake.

***

AFTER SOAKING IN THE bath for a good half hour, my circulation returned, and with it came the dull ache of exhaustion. The heat had worked its way into my muscles, but it hadn't reached the knot in my chest. That felt like it had taken root—a living, pulsing thing was feeding on my sadness.

I wrapped myself in the soft towels Mum had left out, their familiar scent of sunshine bringing a momentary comfort. Padding back into the bedroom, I slipped into the flannelette nightie waiting on the bed.

It was like stepping into childhood, back to a time when Mum could make everything better just by being there.

But now, even surrounded by the familiarity of home, I felt adrift.

I sat on the edge of the bed, staring at the faint outline of my childhood room in the dim light. My fingers toyed with the hem of the nightie, the fabric soft but somehow suffocating. My mind raced, replaying every word, every look, every moment of the last few months with Simon. How could I have missed the signs? Was I really so blind to the cracks in our marriage? Or had I simply refused to see them?

I considered calling Lucy, but the thought of her sympathy—or worse, her pity—made me put the phone back down. Plus, she would tell her husband, Mark, Simon's best friend, and that would be even worse. He'd tell Simon, and I couldn't bear the thought of him knowing how broken I was.

I didn't know how to move on from this. How could you move on from the one person who was meant to be your forever?

A knock on the door startled me out of my thoughts.

"Dinner's ready," Mum called, her voice soft, almost hesitant. It wasn't the icy tone she'd greeted me with earlier, but it wasn't the warm, familiar voice I'd grown up with, either.

Downstairs, Mum and Dad were huddled at the table, their voices low and urgent. They didn't even notice me at first. I cleared my throat, and they both turned quickly, plastering on smiles that didn't quite reach their eyes.

Mum had made my favourite—roast beef and Yorkshire pudding. My stomach growled at the sight of it.

"Oh, Mum, it looks delicious," I said, forcing a smile.

"Just get it down you," she said. "You look like you could do with fattening up."

I nodded, biting back a retort. The last thing I wanted was to stir up whatever had made her so prickly in the first place. Instead, I focused on piling my plate high, letting the warm, familiar food distract me from the ache in my chest. I used to comfort eat as a child, and maybe that was a way forward for me.

"So," Dad said, his voice careful, "what's been going on in your world?"

I hesitated, the words catching in my throat. "It's over," My voice was barely above a whisper. "Simon and..." I shook my head. "My marriage. It's over."

Dad leaned back, his brow furrowing in disbelief. "What could be so terrible, sweetheart? You two have been inseparable since you were kids. Never a cross word between you."

"It's just not working." The lump in my throat made it hard to get the words out.

He shook his head as if trying to make sense of it. "Your mum and I have been married thirty-one years. We've had our ups and downs, sure, but the key is communication. You've got to talk to each other, love."

I didn't have the heart—or the energy—to argue. I just nodded, hoping he'd let it drop.

But Mum jumped in, steering the conversation in a different direction. "Max, you were going to tell me who you saw in the village?"

"Oh, yes!" Dad said, brightening. "Do you remember Stan and Fiona's boy, James?"

"Nerdy James Dunn?" I blurted, wiping my eyes on my sleeve.

Dad frowned. "That's not very kind, Geraldine. And besides, he's done quite well for himself. You've heard of Aaron Clark, the True Crime author?"

I nodded, the name sending a prickle of recognition through me. "Aaron Clark? He wrote that book about the little boy whose parents kept him locked in a box, didn't he?"

Dad nodded, his eyes twinkling. "That's the one. Well, Aaron Clark is just his pen name. His real name is James Dunn."

I stared at him, open-mouthed. "You're kidding."

"Nope. He's back in the village," Dad continued. "Investigating those attacks for his next book."

"Attacks?" I asked. "What attacks?"

"What planet have you been living on, Geraldine?" Dad shook his head. "Four women, all local, attacked and—" He stopped, his face darkening. "Each attack worse than the last. The latest one, Cathy Simpson, was left for dead. Her son found her in time, thank God."

The room felt suddenly colder. I glanced at Mum, who was staring down at her plate, her lips pressed tightly together, clearly uninterested in our conversation. This was so unlike her.

After dinner, I helped with the dishes and then excused myself, heading to my room.

As I lay on the bed, thoughts of everything pressed down on me. Mum's earlier hostility, Simon's betrayal, the news about the attacks—it all churned in my mind, refusing to settle.

I heard Mum's voice drifting up the stairs, her tone clipped and formal. I crept to the door and cracked it open, straining to hear.

"...disappointed in you, Simon. Geraldine is in pieces, and you haven't even called..."

Anger flared in me. I stormed downstairs, my footsteps echoing in the quiet house. Mum was just hanging up the phone when I burst into the kitchen.

"Mum! What the hell are you doing?"

She looked up, startled. "I'm doing what needs to be done! You two are being ridiculous. This isn't something you just walk away from, Geraldine."

"Yes, it is!" I shouted, my voice breaking. "It's over, Mum. Do you hear me? Over!"

My sobs shook me as I collapsed into a chair, my body trembling with the force of my emotions. Mum hesitated, then came over, stroking my hair like she used to when I was little.

"He doesn't love me anymore," I whispered.

"Nonsense," she said softly. "He adores you. You just need to fix whatever's broken, that's all."

But she didn't understand. Nothing could be fixed. Not now. Not ever.

Chapter Two

Geri

I WOKE TO THE distant strains of *Bat Out of Hell* drifting up from the kitchen radio, Meatloaf's unmistakable voice cutting through the quiet house. For a moment, I lay still, staring at the ceiling, the memories rushing back like an unwelcome tide.

The last time I heard that song was with Simon. We'd been driving back from Blackpool, the car windows down, the salt air tangling my hair as we screamed the lyrics into the night. Simon was laughing so hard he had tears in his eyes, his hand drumming the beat against the dashboard.

I closed my eyes, willing the memory away, but it lingered, sharp and painful. Would every song carry this ache now? Would I ever hear something without it reminding me of what I'd lost?

A knock at the door jolted me from my thoughts. "Are you awake, love? I've made you some breakfast," Mum called.

I pulled myself up, still tangled in the nightie that had offered fleeting comfort the night before. "Coming," I mumbled before dragging myself out of bed and padding downstairs.

Mum glanced up as I entered the kitchen, her eyes narrowing as they took in my unkempt state. "The mechanic dropped off your bags, so there's no excuse to mope around like that all day. It's not healthy."

"Okay, thanks. I didn't sleep well," I said, avoiding her gaze. "I was thinking of going back to bed for a bit."

"Oh, no, you don't." Her voice had that no-nonsense tone I remembered all too well. "I've got something I need you to help me with."

"Aw, Mum, I don't want to see anyone," I whined. The words were out before I could stop them, and I cringed at how childish they sounded.

"You won't," she said briskly. "Don't worry."

After breakfast, I managed a shower, feeling marginally more human. As I was towelling off my hair, Mum poked her hand through the bathroom door, wiggling the cordless phone at me. "Call for you, Geraldine."

My stomach flipped as I took the phone. "What do you want?" I snapped, the words sharp and defensive.

There was a pause on the other end. "Erm, I was going to tell you what's wrong with your car, but if it's not a good time..."

I felt the heat rush to my cheeks. "I'm sorry," I said quickly. "I thought you were someone else."

"Well, lady, I'm glad I'm not him." He chuckled. "I just wanted to let you know I've had to order a fuel pump, so it'll be a few days before I can get it back to you."

I thanked him, still blushing furiously, and hung up. Mum's pointed glance as I passed her in the hallway deepened the sting.

The day wore on in fits and starts. Mum roped me into helping her dig the garden, and though I complained at first, the physical exertion proved oddly cathartic. By the time we finished, my arms ached, and my thoughts had dulled to a low hum.

Later, a craving for chocolate drove me to the shops. The walk was brisk, the cool air clearing my head, and for a moment, I felt almost normal again. But the spell broke as soon as I returned. Mum was on the phone, and her words froze me in place.

"Oh, hi, Simon," she said, her voice too bright. "Yes, she's right here."

I snatched the phone from her hand, glaring at her as I pressed it to my ear. "What do you want?" I demanded.

"I just wanted to check on you," Simon said softly. "I miss you."

The words hit me like a punch to the gut. "Oh, I'm wonderful, thank you. How do you fucking expect?"

I ignored Mum's sharp hiss of disapproval as Simon sighed on the other end. "Geri, let's be adults about this. We need to talk."

"There's nothing more to say," I snapped. "Just leave me alone." I hung up, my hands trembling.

Mum's expression was a mixture of shock and disappointment. "Geraldine! What has gotten into you? Call him back and talk to him properly."

"Properly? Why should I?" My voice rose, shaking with anger. "He's the one who walked away, Mum. He's the one who—" My throat tightened, cutting me off.

Mum softened then, stepping toward me with a hand outstretched. "I'm sorry, love. I don't mean to upset you. I just—"

"It doesn't matter," I whispered, retreating to my room.

By the time evening rolled around, Mum had coaxed me out of my sulk with the promise of bingo. "It'll be like old times," she said, her tone almost pleading. "And Beryl's been dying to see you."

I relented, more to escape the suffocating weight of my thoughts than out of any genuine desire to socialise. As I dressed, I caught sight of myself in the mirror—pale and drawn, a shadow of the person I used to be.

Would I ever feel like myself again? Or had Simon taken that part of me with him when he left?

***

"FULL HOUSE!" BERYL SHOT up from her seat, waving her card in the air. Her massive bosom bounced with every enthusiastic movement, and I fought to suppress a laugh. She seemed oblivious to the ripple of muttered complaints that spread through the hall as she waited for the assistant to verify her numbers.

Mum nudged me in the ribs, her grin lighting up her face. "We always share our winnings," she whispered conspiratorially. "That'll pay for the fish and chips."

Her good mood was infectious. For the first time in days, I felt a flicker of lightness creep into my chest. Before long, I was joining in with the banter in the room, swept up in the camaraderie. It felt normal. Something I hadn't felt in a while.

When we finally left the bingo hall, Beryl was practically floating. "Why don't we go to the pub for a bar meal instead of fish and chips?" she suggested, her eyes twinkling with mischief. "Welcome Geri back in style."

I hesitated. The idea of the pub filled me with dread. I'd grown up in this village and I knew what walking into the pub would mean—questions, stares, whispers. "I don't fancy it." I tried to sound casual. "You two go ahead. I'll meet you back at the house later."

"No, if you're not going, Geri, then neither am I," Mum said, her voice resolute.

I sighed, realising there was no way out of it. "Fine, I'll go. But I don't want to stay out all night."

They both beamed and hooked their arms through mine, dragging me along the road toward The Farmer's Arms. Their chatter surrounded me, but my mind was elsewhere. Just then, my phone buzzed in my pocket. Grateful for the distraction, I shrugged away from them and turned toward the village green.

"I'll catch you up," I said, waving the phone at them before answering. "Hi, Luce. I was going to call you later."

"Geri! Where the hell have you been?" Lucy's voice was sharp with concern. "I've been going out of my mind."

"At my parents' house," I said, keeping my voice low. "Didn't Simon tell you?"

"I didn't ask him," she said quickly. "I've called you loads of times since yesterday, and your phone just goes to voicemail."

"Sorry, there's no signal at the house. I'm surprised I've got one now, to be honest."

"What's going on? Mark and I haven't seen Simon, and I haven't told Mark anything. I figured it wasn't my place."

This surprised me. I truly thought Lucy would've blabbed everything to her husband. It's a lot to keep from him, considering he was Simon's best friend. "Not much," I admitted, my voice faltering. "He came home the other night... after you left."

Lucy gasped. "He didn't!"

"He did. I thought he was a burglar. You should have seen me, Luce—I grabbed a lamp like I was in some crime drama."

"Oh my God, what cheek! So, what did you do?"

"Honestly? Not much. I went to bed and left him downstairs."

"And?"

"When I got up yesterday, he looked so... broken. I actually felt sorry for him."

"Well, I wouldn't," she said firmly.

"It's not his fault, Lucy. It's nobody's fault."

She snorted, clearly unimpressed. "You're joking, right?"

"I'm not." I sighed, leaning against the railing of the green. "As angry as I am, I know deep down he can't help it."

"So, what? You're just going to forgive him?"

"If forgiving him would fix everything, I'd do it in a heartbeat," I said, surprising myself with how steady my voice sounded. "But it won't. This isn't something we can just move past."

Lucy was silent for a moment. "If it were me, I'd chop off Mark's bits and feed them to the dog. The dirty bastard."

"Bit harsh, don't you think?" I said, managing a small laugh. "It's not like he cheated with another woman."

Lucy groaned. "Oh, come on, Geri. This is a big deal."

"I know it is. But it's not like he wanted this to happen. I'm not the first woman in the world to discover her husband is gay. And I definitely won't be the last."

There it was—the truth I'd been avoiding saying aloud. My chest tightened as the words hung between us.

Lucy's sharp intake of breath echoed through the line. "Geri... I don't even know what to say. Are you okay?"

"I will be," I said, though I wasn't sure I believed it. "Eventually."

Chapter Three

Geri

THE FARMER'S ARMS WAS the heart of the village, a cosy pub housed within a sprawling stone building that seemed to have stood there forever. Weathered by decades of wind and rain, the building's stone exterior was a patchwork of ivy and moss.

The building had been divided into three distinct interlinking spaces, each catering to a different facet of village life.

The pub was in the middle, its small-paned windows glowing with the warm amber light that beckoned locals and travellers alike, served real ales and bar meals.

To the left of the pub was the village hotel, its modest entrance framed by hanging baskets that overflowed with seasonal blooms.

And on the far right stood the village's only restaurant, its charm lying in its simplicity—a blackboard outside boasted the daily specials in neatly chalked letters.

All three were owned by the same family, their lineage tracing back over a hundred years. It wasn't just a building; but a living piece of the village's history, a cornerstone of its community.

It always surprised me how busy the pub got on a Friday night, especially for a village as tiny as ours. There was an odd comfort in it, though—a kind of predictable chaos.

I recognised faces instantly, nodding and waving in the way you do when you want to acknowledge someone without inviting a conversation. But even that felt heavy tonight. I spotted Mum and Beryl tucked away at the back of the room, poring over the menu, and headed toward them.

"There you are, Geri," Mum called, her face lighting up when she saw me. "Come and sit down. Who was on the phone? Simon?"

"A friend," I replied, pasting on a smile. The last thing I wanted to do was discuss Simon in front of Beryl. The comments from Lucy earlier still burned. She'd been right about Simon, of course—everything she'd said mirrored my own thoughts. But hearing it spoken aloud had struck a nerve, like someone picking at a wound that wasn't ready to heal. Yet I'd tried to defend Simon, regardless of the fact I still smarted from his brutal betrayal.

"Geraldine—is that you?" A voice shrieked from behind me, and before I could react, I was engulfed in a suffocating bear hug.

I twisted in the embrace, barely able to breathe. Debbie. Mad Debbie, as she was affectionately known. Her chatter tumbled out in a flood, most of it drowned by the DJ's sudden assault of '80s hits.

"Come and join us!" she mouthed, gesturing toward a table crammed with women clutching half-empty cocktail glasses and shrieking at one another over the music.

"Can't. I'm with my mum." I mouthed back, adding an apologetic smile. I gestured toward Mum and Beryl, hoping she'd let it drop.

"How long are you here?" she yelled, leaning in.

"A while." I tried to sound nonchalant, though I was already itching to leave.

"Great! Can't wait to hear all your gossip!" she trilled.

"Me too." Her hands dropped from mine, and she tottered back to her friends. I let out a breath I didn't realise I'd been holding and slid into the chair beside Mum.

The menu was a blur as I scanned it, eager to eat and escape. We all chose the chef's special: steak and ale pie. Beryl handed over her bingo winnings to Mum, who navigated her way to the bar, stopping every few steps to chat with familiar faces. I kept my head down, pretending to be absorbed in the menu, hoping to avoid any more impromptu reunions.

"How's Carl getting on, Beryl?" Mum asked as she returned with drinks.

"Not so bad," Beryl replied. "He seems to be settling down. For now, anyway."

Mum turned to me with a smile that was almost conspiratorial. "Did you know it's Carl who's been working on your car? He's Beryl's nephew."

I barely had time to register this before Mum leaned in and whispered, "Be right back—nature calls." That in itself was surprising; Mum usually made such exits with silent dignity. I watched her weave through the crowd toward the loo, wondering if I was being overly sensitive.

Beryl took up the slack, chatting about her nephew. "He doesn't stay anywhere for long," she said as if it were a badge of honour. "This is just a stopgap. He's talking about going to Canada next or maybe back to Australia. I'd rather him settle around here for a while, though."

"Right," I murmured, forcing a smile. My interest in Carl—or his international escapades—was minimal, but politeness demanded I feign some. "And how's Julie getting on?" I regretted it immediately.

"Oh, Julie's wonderful," Beryl gushed. "Baby Jack's nearly six months now, and she's back at the pharmacy part-time. I watch Jack three mornings a week. He's such a darling!"

"Lovely." My tone was flat, and I let my eyes wander to the bar, hoping the food would arrive soon. I didn't need a blow-by-blow account of Julie's perfect life right now. She'd always been a natural at everything—school, career, relationships. Even motherhood, it seems. The thought of her smug face, when she heard about my crumbling marriage, made my stomach churn.

The evening trudged along, marked by small talk and lukewarm pie. Mum, buoyed by a couple of brandies, was unusually lively. Her laughter was contagious even as she stumbled out, waving goodbye to the barmaid with exaggerated elegance.

As we walked home across the green, the cold air biting at my cheeks, I noticed Dad silhouetted in the living room window. His watchful presence was comforting, even as Mum swayed beside me, hiccupping through her explanation of her newly packed schedule.

"You're doing yoga now?" I asked, surprised.

"Yoga on Monday, embroidery on Wednesday, bingo on Friday—and..."

"And?" I raised an eyebrow, waiting.

"Salsa on Saturday. With your dad."

I stopped walking. "You're joking."

She grinned. "We're planning a cruise around the world. I want to salsa with him in Cuba."

When we stepped inside, Dad sprang to his feet as though he'd been lounging on the sofa, not watching us through the window. I smiled. It was sweet the way he loved and protected her.

Mum launched herself into his arms, giggling and swaying like a teenager. "Dance with me, Maxie!" she cooed.

The way they looked at each other made my chest ache. That was supposed to be Simon and me once upon a time.

I climbed the stairs to bed, the sound of their laughter trailing behind me. The hollow weight of loss pressed against my ribs. They still had each other. What did I have?

***

I WAS AWAKE, BUT I kept my eyes shut tight, listening. The house was silent—eerily so. No sound of Mum bustling about in the kitchen, no faint hum of the radio playing her favourite golden oldies. I figured it must still be early, the village not yet stirring.

I rolled onto my side, prying one eye open to peek at the clock. The red digits sent a jolt through me: 10:47 am.

I shot upright, my head spinning from the sudden movement. Mum never let me sleep in this late. She had a lifelong philosophy that lying in bed past eight was both unhealthy and an unforgivable waste of daylight. The rare exception was when I'd been sick as a child—and even then, she'd hover around, plumping pillows and bringing me cups of weak tea to ensure I wasn't malingering.

Still groggy, I scrambled out of bed, pulling on a hoodie over my pyjamas as I went downstairs. The house felt strange—unnaturally still like it was holding its breath.

The living room curtains were drawn shut, the air stale and heavy. That was unusual for Mum, who prided herself on "airing the house" first thing every morning, regardless of the weather. Unease prickled the back of my neck, but I shook it off. Maybe she wasn't feeling well. Or maybe Dad had insisted on having a quiet morning for once.

However, I hadn't been home for a while—maybe this was the new normal.

I wandered into the kitchen, filling the kettle out of habit and popping two slices of bread into the toaster. The familiar motions grounded me, even as a niggling sense of wrongness lingered. What was I expecting? A note? A sign?

The kettle began to gurgle as I stepped into the lounge and pulled back the curtains. Light flooded the room—and that's when I heard it. A low groan.

I froze, my fingers gripping the fabric of the curtain. The sound came again, louder this time, a strained, guttural noise. My heart thudded painfully as I turned scanning the room for the source.

"Mum!" I gasped, relief washing over me when I spotted her sprawled on the sofa. But the relief was short-lived. She looked dreadful, her skin pale and blotchy, her hair sticking to her damp forehead.

"Close the curtains, Geri," she croaked, shielding her eyes with one hand. "Please."

I let the curtain fall, stepping closer. "Mother..." I couldn't hide the smirk tugging at my lips. "Do you have a hangover? Would you like a hair of the dog?"

She groaned again, waving a weak hand in my direction. "It's not funny. I feel like death."

I bit back a laugh, sitting on the armrest of the chair opposite her. "Where's Dad?"

"Golf," she muttered, her voice muffled by the cushion she'd buried her face in.

The toaster popped in the kitchen, the cheerful sound jarring against the heavy silence of the room. I stood, glancing back at her as she moaned softly. "Can I get you anything? Tea? Toast? A miracle cure?"

"Lucozade," she mumbled, her voice hoarse. "Get me a bottle from the shop, will you? And close those bloody curtains."

I folded my arms, leaning against the doorframe with a grin. "It's nearly half-eleven. What will the neighbours say?"

"I don't care," she snapped, though the bite in her tone was undermined by her pitiful state. "Just get me the Lucozade."

I laughed, but the sound felt hollow. Something about seeing her like this—so uncharacteristically fragile—unnerved me. It wasn't just the hangover. It was the curtains, the silence, the way the house felt off-kilter as if some invisible force had slipped inside and shifted things ever so slightly.

After I ate my toast, I ran upstairs, threw on a pair of jeans and a jumper, and headed to the village store.

Chapter Four

James

JAMES SNAPPED HIS LAPTOP shut with a faint sigh, the click of the lid echoing in the small, sterile hotel room. He eased to his feet, the stiffness in his joints reminding him he'd been hunched over for hours. His back protested as he straightened, vertebra by vertebra, the tension unwinding in a way that was almost satisfying.

Katrina's voice echoed in his head: "You'll end up with a hunchback, you know." She'd said it often enough, usually accompanied by that sharp little laugh of hers. To prove her point, she'd installed an alarm on his laptop. Every hour, it would chirp insistently, reminding him to stand up, stretch, drink water, or—as she so eloquently put it—"go for a wee."

The alarm had been her way of looking out for him, though it had the opposite effect. Each beep was like a hammer striking his focus, shattering his sentences mid-thought. It didn't take long before he'd threatened to toss the laptop out of the window if she didn't remove the bloody thing.

Katrina, his ex, had been a good woman in many ways. Thoughtful, organised, dependable. But her need for control had suffocated him. She'd wormed her way into his life, rearranging it into neat, predictable order. Some might have found comfort in it, but James wasn't one of them. He thrived on chaos—writing when inspiration struck, sleeping when exhaustion overcame him, and eating... well, whenever he remembered. Schedules weren't his thing, and Katrina's attempts to impose them only highlighted how fundamentally mismatched they were.

Breaking up with her had been messy. She'd crumpled into his arms like a character from one of his grandfather's cowboy films, clutching at his shirt as though he were the only thing keeping her upright. Then came the tears—loud, hiccupping sobs that made his skin crawl. He wasn't heartless, but there was something about a woman crying that turned him into a fumbling idiot. He'd patted her back awkwardly before bolting like a spooked horse.

They'd only crossed paths twice since. Once, when she turned up with her two burly brothers to collect her things—an encounter that had him bracing for a punch that never came. The second time was in Tesco, where their trolleys collided in the bread aisle. She'd stared at him, eyes wide and glittering, like she might throw a baguette at his head. He'd mumbled a vague apology and abandoned his shopping trolley on the spot.

Now, staring out the hotel window, James felt a pang of nostalgia, or maybe guilt. Below, two men were squaring off by their cars, shouting and gesticulating like actors in a soap opera. Normally, he'd ignore such theatrics, but boredom had him craning his neck to see. The altercation fizzled out quickly, one man storming off, the other retreating to his vehicle. Just another dull day in the village.

James had been back there for a week, and frustration simmered just beneath the surface. Despite his best efforts, he was no closer to uncovering who was behind the recent spate of attacks that had gripped the small community. Every lead seemed to dry up as quickly as it appeared, and the people here, though polite enough, weren't exactly forthcoming with information.

The local police weren't much better. Or rather, Vinny wasn't. Officer Vincent Martin, the closest thing this village had to law enforcement, had been less than accommodating. It didn't surprise James; the two of them had a history, one rooted in petty childhood grievances that Vinny, apparently, still carried like a badge of honour.

James had tried to let bygones be bygones. When he first arrived, he'd even made an effort to approach Vinny with the kind of professional detachment his work required. He'd turned up at the station with a notebook in hand, hoping to extract some information—anything that hadn't already been splashed across the news. But Vinny's reception had been icy at best.

Vinny had leaned back in his squeaky chair, a smug smirk pulling at his lips as James outlined his questions. "Can't share details of an ongoing investigation," he had said, his tone dripping with mockery. "You know how it is, mate. Don't want the press getting the wrong idea."

"Vinny, come on." James forced his voice to stay even. "This isn't for the press. It's for the book."

"Ah, right. The book," Vinny had said, as though the word tasted sour. "True crime, yeah? Always thought that meant writing about what's true, not digging up rumours."

It had taken every ounce of James's self-control not to snap back. Vinny had always been good at baiting him. Back in school, it was name-calling and pranks. Now, it was passive-aggressive jabs disguised as professional propriety.

The truth was, Vinny didn't want James here. He didn't like outsiders poking around, and despite James having been born and raised in this village, he knew that Vinny now saw him as one. Years spent living in the city had changed the way the locals looked at him. He was no longer "Jimmy from down the lane." He was "that writer bloke"—an outsider prying into their lives for his next big story.

Still, James couldn't afford to give up. This case wasn't just another chapter in a book. It was personal. The victims were people he'd grown up with—some of them friends, others acquaintances. Their names and faces haunted him in a way that no other story ever had. He owed it to them to find answers, even if it meant going it alone.

He tried not to dwell on his last conversation with Vinny, but the man's parting words stuck like a thorn in his side: "Leave the investigating to the professionals, James. Don't go playing detective—you'll only get in the way."

James had walked out of the station that day with clenched fists and a gnawing sense of unease. He didn't trust Vinny to handle this properly—not with the way he'd brushed off James's questions and ignored obvious leads. If anything, it seemed like Vinny was actively trying to keep him in the dark.

Back in the present, James stared out the hotel window, the grey sky mirroring his mood. He had work to do, but the growing sense of futility was hard to ignore. If he wanted answers, he'd have to dig them up himself. And if Vinny wouldn't talk? Well, James had never been one to let a closed door stop him.

James was about to turn away when movement across the green caught his eye. His stomach did a somersault. The woman striding toward the shops—could it be? No. It wasn't possible. He'd spoken to Geraldine's father just days ago, and he hadn't mentioned she was in town. But as she drew closer, there was no mistaking her. Same golden-brown hair, same confident gait, though her figure had matured into something more striking than he remembered.

Suddenly galvanised, James dashed to the bathroom. He scrubbed his face, brushed his teeth, and ran a comb through his unruly hair. A quick spritz of deodorant, and he was ready—or as ready as he could be. He grabbed his jacket and wallet, muttering under his breath to calm the flutter in his chest.

By the time he hit the street, he'd forced himself into a casual stroll, aiming for nonchalance. There weren't many shops in the village, and it didn't take long to spot her. She was in the general store, flipping through magazines. James hesitated, his heart thudding like it hadn't in years. He sidled over, pretending to browse the shelves. His eyes landed on a Classic Car magazine—safe territory compared to the risqué tabloids and top-shelf offerings.

She didn't notice him. Minutes ticked by, and James realised he'd read the same page three times without absorbing a single word. He replaced the magazine and retreated to a safer vantage point, where he could observe her without drawing attention.

She was even more stunning up close. Her hair caught the light as she moved, and her eyes—those eyes—still had the power to disarm him. He was so absorbed that he didn't hear the elderly woman approach until she cleared her throat pointedly.

James turned, startled, and found himself face to face with the so-called witch of the village. She hadn't changed much—same steely gaze, same uncanny knack for making him feel like a guilty schoolboy.

"Afternoon," he muttered, nodding. Her disapproving glare followed him as he moved away. Having a rapist in the village put every male under scrutiny.

By the time Geraldine reached the checkout, James was on the verge of giving up. He loitered in the last aisle, debating whether to make his presence known or slip away unnoticed.

He moved closer, standing just behind her when she turned on the spot and ran straight into him.

Chapter Five

Geri

THE VILLAGE SHOP WAS quaint and familiar, shelves stocked with all the essentials and more magazines than anyone could reasonably read. I browsed leisurely, flipping through a glossy magazine with a picture of some pop star on the cover. My basket held a couple of chocolate bars, an indulgence for later. When I finally approached the counter, a thought struck me.

Mum's energy drink

I turned abruptly and without warning, collided with a wall of muscle standing directly behind me.

"Oops, sorry," I stammered, stepping back.

"That's okay, Geraldine," came the resounding reply.

I froze. "Sorry?" I echoed, my brain scrambling to place his face.

"Yes, so you already said." He grinned, enjoying my confusion.

"I meant... how do you know my name?" I asked, trying to sound less rattled than I felt.

He laughed, a low, rich sound that seemed oddly familiar. "Don't you recognise me?"

I stared at him, scanning for a memory, but nothing clicked. I wasn't going to admit that, though. Instead, I opted for a safe, vague approach. "Oh, of course. Hi! How are you?"

He didn't look convinced, but his smile widened. "Not too bad, I guess. All the better for bumping into you, though."

I cringed inwardly. Was he serious? That line belonged in a bad romance novel.

The girl at the counter cleared her throat loudly, interrupting the moment. "Oh, well, I'd best be off," I muttered, clutching my basket. I hurried down the aisle, suddenly hyperaware of his gaze on me, and grabbed the energy drink.

As I left the shop, I spotted him leaning against an old Ford. Its patchwork of mismatched panels giving it a rainbow-like appearance. He looked up as I passed, his grin still firmly in place.

"Can I give you a lift?" he offered casually.

I shook my head. "Oh no, that's okay. I need the exercise." I turned and started across the village green, hoping to escape the odd tension of the encounter.

"Do you mind if I walk with you, then?" he called after me.

I paused, glancing over my shoulder. "Um, no, of course not, but... what about the car?"

He chuckled, falling into step beside me. "Not mine."

I tilted my head, baffled by his random humour. His arm brushed against mine as we walked, and a strange current of static energy zipped through me. I shivered, though the weather wasn't cold in the slightest.

"How's your mum doing?" he asked.

"She's well, or she was until last night," I replied, holding up the bottle. "She had a bit too much to drink."

"And yours?" I added, aiming to keep the conversation flowing while I tried to figure out who this guy was.

"My mum died fifteen years ago, Geraldine," he said softly. Then his expression shifted, and his grin returned. "You don't have a clue who I am, do you?" His raspy chuckle made me feel weak at the knees.

I faltered, guilt twisting in my stomach. "I, um... you do look familiar," I hedged, "but I can't place you. I'm sorry about your mum, though."

"It's alright." He studied me for a moment, his gaze both amused and sharp. "Do you often let strangers tag along with you like this? You need to be careful, you know. There's a lunatic out there."

"You sound worse than my dad," I shot back. "Who are you, anyway? The local detective?"

As the words left my mouth, something clicked. His face, his laugh—they suddenly aligned with a memory. "Oh my God! James. James Dunn!" My eyes widened. "I can't believe how much you've changed. You used to be so skinny and weedy. Now look at you!"

He laughed, the sound deep and rich. "No need to get personal, little lady."

"I don't mean fat," I clarified quickly. "I just mean... massive! What happened?"

"I grew up, Geraldine. And so did you," he said, his gaze flickering over me in a way that sent a warm flush to my cheeks. "I heard you married Simon McIntyre, lucky sod."

"Who, him or me?" I was blatantly flirting with him now, and it felt good.

"Him, of course." He smiled again, and my stomach clenched.

"Well, we're not together anymore, but I'd appreciate it if you'd keep it to yourself for now."

"I'm sorry to hear that. I thought you guys were tight."

"Me too, but there you go. Anyway, how about you? Do you have a Mrs Dunn and a few baby Dunns on the scene?"

He raised his gorgeous eyes to the sky. "Gosh, I wish. I haven't had the time or the inclination, to be honest with you. I get bored easily, and anyway, the love of my life married somebody else, so it seems bachelorhood is my destiny."

He stopped walking, and I realised we'd already reached my parents' cottage. I turned at the gate, feeling strangely reluctant to part ways. "Well, thanks for walking me home, James. It was nice to see you again after all this time."

"And you too, Geraldine," he replied. Then, to my surprise, he bent and kissed the top of my head. The gesture was innocent, almost brotherly, but it set my heart racing.

I watched as he walked away across the green.

I had barely hung up my coat when a knock sounded at the door. Opening it, I found James standing there, his lopsided grin firmly in place.

"Do you want to go for a drink with me?" he blurted. "Tonight, or tomorrow. Up to you."

"I, um..." I hesitated, caught off guard.

He looked flustered, suddenly less confident. "I'm sorry, probably not, eh? It's too soon after—"

"Yes. I'd love to." The words tumbled out before I could stop them.

His face lit up. "Oh. Alright, erm... great! Pick you up at eight, then."

I nodded, watching as he backed down the path and retreated across the green. His awkwardness was oddly endearing.

Closing the door, I sank onto the bottom step, replaying the moment in my mind. For someone so self-assured, James Dunn had been surprisingly flustered. And I couldn't help but smile.

Chapter Six

Geri

"HERE YOU GO, MUM. This will make you feel better," I said, setting a glass down on the coffee table. Mum lay sprawled on the sofa, her face a patchwork of pale and blotchy. She looked terrible.

"You took your time," she snapped, her voice clipped and sharp.

I blinked, startled by her sudden hostility. "I was as quick as I could be. Jeez, Mum, how about a bit of gratitude?"

She pushed herself up slightly, reaching for the glass. After taking a slow, deliberate sip, she placed it back on the table with a clink. "Who was at the door?"

"James Dunn." I tried to temper my excitement, but the words came out in a rush. "I bumped into him at the shop. I didn't even recognise him at first—he's changed so much."

"So that's what kept you. Reminiscing with an old flame while I lay here dying?"

"You're hardly dying, Mum," I muttered, rolling my eyes.

"Anyway, do I have to remind you that you're a married woman? And before you start spouting that nonsense about being 'over,' mooning over other men is hardly a solution. It's only been a couple of days."

"Mother!" My voice rose before I could stop it. "I think last night's alcohol has scrambled your brain. First, James Dunn was never an 'old flame.' Second, I was not mooning over anybody. And third, Simon and I are most definitely over. Is that clear?"

She groaned, pressing her fingers to her temples. "Stop yelling, Geraldine."

"Then stop bloody moaning. Honestly, the sooner you accept that Simon is history, the better for all of us."

The conversation stung more than I wanted to admit. Mum had a way of ruining the rare moments that sparked a flicker of joy in my otherwise messy life. And yet, I couldn't stop myself from replaying my meeting with James—savouring every detail.

His chocolate-brown eyes had held a warmth I hadn't seen in anyone in months. His strong, muscled frame and rugged good looks, topped with close-cropped curls and a shadow of stubble, made my stomach churn in a way I hadn't felt in years. He was nothing like Simon, and maybe that was why I found him so magnetic.

Simon had been clean-cut perfection: deep blue eyes, golden-brown waves, and a trim build that matched his impeccably curated life. And yet, he'd shattered me. After six years of marriage, his secret had detonated everything I thought I knew.

I still felt raw when I thought about it. Simon, with his pleading voice and desperate promises. "We can keep things as they are, Geraldine," he'd said. "Why ruin what we have?"

What we have! As though it were a garden shed we could patch up with some paint and a few nails. What he really wanted was for me to keep playing housewife while he snuck off with Kevin—his boss and fellow closet-dweller.

I'd had half a mind to tell the world, but I couldn't. Not out of respect for Simon but because my own pride couldn't withstand the fallout.

"Right, Mum," I said, pulling myself back to the present. "I'll start on lunch. What time's Dad back?"

"Anytime now. Don't make a mess in my kitchen."

"Mother, I'm perfectly capable of making a sandwich without turning it into a catastrophe. What's the matter with you anyway? Do you have another migraine? Because you're being nasty again." It was hard work trying to keep up with her ever-fluctuating moods.

She opened her mouth to retort but then closed it again, her expression softening. I watched as she slowly let go of whatever barb she'd been preparing to hurl.

"Why don't you go have a shower?" I suggested gently. "You'll feel better."

Mum nodded, draining the glass before trudging up the stairs.

By the time Dad returned, the house felt almost normal again. Lunch was ready, and Mum had reappeared looking more like herself, though her pallor still lingered. We ate quietly, exchanging small talk, and I felt the knot in my chest loosen.

Later, I retreated to the garden with a magazine and a bottle of fizzy orange. The sun was warm on my face, and the rhythmic hum of the bees was lulling me into a delicious daze when a faint rustling pulled me back to reality.

I opened one eye and nearly jumped out of my skin. A man sat next to me, flipping through my magazine as though he owned it.

"What the hell?" I spluttered.

He glanced up, unbothered, and took a leisurely draw from a stupid plastic cigarette. "Oh, hi. You must be Geraldine. Your mum said I'd find you out here. You looked so peaceful I didn't want to disturb you."

"You didn't want to disturb me, so you decided to help yourself to my magazine?"

"Seemed logical," he said with a shrug.

"Who the hell are you?"

He grinned, a cocky tilt to his lips. "Carlos John Robertson the third." He stood, executing an exaggerated bow before grabbing my hand and brushing it with his lips.

I yanked my hand back. "What are you even doing here?"

"Your car's fixed. I brought it back. You're welcome, by the way."

"Ah, so you're Beryl's nephew. That explains a lot."

He put a hand to his chest, mock wounded. "What's that supposed to mean?"

"It means I understand why Mum let you wander out here. But next time, maybe shout before sneaking up on people."

He chuckled. "Noted. Anyway, I'd better head off." He handed me my car key.

I also got to my feet. "Thank you. How much do I owe you?"

"We can discuss it over dinner tonight?"

I laughed despite myself. "Nice try, but I'll just have the bill, please."

"It's a little inconvenient but I'll do anything for your mum. She asked me to entertain you while she and your dad go out." He smirked. "So tonight, seven. I'll see you then."

"I'm sorry to burst your bubble, but I've already made arrangements for tonight."

"It'll have to be tomorrow night, then." He winked, and with that, he was gone.

Back inside, Mum was humming along to the radio. "Carl found you, did he?"

"Yes. And thanks for playing matchmaker, Mum. That wasn't mortifying at all."

"Oh, don't be silly. I thought you might like the company."

I sighed, flopping onto the couch. "For the record, I already have plans tonight."

Mum arched a brow. "With James Dunn, I presume?"

Her tone was a warning, but I ignored it. She could think what she wanted. I wasn't about to let her ruin my day.

***

A couple of hours later, I heard Mum humming a tune in the bathroom while she prepared for her night out.

Downstairs, Dad was in his usual spot, watching football highlights on the TV. The soft glow of the screen lit up his weathered face, his brow furrowing slightly as a missed goal replayed in slow motion.

"Hi, sweetheart. How was your day?" he asked, glancing up with a smile.

I leaned down to kiss his freshly shaved cheek before snuggling up beside him on the sofa. The faint scent of his aftershave—clean and familiar—wrapped around me like a safety net. He draped a strong arm over my shoulder, pulling me closer.

"Boring," I admitted. "I need to sort myself out, Dad. Maybe look for a part-time job. I could do with the cash."

He didn't say anything right away—he just gave a slow nod. "Have you spoken to Simon?"

I hesitated, staring at the muted TV as a player celebrated a goal with an exuberant slide across the pitch. "No. I suppose I should call him, but I really have nothing to say."

Dad tightened his hold around me, resting his chin lightly on the top of my head. "Is it that bad, darling?"

I swallowed the lump forming in my throat. "Yes," I whispered. "It is."

The creak of the stairs announced Mum's arrival, and I turned my head, the words dying in my throat.

She looked stunning. Her wine-coloured, multi-layered skirt swished gracefully with each step, and her silky white cap-sleeve top shimmered under the soft light. Black sandals with modest one-inch heels completed the outfit, along with a lacy scarf draped over her slender shoulders.

"Wow, Mum, you look lovely," I said, meaning it.

She paused at the bottom step, her hand resting on the bannister, a playful glint in her eye. "Not bad for an old timer, am I?"

"Not bad at all." I grinned.

Dad's reaction, however, was the showstopper. His eyes lit up with genuine admiration, his smile broadening as he rose from the sofa. "As always, Grace, I'll be the envy of every man in the place tonight. You look beautiful." Taking her hand, he leaned in and pressed a kiss to her neck, making her giggle like a teenager.

I watched them, a pang of envy mixing with a strange pride. Even after all these years, they were still so deeply in love, so effortlessly attuned to each other.

When I was younger, I used to dream about finding a love like theirs. Something all-consuming but steady, passionate but comforting. I thought I'd come close with Simon. I thought we'd been building that kind of life together.

How wrong can a girl be?

Now, all I had to show for our marriage was this gnawing emptiness in the pit of my stomach, a hollow ache where my dreams used to be.

But it wasn't the kind of heartbreak I'd always imagined. It wasn't raw. It didn't knock the breath from my lungs.

Maybe that was the worst part.

Did that mean I hadn't truly loved him?

No. I had loved Simon—I still did. But maybe I wasn't in love with him.

Chapter Seven

Geri

ONCE MUM AND DAD had left, I bolted upstairs, excitement fizzing through me like a shaken-up cola. Tonight, I had a hot date with Mister-sexy-pants himself—James Dunn.

A long, steamy shower later, I stood wrapped in a towel, avoiding the full-length mirror in the bathroom. It was the kind of mirror that demanded a level of confidence I hadn't quite mastered. Only someone like my mother, who had the figure of a 1950s movie star, would think a full-length mirror belonged in a space where you had to be naked.

I told myself not to look. And, like always, I looked anyway.

My reflection greeted me, its honesty unkind. My face wasn't bad, I thought. Cute, even, in a youthful way—not the smouldering, sophisticated allure I sometimes wished for, but it was okay. My long neck and delicate shoulders were perhaps my best features. But as my gaze travelled lower, the critique began.

My breasts were heavy, more frumpy than perky. They didn't even have the decency to cooperate and form a proper cleavage, instead retreating toward my armpits like rebellious teenagers. Then came my stomach and waist—not awful, but definitely softer than I liked. My legs—thankfully slim and long, a feature I silently thanked the genetic lottery for.

Finally, I twisted to inspect my backside. A giant plump peach stared back at me. It made me chuckle, reminded of *James and the Giant Peach*, my favourite childhood book. Considering I was about to go on a date with James, it felt oddly fitting.

I sighed, pulling away from the mirror. This self-critical ritual had become second nature, a habit born from years of trying to decipher why Simon had found excuses to avoid intimacy. Now, I know it had nothing to do with me and my curves.

With a deep breath, I headed to my room to tackle the next challenge: what to wear. My limited wardrobe wasn't exactly date-ready. After some deliberation, I settled on my trusty jeans, pairing them with a fitted red blouse and a black jacket to add a touch of flair.

I found a pair of black heels in the bottom of the wardrobe. Although they were slightly outdated and a little too high, they completed the outfit. They pinched my toes but made my legs look fantastic. A slick of red lipstick sealed the deal. I blew myself a kiss in the mirror, confidence finally blooming.

When the doorbell rang, I gave my push-up bra a final adjustment and descended the stairs.

James stood on the doorstep, his dark grey slacks and striped shirt fitting him like a glove. His messy hair had been tamed, though not too much. He still had that rugged edge.

"Wow," I breathed. "You look amazing. Am I underdressed?"

"You've got to be kidding," he said, his eyes scanning me, lingering just a second too long on my neckline. "You look stunning."

He took my hand, leading me to his sleek silver Toyota parked at the curb.

"I half-expected you to be in that rust bucket from earlier," I teased as he opened the door for me.

He laughed, shaking his head. "I told you—that wasn't mine. It was just something to break the ice. Honestly, if you'd accepted the lift, I'd have had to explain myself all the way to the hotel."

"Idiot," I said, grinning. "So, where are we headed?"

"There's this new Mexican restaurant in Penrith. The hotel receptionist recommended it—apparently, it's fantastic."

"Sounds great," I said, though I couldn't remember if I'd ever tried Mexican food.

"You do like Mexican food, right?" He glanced at me, a flicker of concern in his eyes.

"If it's food, I'll like it," I said confidently.

"I love a woman who appreciates her food." He flashed me a grin that made my stomach flip. Those dimples!

"You'll want to marry me by the end of the night, then," I joked, the words tumbling out before I could think better of them.

His smile faltered, just for a moment, and my cheeks flamed.

"I mean," I stammered, "when you see how much I enjoy food, you'll be impressed, that's all."

His grin returned, the momentary tension dissolving. "Got it. You're a foodie. I like that."

I let out a breath I hadn't realised I was holding and sank into the seat, vowing to keep the rest of the conversation far away from the M word.

When we arrived at the restaurant, I tottered towards the bathroom in my too-high heels, the faint pinch of discomfort a reminder that beauty often demanded sacrifice. In the dimly lit mirror, I reapplied my lipstick, the bold red made me feel daring and confident, even if my nerves rattled like a tambourine. I tugged at the neckline of my blouse and gave the girls another hitch in my push-up bra. Despite its best efforts, gravity always seemed to win the battle, eventually.

James was already at the table when I returned, rising swiftly as I approached. He pulled out my chair, a gentlemanly gesture that was almost shocking in its rarity.

"Thank you," I said, smoothing my jeans as I sat.

We ordered beers while perusing the menu, The lively beat of the restaurant's music pulsing through the air made it impossible not to tap a foot or sway a little in rhythm.

"Would you like a glass, Geri?" James asked as the waiter set down our drinks.

"No, thanks," I said, taking a swig straight from the bottle. It felt more relaxed, less fussy.

James smiled, and I got the feeling he was totally interested in anything I had to say, however mundane or boring.

The menu was overwhelming—every dish sounded like a slice of heaven. "I don't know what to choose. It all looks amazing," I admitted the options blending together in a sea of unfamiliar names.

"How about we share a few things? That way, we can try some of everything," James suggested.

"That sounds perfect. You decide—I trust you."

The waiter returned, taking James's confident order while I silently marvelled how at ease he seemed. Once the food was on its way, the conversation turned, and the nerves I'd been keeping at bay began to creep in.

"So, what brings you back to Cumberside?" I asked, forcing myself to focus on him instead of my worries about saying the wrong thing.

James leaned back in his chair, his expression softening. "Work, mostly. But I've been meaning to come back for a while. My dad moved to Glasgow a few years ago, so I don't get out this way much anymore. But I've missed it."

There was a warmth in his voice as he spoke, a wistfulness that made my chest tighten. His eyes sparkled under the restaurant's soft lights, and the dimples in his cheeks deepened with every smile. I couldn't stop staring, a rogue thought flashing through my mind—I wanted to bite that bottom lip of his.

Realising I'd been too quiet for too long, I cleared my throat. "And where are you living now?"

"Nottingham way. Robin Hood country."

I laughed at his attempt at a cockney accent. "Oh, nice. I didn't even know your dad had moved."

"Yeah, he remarried a while back. He and Mary seem happy. I might visit them one weekend before I head home—it's only a couple of hours away from here."

"That's nice," I said, though my stomach flipped at the idea of him leaving so soon after just coming back. "So, where are you staying?"

"At the hotel. It's decent—clean and warm. The food's average, but it does the job."

I hesitated before broaching the next topic, but curiosity won out. "Are they any closer to catching the rapist?"

James's expression darkened slightly. "I shouldn't talk about it, really, but ... no. Not yet. However, I've been doing my own investigation, and I think there's a connection to some other attacks in the Penrith area over the past decade—nothing as severe as rape, but there are similarities."

"Have you mentioned it to Vinny? He's still the village cop, isn't he?"

"He is," James said with a wry grin. "But let's just say he's not exactly receptive to new ideas. He's not the easiest guy to deal with."

"I've always got on well with him," I said.

"You would. You're not intimidating."

"And you are?" I teased.

James shrugged. "Apparently."

"Do you have any idea who it might be?" I pressed, lowering my voice.

"No," he admitted. "The guy's careful. He wears dark clothes, a balaclava, and doesn't say a word. He also uses a condom, which is rare. There's no DNA, no identifying marks left behind. It's calculated. He watches his victims first and stakes out their homes. It's sick."

A shiver ran down my spine. "Terrifying to think he could be someone we know."

James nodded grimly. "Quite possibly."

Sensing the tension rising, he forced a smile. "Let's talk about something else. This is depressing, and I don't want to ruin the night. What about you? What brought you home?"

I hesitated, then decided to be honest. "Simon's been having an affair. Someone from work."

James winced. "Ouch."

"Yeah. Ouch," I said, the memory still raw. "I had no idea. It blind-sided me completely."

"His loss," James said firmly, his tone leaving no room for argument. "He's an idiot."

I smiled, my chest tightening with emotion. "Thanks."

"Right, no more talking about that. Tonight is about having fun." He signalled for another round of drinks, though I noticed he'd barely touched his.

As the waiter brought out a colourful array of dishes, the music swelled, and everyone in the restaurant seemed to vibrate with energy. A group of performers had taken to the stage, their traditional

Mexican attire vibrant and striking. The men wore tight black suits adorned with silver details, while the women twirled in bright red dresses layered with frills.

The atmosphere was infectious, with laughter and music blending into a symphony of joy. At a nearby table, a red-haired woman with a laugh like a cackling witch had James and me in stitches every time she let loose.

I tried to maintain some semblance of decorum with the delicious food, though the temptation to devour everything was strong. The flavours were a revelation—spicy, rich, and utterly delicious.

"Another drink?" James asked, gesturing to my empty bottle.

I nodded, realising too late how easily the beers were going down. But tonight felt like a celebration, and I wasn't about to let anything ruin it.

Once the plates were cleared, the restaurant transformed into a buzzing carnival. The dancers leapt off the stage, weaving between tables in a whirlwind of colour and energy, coaxing diners to join them. A guy near us with the rhythm of a brick wall gamely gave it a go, his awkward stomping reminding me of *Odd Bod* from the Carry On films. His stiff movements and blank expression had me in stitches, but his obvious joy was infectious.

After a while, the band took a breather, and the room settled into a more mellow hum. It was a relief to hear James's voice without shouting above the din.

"Thanks for tonight," I said, leaning forward slightly. "I haven't had this much fun in ages."

"Me neither." His smile was warm and genuine.

"The food was incredible. I think I overdid it, though." I stretched back and sighed, feeling comfortably stuffed.

James waved at a waiter, ordering another round.

"What are you drinking?" I asked, noticing his untouched glass from earlier.

"Just Cola. I don't drink more than one if I'm driving," he said with a casual shrug.

"I don't usually drink this much either, but I'm loving the beer here," I admitted.

"What's your usual drink?" he asked, his gaze locked on mine.

"Gin and Tonic. You?"

"I'll have the odd lager occasionally, but I'm not much of a drinker."

The band returned, tuning their instruments, and the energy in the room started to climb again. I excused myself to visit the ladies, where I had a minor crisis over my shoes and my bra. The heels were killing me, and my bra had given up its earlier promise of defying gravity.

An idea struck as I stared at my reflection, annoyed at the wayward state of things. Back in the cubicle, I grabbed two small wads of toilet paper and stuffed the outer edges of my bra. It worked like a charm. Feeling triumphant, I reapplied my lipstick and mascara, checked my hair, and wobbled back to the table.

The room had taken on a new mood. Waiters lined the perimeter, linking arms, while James clapped along to the upbeat rhythm of the band. His chocolate-brown eyes sparkled when I sat down, and I felt a little flutter in my chest.

The music shifted to a tune I recognised immediately. Da dada de dada de dada ... I couldn't help myself. "More reasons, more reasons, more reasons to shop at Morrison's," I sang under my breath.

James belted out a laugh. "I was about to do the same thing! I can't believe you beat me to it."

The waiters began clapping, leading the entire room to join in time with the music. Then, as if choreographed, they picked up bottles of tequila and filled shot glasses for every table.

"Tequila!" they shouted in unison before downing their drinks and slamming the glasses onto the tables.

I winced as I knocked mine back. The sharp burn in my throat reminded me of paint thinner. Out of the corner of my eye, I noticed James discreetly sliding his glass over to me.

Before I could say anything, a waiter pulled my chair out, hauling me to my feet.

"James!" I called out, but he was already in the clutches of a stunning woman in a red dress. Her bright smile and confident grip left no room for argument.

The music surged, and I was spun around the room at a dizzying pace. By the time the song ended, I was breathless and dishevelled, staggering back to the table and gulping down my beer.

"This place is wild!" I laughed, my cheeks flushed from the exertion.

"I'm glad you're having fun." James's own face was slightly red.

"It's amazing." My laughter bubbling up again.

The waiter returned, and I braced myself for another dance partner, but this time, they zeroed in on James.

He shot me a pleading look as they dragged him toward the stage, and I shrugged helplessly, grinning like a Cheshire cat.

On stage, they dressed him in a comically small waistcoat, a wide-brimmed hat, and a multicoloured blanket slung over his shoulder. He looked utterly ridiculous.

I reached for my phone, taking several photos and a video.

Despite his initial embarrassment, James got into the spirit, stomping and thrusting his hips to the beat with theatrical flair. Every so often, he glanced my way and winked, his cheeky expression only making me laugh harder.

By the time he returned to the table, my sides were aching, and tears were streaming down my face.

"You're a natural," I teased, still catching my breath.

"Don't you be putting those photos all over social media," he said, collapsing into his chair. But the grin tugging at his lips gave him away.

"Too late!" I teased.

The band played on, the restaurant alive with energy, laughter, and the kind of joy that makes you forget the outside world entirely. Tonight felt magical, and for the first time in a long time, I felt like I could let go.

The night had spiralled into chaos by the time it was time to leave. Several tequila shots, an uncountable number of beers, and endless dancing had left me unable to walk straight. James, ever the gentleman, tried to keep me upright, but I was a hopeless case, leaning my full weight against him as we wove through the tables.

I insisted on saying goodnight to every waiter in the place, planting sloppy kisses on their cheeks and giggling like a schoolgirl. Outside, the fresh air hit me like a wall, and the world started spinning faster than the dance floor.

James sat me down on the pavement edge, propping me against a lamppost while he went to fetch the car. My stomach churned uneasily as I leaned my head back, fighting the nausea.

"Geraldine?"

The voice was familiar, even in my beer-soaked haze. I opened one eye, squinting up at the figure standing over me. A plastic cigarette dangled from his mouth, and his smirk was unmistakable.

"Oh, hello," I drawled, trying to sound composed. "If it isn't Carlos-Humpty-Dumpty the Third." I tried to stand, but my heel caught in the pavement grid, sending me tumbling against Carl. The next thing I knew, we were both sprawled on the ground, me perched on top of him, laughing uncontrollably.

James pulled up at that exact moment, his silver car gleaming under the streetlights. He got out, taking in the scene with an unreadable expression.

"Ah, my knight in shining armour!" I called, raising my arms dramatically toward James as Carl dusted himself off.

James approached, trying to help me stand, but my broken heel rendered me useless. He sighed, scooped me into his arms, and carried me to the car.

"Oh, my hero," I slurred, draping an arm around his neck.

Carl, ever the opportunist, leaned in through the open window as James buckled me into the passenger seat.

"See you tomorrow, Geraldine, for our date." He winked, mischief dancing in his eyes as he tucked the cigarette behind his ear.

"Goodnight, Carl-Lagerfeld the Third," I called after him as James shut the door, his jaw tightening.

The ride home was awkward. I was a giggling, singing nuisance, while James remained stoically silent, his hands gripping the wheel.

"Are you mad at me, James?" I tried to meet his eyes.

"No," he said flatly.

"Then why aren't you talking to me?"

"Because I have nothing to say to you."

"Is it because I got a little tipsy?"

He shot me a side glance. "No, it's not because you're a little bit tipsy. Or because you're a lot tipsy. Or because you're completely legless."

"Then what?"

"Because you were fawning all over a stranger and making dates with him the second my back was turned."

"Oh, that?" I waved a dismissive hand. "Carl isn't a stranger. And for the record, I already planned to go out with him tomorrow. I'm a free agent, James. I can do what I like." My tone turned haughty, my words slurring as I tried to sound self-assured.

The silence stretched again, heavy and uncomfortable.

"Are you sulking?" I asked after a moment, breaking the quiet.

"No," he snapped.

"Sure, looks like sulking to me."

"I don't sulk."

"You're doing a hell of an impression."

He glanced at me, his lips twitching despite himself. "Do you have any idea how you looked straddling that punk back there?"

"I can imagine," I said, laughing.

"I thought you'd tackled him to the ground."

"You must think I'm really easy."

"What else was I supposed to think?"

By then, we were both laughing, the tension dissolving into a shared absurdity.

When we pulled up outside my parents' house, I leaned over to kiss him goodnight. My aim was off, landing just on the corner of his mouth. As I leaned back, he reached for me, his fingers brushing the neckline of my top.

"James!" I gasped, scandalised.

"Relax, Geraldine," he said, pulling back with a smirk. "You lost something."

Before I could respond, he plucked one of the tissue wads I'd had in my bra and held it up like a trophy.

I was mortified, snatching it from him and bolting from the car. My broken heel made my exit less graceful than I intended, but I hobbled up the garden path with as much dignity as I could muster.

I heard the car door slam and seconds later, James was beside me.

"Geri, wait," he said, catching my arm. "I'm sorry."

I turned to face him, and for reasons I couldn't fully explain—maybe the tequila, maybe the humiliation, maybe just the pull of his damn beautiful face—I stood on my tiptoes and kissed him. Hard.

For a moment, he kissed me back, and it felt like the world was right again. But then his hands pressed against my shoulders, pushing me back.

It wasn't until he bit my lip that I realised he was trying to stop me.

Staring at him, my vision blurred with tears. Humiliated and rejected again, I fumbled with my key, let myself inside, and slammed the door behind me.

I pressed my back against the door, letting the sobs escape as the night's events crashed over me. Another man, another knock-back.

Outside, I heard James's footsteps retreating, his car engine starting up. He was gone, and I was left alone with the echoes of my drunken bravado and the sting of his rejection.

Chapter Eight

James

JAMES STRODE BACK TO his car, each step heavy with frustration and self-reproach. The evening, which had begun like a dream, had unravelled into a mess of awkwardness and regret. He slid into the driver's seat, gripping the steering wheel so tightly his knuckles whitened.

The date had been everything he'd imagined—and more. Geraldine looked stunning, her red blouse accentuating her vivacious energy. It had taken every ounce of self-control not to let his gaze linger too long on the curve of her smile or the sparkle in her eyes. And her laugh—it was infectious, the sound that could lift a room. He'd been utterly captivated.

He couldn't help but smile as he thought back to the moment when the waiter swept her onto the dance floor. Her expression, a mix of shock and giddy excitement, was priceless. She'd been a whirlwind of energy, twirling, laughing, and radiating a charm that left everyone around her in stitches.

But the glow of the memory faded as the night's sour ending replayed in his mind.

He didn't mind that she'd had a few too many drinks. Geraldine was fun and unapologetic, and he admired that about her. He wasn't one to judge. Just because he didn't drink didn't mean he expected others to follow suit. His choice had always been personal, rooted in painful memories of the night a drunk driver took his mother's life.

Still, her exuberance wasn't the issue. What had gnawed at him was the sight of her, tipsy and laughing, sprawled across some bloke on the side of the road. The sharp pang of jealousy had hit him like a gut punch. He'd felt foolish for how much it bothered him—especially since she didn't owe him anything. They'd only just met up again.

And then there was the kiss.

When Geraldine leaned in, her lips warm and insistent against his, he'd frozen. It wasn't like he hadn't imagined this moment before. As a teenager, he'd spent countless nights dreaming of Geraldine, replaying scenarios where she kissed him like that, where she looked at him the way she had tonight. Even as an adult, after his split with Katrina, his thoughts had drifted back to Geraldine, the idea of her always more compelling than the reality of anyone else.

But when it actually happened, when her kiss burned with the kind of passion he'd fantasised about for years, he'd panicked.

And then, of course, he'd done the unthinkable. He'd bit her fucking lip.

He groaned aloud, leaning his head back against the car seat. "What the hell is wrong with me?" he muttered aloud.

He parked in the hotel car park. His thoughts in a blur, he debated heading to the pub to drown his sorrows. The muffled laughter and rowdy chatter of Saturday night revelry spilled into the lobby as he approached the internal entrance from the hotel reception. But the thought of forcing a smile or making small talk was unbearable.

Instead, he changed direction and went straight to his room.

Once inside, James kicked off his shoes and collapsed onto the bed. He considered pulling out his laptop to work on the case, but his mind was too tangled for clarity. Writing required focus, and right now, all he had was a looping reel of Geraldine's kiss, her fiery laughter, and the way her face had crumpled when he pushed her away.

The television flickered to life as he switched it on, its mindless chatter a small distraction from the ache in his chest. He lay back, one arm covering his eyes, replaying the night's events over and over.

He knew he'd need to fix this. Geraldine deserved an apology. But for now, he let the noise of the television fill the room, trying to drown out the sound of his own thoughts.

Chapter Nine

• • •

THE PUMPING BASS FROM the pub reverberated faintly through the
damp night air, a muffled rhythm of duf-duf-duf.

The man stood in the shadow of the side street, his eyes were fixed
on the entrance, his breath visible in the chill.

He didn't know how the evening would end—it hinged entirely on
whether Samantha would leave with the man she'd been clinging to
earlier or make her usual drunken walk home alone.

He'd watched her earlier, laughing too loudly, pressing herself
against some out-of-towner who reeked of desperation. Samantha had
no class no sense of self-preservation. She'd practically dared the world
to come after her. Tonight, he might oblige.

His watch told him it was nearly closing time. The muffled music
cut out abruptly, and the bar's lights brightened, illuminating the
faces of patrons as they spilled onto the street. Groups of women
teetered arm in arm, their laughter bouncing off the buildings. Two
men stumbled into a half-hearted scuffle, egged on by a jeering crowd.

Then he saw her. Samantha. Staggering out the door, clutching the
arm of her earlier conquest.

"Damn it," he muttered, scuffing his shoe against the kerb. He shrank deeper into the shadows, his breath quickening.

But as luck would have it, their conversation drifted to him on the night breeze. The man was saying goodbye, muttering something about an early morning. Relief flickered across Samantha's face as they parted ways.

She started along the pavement, her heels clicking against the concrete, alone—just as he'd hoped.

He slipped into his car and kept a cautious distance as she made her way through the village. The streets thinned out, the sounds of the night retreating with each step she took toward her tiny cottage. She didn't glance over her shoulder, didn't falter—confident in her belief that she was untouchable.

She'd bragged about it just last week. "That so-called rapist doesn't scare me," she'd said in a voice dripping with defiance. How foolish.

He bypassed her, scooting along another street and doubling back, parking his car just beyond the entrance to the narrow lane leading to her cul-de-sac. There were no street lights that far out of the village, the only light coming from the faint glow of her porch.

He didn't have much time. He moved. Fast, careful, deliberate, silent. He crept around the back, testing the doors and windows. Locked. She'd been more cautious than he'd expected.

But the front door? That was a surprise. It swung open with a faint creak as he turned the handle.

Inside, the house was quiet except for the low hum of the boiler.

He moved quickly, checking the rooms, ensuring the house was empty. He knew her son stayed with his father on the weekends.

Moments later, she let herself in and turned on the TV before heading for the kitchen. The sound of the kettle boiling told him he had a few minutes grace before he needed to hide.

From his vantage point at the top of the stairs, he listened as she made a phone call, her voice carrying up to him. She recounted her evening in vulgar detail, each word laced with intoxicated bravado. His lip curled in disgust.

Finally, the conversation ended, and the house fell quiet, apart from the steady hum of the TV in the background. He waited, breath held, until she turned it off, and her footsteps echoed in the hallway below.

She was coming upstairs.

He retreated into her bedroom, positioning himself behind the door, and pulled down the mask. His pulse raced as the doorknob turned, but he hesitated. As Samantha entered, her carefree humming came to an abrupt stop.

Her eyes met his. Confusion. Fear. Slowly, realisation dawned on her face.

"Who the fuck are you, and what are you doing here?" she demanded, her voice rising in pitch.

He took a step forward, her fear feeding his resolve. But something in her gaze shifted. Samantha wasn't the trembling, helpless woman he'd envisioned. Her fear gave way to anger, her voice steadier than he anticipated.

"You have no idea who you're messing with," she spat, backing toward the door.

For a moment, uncertainty flickered through his mind. This wasn't going to go as planned.

Chapter Ten

Geri

My head throbbed like a drum being beaten by a sadistic child. Every movement sent a fresh wave of pain radiating through my skull. Somewhere beneath me, I could hear Mum banging pots and pans in the kitchen, each clang like a hammer blow to my temples. All I wanted was to crawl back under the duvet and disappear into oblivion. But my mouth was so dry it felt like I'd swallowed a handful of grit, and my tongue stuck to the roof of my mouth every time I tried to swallow. I needed water—or milk—anything to bring me back to life.

Dragging myself out of bed, I squinted at the harsh light of day streaming through the curtains. My limbs felt as though they were filled with lead, and I shuffled down the stairs, bracing myself against the railing for support.

Mum was kneeling in front of the open oven, scrubbing furiously at something that looked like burnt cheese, when I stumbled into the kitchen. She looked up as I entered, her face a mixture of disappointment and mild concern.

"Oh, Geraldine," she said, pulling herself up and snapping off her rubber gloves with a dramatic flourish. The sharp sound pierced straight through my brain, making me wince. "What have you done to yourself?"

I slumped into a chair, my forehead resting against my palm. "I need something for my head, Mum. And a glass of milk, please."

She gave me a pointed look as she opened the cupboard. "I could swing for that bloody James Dunn for getting you in this state, I really could."

"I'm a big girl, Mother," I said, trying not to groan as she slammed the cupboard shut. "I got myself into this state. Not him."

"He should know better," she snapped, pouring the milk with the kind of precision that suggested she was taking her frustration out on the carton.

"Why? He didn't drink—I did." I reached for the glass and the blister pack of paracetamol she handed me. "End of discussion. And anyway, weren't you hung over just yesterday?"

"That," she said with a sniff, "was something I ate."

"Sure, it was." I swallowed the pills dry before chasing them with a gulp of milk. "Let's just drop it, okay? I'm going back to bed." I thought she might complain about that, but she kept strangely quiet.

I was halfway up the stairs when I remembered something. "Muuuum!" I called out, my voice echoing in the hallway.

She appeared below, looking exasperated. "What now?"

"Could you call Carl and cancel tonight? I'm not in the mood."

She rolled her eyes but nodded. "Fine."

The rest of the day passed in a haze of nausea and fatigue. Mum brought me a bacon sandwich mid-morning, and though it helped settle my stomach, the persistent ache in my head refused to budge. I drifted in and out of sleep, cocooned in my duvet, trying to stave off the nagging feeling of guilt and regret. By late afternoon, I was feeling marginally better and ventured downstairs.

Mum was in the kitchen, humming as she fussed with a casserole dish, and I could hear Dad belting out a tuneless rendition of "Sweet Caroline" from the bathroom upstairs. I flopped onto the couch, letting the soft cushions envelop me. My body still felt like it had been run over by a truck.

Dad eventually came bounding down the stairs still half-singing, half-shouting the chorus. He was wearing his best suit, the one with the slightly too-short sleeves. Moments later, Mum appeared in the kitchen doorway, dressed in a floral dress and a pair of low heels. They both looked cheerful. Too cheerful.

"Are you going out?" I asked, narrowing my eyes at them.

"Yeah, love. Some friends of ours are having a little get-together," Mum replied, checking her lipstick in the reflective glass of display cabinet.

"Oh. I thought you were making dinner." I sat up straighter.

"I was—we're all bringing a dish. There's plenty of food in the fridge if you're hungry."

I barely registered the rest of her explanation. My mind was too focused on my empty stomach. Only when I noticed both of them staring at me expectantly did I snap back to reality. "What?"

"You were miles away," Dad said with a grin. "Your mum couldn't get hold of Carl, so he'll probably be here in an hour or so. You'd better get ready."

"What?" My voice came out louder than I intended. "Oh, for God's sake. Doesn't he have a mobile?"

"Don't take the Lord's name in vain, Geraldine," Mum chided, straightening her dress.

"You're not even religious, Mum."

"Doesn't mean I like hearing it," she said tartly. "And for your information, I tried his mobile. He didn't answer. Now, go on. Get ready. It won't kill you to go out with a nice young man for a change. Maybe Simon will hear about it and realise what he's lost."

My stomach sank. Of course, this was about Simon. It was always about Simon.

I had no choice but to get ready. Resigned, I trudged upstairs, muttering under my breath. After a quick shower, I threw on my trusty black slacks and a blouse, blow-drying my hair half-heartedly.

Mum popped her head around the door just as I was finishing. "We're off now. Don't wait up, love!" she chirped.

"Yeah, see you," I called back, forcing a smile.

Alone again, I stared at my reflection in the mirror. The person looking back at me seemed like a stranger—hollow eyes, tired skin, and a heavy heart. I'd need a mountain of makeup to pull this off.

At six forty-five, I was ready. More than ready, actually—I was genuinely pleased with my reflection in the full-length mirror. My black slacks fit perfectly, and my cream blouse, soft and flowing, felt like a small armour of dignity. I'd even managed to tame my unruly hair into loose waves that framed my face. For a brief moment, I allowed myself to feel a flicker of confidence.

As I made my way downstairs, the doorbell rang. I grabbed my jacket off the bannister, expecting to find Carl waiting on the other side. But when I opened the door, I froze, the smile slipping from my face.

It wasn't Carl.

It was Simon.

"Hi, Geri. Can I come in?" His voice was soft, almost hesitant. His presence felt like a slap to my carefully composed façade.

Before I could respond, he stepped into the hallway, closing the door behind him. The familiar scent of his aftershave hit me, a mix of nostalgia and bitterness.

"You look lovely," he said, his eyes flicking over me. "Are you going out?"

"Not that it's any of your business," I snapped, the words sharp on my tongue, "but yes. I have a date."

He flinched, just slightly, but enough for me to catch it. Good.

"I don't know why that should bother you, Simon," I continued, my voice laced with bitterness. "At least I waited until we were officially over. Now, what are you doing here?"

He hesitated, shoving his hands into the pockets of his coat like a chastened schoolboy. "We need to talk. You won't take my calls, so, what choice did I have? Are your mum and dad out?"

I crossed my arms. "Yes, but not for long. So just say what you need to say and then go. Please."

He moved into the lounge, as though he still had the right to be comfortable in my space. The clock above the mantelpiece ticked loudly in the silence as I followed him inside. The time read 6:50 pm. Of all the moments he could have chosen, it had to be now.

"Well?" I prompted, standing rigidly while he settled into the armchair like he belonged there.

"This week's been awful, Geri," he began, his voice laden with self-pity. "I haven't been to work, haven't faced anyone. I don't know what to tell people—we need to get our story straight."

And there it was. His concern wasn't for me or the wreckage of our marriage. It was appearances.

"I knew it," I said, shaking my head. "All you care about is what people think of you. I told you I wouldn't tell anyone, and I haven't—except for Lucy. And she promised she wouldn't even tell Mark. That's your job, Simon. He's your best friend, for God's sake."

"That's not all I'm bothered about," he said quickly. "I've missed you."

I let out a hollow laugh. "Why? Won't Kevin do your laundry?"

"Don't be cruel, Geri. It's not like that."

We sat in silence, a chasm of unspoken words between us. I could feel the weight of his gaze, but I refused to look at him.

Finally, I stood. "Well, if that's all, I'll see you out."

"There's one more thing." His voice stopped me mid-step. "I just... I need to know—is there going to be a baby?"

The question hit me like a slap. I turned slowly, my jaw tightening. "Pardon?"

"Are you pregnant?" he asked, his voice hesitant but steady.

My hands curled into fists. "Do you honestly think I would have a baby after everything? If there was a baby—and believe me, I sincerely hope not—I wouldn't keep it. A child needs two parents, Simon, not just one."

The words came out louder than I'd intended, and my whole body shook with anger. How dare he? How dare he even ask?

"So you're not sure," he pressed, oblivious to the storm brewing in me.

"Are you deaf?" I exploded. "There is no baby, Simon. There is no marriage. And there's absolutely nothing left to say. Now, get out!"

He stood, but instead of leaving, he took a step closer. His hands reached for mine, and I let him take them, too stunned by his audacity to pull away.

"If there is a baby," he said quietly, "I'd take it. You wouldn't want for anything. I'd make sure you were looked after."

His words cut deeper than I thought possible. I ripped my hands from his grasp. "You selfish bastard. This was your plan all along, wasn't it? You wanted me pregnant before dropping the bomb about Kevin. How stupid was I not to see it?"

"That's not true," he said, his voice breaking. "I didn't want to hurt you, Geri. I do love you."

"No, Simon," I said, my voice low and cold. "You love yourself. Now get out of my house."

For a moment, he looked like he might argue, but then he nodded and walked to the door. I stood frozen until I heard his car drive away.

Then the tears came. Hot, angry, unstoppable. I buried my face in the couch cushions, muffling my sobs.

"Geraldine?" A soft voice broke through my despair.

I looked up to see a pair of brown loafers and blue jeans. Carl. I'd completely forgotten about him.

"The front door was open, are you alright?" He knelt beside me, his hand warm and reassuring as he stroked my back. "It's okay. Get it all out."

"I'm sorry," I choked out. "I was ready, but now I'm a mess. I don't think I can go anywhere tonight."

"That's okay," he said softly. "We'll stay in."

"No, I don't want to ruin your evening—"

"Hey," he interrupted, brushing a strand of hair from my face. "I'm here for you, not some fancy dinner. Now go freshen up. If you still don't fancy going out after you've reapplied your lippy, I'll let you pick the takeaway."

I smiled despite my mood.

***

I DID AS CARL suggested, and, as much as I hated to admit it, he was right. Splashing water on my face, fixing my lipstick, and brushing my hair made me feel like a new person—or at least someone who could fake it for an evening.

He drove us to a cosy pizza bar in Kirkby Mayor, which had mismatched chairs and red-and-white chequered tablecloths. It smelled of garlic and melted cheese, and the warmth of the wood-fired oven seeped into the air, softening the edges of my earlier mood. By the time we'd ordered our pizzas, I was starting to relax, even warming to Carl's easy humour.

Carl slapped both palms onto the table with a loud thud, breaking me out of my thoughts. "Right, spill."

I blinked at him. "Spill what?"

He shrugged dramatically, glancing around the room as if seeking an audience. "You and the husband. What were you arguing about? Don't leave me hanging."

"It's a long story," I said, fiddling with the edge of the napkin in front of me.

Carl leaned back in his chair, spreading his hands wide. "Perfect! Long story for a place that takes forever to make pizza. We've got time."

I couldn't help but laugh. "We've separated—he's seeing someone else."

Carl's face darkened instantly. "Wanker!"

"Exactly," I muttered, dabbing at the corners of my eyes before any stray tears could fall. "And now he wants a baby."

"With you?" Carl's eyebrows shot up as he shook his head in disbelief. "You've got to be joking."

I laughed bitterly. "Not now, no. But we were trying before everything went to hell. He just wanted to know if I'm pregnant. And if I am, he wants the baby."

Carl's expression shifted from disbelief to pure confusion. "Hang on. Most blokes in his situation would be running for the hills. Pregnant exes don't exactly scream 'fresh start.'"

"Yeah, well," I said, shaking my head. "Simon's not most men."

"No kidding."

"If I tell you something, will you promise to keep it between us?"

I raised an eyebrow. "Ooh, scandal—gossip." He rubbed his hands together in anticipation.

I blinked, shocked, and closed my lips in a tight line.

"Fine, fine." He laughed, holding his hands up in mock surrender. "If you tell me something, I promise it'll go no further. Scout's honour."

"You were even in the scouts?" I asked, sceptical.

"Of course!" He held up three fingers in a precise salute. "Dib, dib, dib."

I chuckled, rolling my eyes. "What does that even mean?"

"'Do your best,' obviously. See? Stick with me, kid—you'll learn stuff."

"Such an education," I teased. "Amazing."

Our pizzas arrived, saving me from his growing smugness, but not before my stomach growled loud enough to turn heads.

Carl grinned. "See? I told you—you need feeding up."

I blushed, embarrassed. "Alright, alright. You win this round."

He let me take a few bites before leaning in again. "So come on, Geri. Stop dodging. I'm dying to know."

I sighed, setting my slice of garlic bread down. "Fine. But it's not easy to talk about."

He nodded, his expression softening. "No rush. Take your time."

I stared at the flickering candle on the table before answering. "Simon's gay."

Carl froze mid-reach for his pizza. "You're shitting me!"

"I wish I was," I said, taking another bite to stave off the lump in my throat. "I just found out last week."

"How?" he asked, leaning forward, his eyes wide—serious for once. "What happened?"

I swallowed hard, the memory still raw. "He was working late, so I thought I'd surprise him. I showed up at his office with supper, but the place was dark, all locked up. His car was still there, though, so I figured he must be next door at this little Italian place."

Carl's expression tightened as if bracing for impact. "And?"

"And there he was, sitting with his boss," I said, forcing the words out like they were nails in my mouth. "They were holding hands, staring at each other like they were the only two people in the world. I didn't know whether to cry or laugh. It all just... clicked."

Carl leaned back, exhaling slowly. "Bloody hell. That's a lot to take in."

"It was," I admitted. "But honestly? It explained so much. The distance, the late nights, the way he always seemed so... so tense. I'd even met his boss before. He came to dinner at our house once. I really liked him."

"Clearly not as much as Simon did," Carl quipped, though his voice was gentle.

"Clearly," I said, managing a small smile.

Carl shook his head. "You're handling this way better than I would, you know."

"Am I?" I asked, gesturing to myself. "Because from where I'm sitting, I'm barely keeping it together."

"Trust me," Carl said, his voice firm. "You're stronger than you think."

And for the first time in a long while, I almost believed him.

Chapter Eleven

Geri

WE ATE OUR PIZZAS in companionable silence. Each bite felt comforting and grounding after the emotional whirlwind of the day. It was a world away from last night's date, but no less enjoyable. If anything, it was refreshing to spend time with someone like Carl—easy going, full of charm, and blessed with a wicked sense of humour that kept me on my toes.

Carl was a few years younger than me, but he carried himself with the kind of confidence that made you forget the age gap. His brown hair was combed into a neat quiff, and his mischievous eyes seemed to dance with every joke or teasing remark. There were faint creases at the corners of his eyes—definite laughter lines—and his teeth were so straight and white they could have graced the cover of a celebrity magazine.

I liked him. I liked him a lot. But there was no spark—the kind that left you breathless or made your pulse race.

When I thought back to last night with James Dunn, I felt an entirely different kind of warmth creep into my cheeks. My stomach twisted as I remembered how I'd practically launched myself at him, only to be gently but firmly rejected. Pity he didn't feel the same way I did. I'd probably ruined whatever semblance of friendship we'd had.

Carl seemed to read my mind because he leaned forward, his expression turning curious. "So, who was the guy from last night?"

I blinked at him and shrugged. "What guy?"

He rolled his eyes, grinning. "Tall, dark, and broody? The one who looked like he wanted to kick my teeth down my throat. The one who picked you up off the floor."

I shook my head, trying to keep my voice casual. "Oh, that guy. That's James. He's just a friend. We all grew up together."

"Just a friend?" Carl raised a sceptical eyebrow. "He didn't look at you like you were just friends. Not with that expression on his face."

I laughed, waving him off. "Trust me, Carl, it's nothing like that. He dropped me off, we said goodnight, and that was it."

"Good." Carl leaned back in his chair with a satisfied smirk.

"Why good?" I asked, amused by his smugness.

"Because you're my girl now," he declared, grinning broadly.

I couldn't help but laugh. "As if."

"I'm serious! I'm not a bad catch, you know." He feigned hurt.

"I know that. You're just not my type," I teased. "But I do need a friend if that'll do you?"

Carl held up a hand. "If that's all you're offering, I'll take it. For now. But be warned—you're liable to fall madly in love with me."

"You're impossible." I shook my head, laughing. "So, tell me your story."

"Nothing much to tell, really," he said, shrugging and tapping his fingers lightly on the table.

"Bullshit," I said, narrowing my eyes at him. "Beryl told me you've travelled a lot."

He shrugged again, avoiding my gaze. "I get itchy feet. You know how it is."

"Not really," I said honestly. "I lived in the same house I was born in until I moved out six years ago. And when everything fell apart? Straight back to Mum and Dad's. Not exactly adventurous."

Carl smiled, his fingers still drumming lightly. "There's no place like home."

His tone was warm, but something about the way his fingers tapped nervously made me push further. "So, where were you born? Where do you call home?"

He hesitated, his fingers twitching as though they had a mind of their own. "Bristol," he said finally. "That's where I was born. My mum and I lived there until she passed away last year. Before that, I was in Australia for almost three years. I came back when she got sick."

I softened at his words. "What about your dad?"

"Never knew him," he said, his voice quieter now. "It was always just me and Mum."

"You must miss her," I said gently.

His eyes clouded for a moment, and I panicked, unsure how to handle a man on the verge of tears. Thankfully, the waitress appeared just then, clearing away our plates and giving Carl a chance to pull himself together. She asked if we wanted dessert, but we both declined and asked for the bill.

"I'm desperate for a ciggie," he said, clearly agitated.

"Oh, yes. I thought there was something different about you—where's your plastic cigarette?"

"Dunno. I must've dropped it last night. I need to get another."

When the waitress returned, I reached for my purse. "I'll get this."

Carl shook his head. "Oh no, you won't. I asked you out, so I'm paying."

"Fine," I said, grinning. "But what about the bill for my car?"

"Your dad took care of that," he said, flashing a cheeky grin.

"You conniving sod!" I laughed. "You tricked me into coming out with you."

"Maybe," he admitted. "But I knew you wouldn't refuse if you thought you owed me."

"Well, as punishment, you can pay for dinner," I said, shaking my head in mock disapproval.

"Deal." He smiled. "So, what do you want to do next?"

I thought for a moment. "What are my options?"

"Well," he said, leaning forward with an exaggeratedly serious expression, "I could take you home and give you a full-body massage... or we could head to the pub."

"Pub it is," I said without hesitation.

"Thought you'd say that," Carl said, pretending to punch the air in mock disappointment.

Leaving the restaurant, I realised how much lighter I felt. Carl's company was easy and uncomplicated, exactly what I needed. For the first time in what felt like forever, I let myself enjoy the feeling of freedom.

***

As we arrived back in Cumberside, I was struck by the throng of people on the footpath, spilling out onto the green in murmuring clusters. The air was thick with unease, their voices rising in hushed urgency as the police blue lights flickered in the distance. Carl parked the car and glanced at the crowd, his brows knitting together.

"What's going on, mate?" he asked a man standing on the pub steps.

The man shook his head, his face pale under the streetlights. "Another woman attacked—same as the rest."

Carl exhaled sharply. "What's this place coming to?"

"Dunno, mate. Dunno." The man sounded weary.

Carl gave the man's shoulder a pat and then gestured for me to follow him into the pub. Inside, it was startlingly quiet compared to the chaos outside. Only a few locals propped up the bar, their voices subdued, and a pair of men played darts at the far end. The thud of the darts hitting the board was the loudest sound in the room.

"I wonder who it was this time," I murmured, feeling a chill creep over me.

"We'll know soon enough." Carl's tone was dark. "News like this doesn't stay secret in a village for long."

I nodded, unsettled. "It feels weird, though—this is the first time something like this has happened since I've been back."

Carl offered a faint smile, trying to lift the mood. "If you want to ditch the pub and take me up on that massage instead, I'm happy to oblige."

"No, thanks!" I laughed, shaking off some of the tension. "How about a game of pool?"

"You're on," Carl said, brightening. "But be warned—I was the snooker champ at the after-school program in Bristol back in 2006."

"Ooh, I'm trembling," I teased, grinning.

"Hey, cheeky," he said with mock indignation.

"Anyway, you must've been a baby in 2006," I said, eyeing him playfully.

He raised his eyebrows. "How old do you think I am?"

I shrugged. "I don't know now, but I was thinking twenty-two? Twenty-three?"

"Bullshit!" He laughed. "Honestly, guess again."

I frowned, studying him. "Alright, go on then—how old?"

"Thirty-one next January," he said with a smirk.

"You're joking!" I said, in surprise. "Well, there goes my excuse not to date you—I was going to say you're too young."

We both burst into laughter, the easy banter lifting the mood even further. Carl ordered a pint of beer, and I stuck to orange juice—no way was I risking another alcohol-fuelled disaster like last night.

We started our game, and it didn't take long for Carl to establish himself as the clear winner. My attempts at pool were laughable at best, and we were soon doubled over in hysterics at my hopeless efforts.

"Alright," Carl said, leaning on his cue with a wicked grin. "If I win the next game, I'm taking you home and having my wicked way with you."

"Oh, how could a girl possibly refuse when you're so masterful?" I scoffed, rolling my eyes.

But Carl's grin faltered, his gaze shifting over my shoulder. His playful demeanour evaporated, replaced by something wary. I turned slowly, my heart sinking.

James stood a few feet away, looking gorgeous in a fitted grey t-shirt and pale blue jeans. His dark hair was tousled, and his face was set in a thunderous expression.

"Oh, hi, James," I said, trying to sound casual. "I didn't see you there."

"Geraldine," he said with a curt nod, his voice tight.

"You remember Carl?" I said, glancing between them. Carl's face was a picture of amusement, while James barely acknowledged him.

"Unfortunately." James's tone was icy.

An awkward silence settled between us, broken only by the distant thud of darts hitting the board.

"I wanted to say I had a great time last night," I said, trying to ease the tension.

James didn't respond, his expression unreadable.

"Do you want a game?" I gestured to the pool table.

"No, thanks," James said. "Sounds like you've already made a bet I wouldn't want to be part of."

My face flamed as his words sank in. Of course, he'd overheard Carl's joke about taking me home. I could feel the heat rising in my cheeks as I stammered, "It was just a joke—" I eyeballed Carl, and smiled before turning back to James. "Did you hear about the attack?" I was desperate to change the subject.

James nodded, his expression darkening. "Yeah, I just got back from the hospital. She's shaken up but alive. Thank God he didn't cut her this time. She's badly beaten and was left tied up since last night."

"Oh, my God. Who was it?" I asked, my stomach churning.

"Sammy Palin," he said. "Stephy's younger sister—you remember her?"

It took me a moment to place the name. "Oh, yeah. She's a couple of years younger than us, isn't she?"

James nodded, his mouth tightening. He downed what remained in his glass before placing it on the bar with a thump. "Goodnight, Geraldine. Carl." His voice was clipped as he turned and walked out.

Carl burst into laughter the moment James was out the door, his laughter so loud it turned heads.

"Shush!" I hissed, glaring at him. "What the hell's so funny?"

"His face!" Carl managed between guffaws. "I felt like a naughty schoolboy."

"He's not that bad," I said, though I couldn't suppress a small smile.

After a few more games, we called it a night. Carl, ever the gentleman, let me win the final round, sparing me from becoming his "trophy." As if.

We left the pub, the chill night air wrapping around us as we headed to his car. Across the green, the flicker of blue lights caught my eye.

"Is that Auntie Beryl's house?" I asked, pointing.

"What the…" Carl muttered, climbing out of the car and running toward the commotion. I followed, my heart pounding.

When we reached the house, a police officer was banging on the door. Carl called out, "Hey!" and the officer turned. My breath caught as I recognised him—Vinny, from school. Except now, the puppy fat was gone, replaced by lean muscle and a jawline straight out of a Hollywood blockbuster.

"Ah, Carl," Vinny said, his expression unreadable. "I'm going to need you to come with me to the station. We have a few questions regarding the recent assaults."

Carl's face fell. "What? You've got to be kidding me—why would you want to talk to me?"

Vinny's grip tightened on Carl's shoulder. "I'd advise you to cooperate."

"It's obviously a mistake," I said quickly. "Just go with him, Carl. You'll be okay."

But as Carl's laughter faded and he allowed himself to be led to the car, a cold weight settled in my stomach. Something about this didn't feel right.

Chapter Twelve

Geri

I STOOD IN THE driveway, the icy chill of the night air biting through my coat as I watched the taillights of the police car fade into the distance, taking Carl with it. My arms hung limply by my sides, my thoughts a tangled mess of disbelief and fear. What had just happened? Vinny's face flashed in my mind—serious, almost regretful. Why did he have to take Carl in? What was he hiding?

Inside, the house was eerily quiet. Auntie Beryl's bungalow loomed in the shadows, its curtains drawn tightly shut. She must have been sound asleep—otherwise, there was no way she wouldn't have come outside after the commotion Vinny made. She wasn't one to miss a neighbourhood drama. I decided not to disturb her tonight. No good would come of waking her. Besides, Carl would likely be back by morning. Wouldn't he?

I turned toward my house, surprised to see warm light spilling from the lounge windows. At this hour, I'd expected everyone to be in bed. As I opened the door, the familiar smell of home greeted me. But the atmosphere felt anything but familiar.

Mum and Dad were sitting in the lounge. Mum perched stiffly on the edge of the armchair, her face set in a scowl, while Dad leaned back on the sofa, his hand resting on his forehead. The tension was palpable, like static in the air before a storm.

"Hello, you two," I said, stepping into the room. "I thought you'd be in bed by now."

Mum's head snapped toward me, her eyes narrowing. "Oh, here she is—our resident loose woman," she sneered, her voice dripping with venom.

I froze, the words slicing through me. "Mum, what—"

"Enough, Grace," Dad interrupted sharply. His tone was firm, but his weariness was evident. "If you're angry, take it out on me, but leave our daughter out of it."

"What's wrong? What's happened?" I asked, my voice trembling.

Dad stood and walked toward me, his hand gently brushing against my hair before he kissed my cheek. "Your mum's just got one of her headaches again. Nothing to worry about, love. Why don't you head up to bed?"

"Is she all right? Can I do anything?" I glanced at Mum, but she avoided my eyes, staring daggers at the floor instead.

"I am here, you know!" she snapped, her voice rising. "Both of you jabbering away like I'm deaf!"

Dad ignored her outburst and lowered his voice. "No, she's had her medication. She'll be fine soon. Go on, love. Get some rest." He ushered me toward the stairs.

At the bottom of the staircase, I hesitated. "There's been another assault, Dad. Carl's been taken in for questioning. Should I—should I do something?"

He frowned deeply. "Carl? No way. Not in a million years. That lad wouldn't have anything to do with something like this."

"That's what I said. But Vinny must have had a reason, right?"

Dad sighed, rubbing his temples. "Let's see what tomorrow brings. Best you get your head down. We'll know more in the morning."

As I climbed the stairs, I paused again. "Dad? Is everything okay with Mum?"

He looked over his shoulder toward the lounge door as though making sure she couldn't hear. "To be honest, I don't know. These headaches are getting worse, and some of the things she says..." He shook his head. "Grace isn't herself lately. She called one of Beryl's friends a slapper tonight."

I stared at him, horrified. "She didn't."

He nodded. "She did." He gave me a weak, tired smile. "Goodnight, Geri."

***

THE NEXT MORNING, I went to Auntie Beryl's house, tapping on her kitchen window. Through the glass, I could see her bustling around the sink, her grey curls bobbing as she scrubbed dishes. She turned at the sound, smiled warmly, and gestured for me to come in.

"No need to knock, lovey," she said, stepping back to let me through the door. "Come on in."

Her house was exactly as it always was—a chaotic treasure trove of knick-knacks, family photos, and mismatched furniture. Mum would have a coronary if she ever had to sit in this room for more than five minutes. But Auntie Beryl's clutter wasn't dirty—far from it. Every surface gleamed, each trinket polished to perfection.

"So, where is he?" she asked, glancing past me toward the door.

"Who?"

"Who indeed," she chuckled, raising an eyebrow. "Carl. I saw his bed wasn't slept in. Although I didn't think your mum would allow any hanky-panky under her roof."

I flushed. "Carl's not here?"

She frowned, her face clouding with confusion. "No, love. Wasn't he with you?"

"He was, but…" I hesitated. "He got taken to the police station last night. Vinny said he needed to ask him some questions about those attacks."

Her watery grey eyes widened in alarm. "Our Carl? Taken in?" She wiped her hands on her floral pinafore, her movements quick and nervous. "What for? He wouldn't hurt a fly, lovey. You know that."

"I know," I said quickly. "That's what I told Dad. I think maybe Vinny just needs his help with something. Maybe Carl saw something at the pub."

She nodded slowly, though her face betrayed her worry. "Aye, that'll be it. He's just helping out. Our Carl wouldn't be mixed up in anything nasty."

***

A wave of unease washed over me as I reached the hotel. James was my only hope of figuring out why Carl had been hauled off by Vinny, but I wasn't sure if he'd even take me seriously.

The reception desk was manned by none other than Shelly Spears, or as she'd been cruelly dubbed during our school days, "Shelly-pig-face-Spears." Kids could be monstrous, but adulthood had been kind to Shelly. Her nose, now a delicate slope, was a clear improvement.

Her poise and polished look made her almost unrecognisable, but her wide, pretty, dark eyes gave her away.

"Shelly! Fancy seeing you here," I said, genuinely surprised.

She glanced up, a flicker of recognition in her expression. "Geraldine," she said coolly, nodding. "Back in the area, I see. We all gravitate back here at some time or other—including you."

"That's true," I agreed. "I'm surprised how many of us from school ended up staying—or coming back. For all its faults, it's nice to be home."

Her smile softened. "You're looking well, Geri."

"Thanks, Shell. So are you." I hesitated. "Listen, I need to talk to James Dunn. Is he in? Could you tell me his room number?"

Her professional smile faltered slightly. "I'm not supposed to give out room numbers, you know. But I can call him for you."

I sucked in a breath, weighing my options. "The thing is, Shell, I'd rather just pop up myself. It's only me. You know I won't do anything to get you in trouble."

She hesitated, her gaze scanning my face, searching for any sign of deceit. Finally, she relented with a small sigh. "Sixteen," she whispered. "But you didn't hear it from me."

"You have my word," I said with a grateful smile.

Following her directions, I climbed the stairs to the first floor. The hallway was lined with identical doors, but number sixteen stood at the far end. As I approached, two chambermaids were loitering near James's door, their giggles giving them away. They froze when they noticed me and quickly scurried off with their trolley.

I knocked lightly.

"Not today, girls," James called from inside, his voice carrying a note of irritation. A moment later, the door opened, and he blinked in surprise when he saw me. "Oh, it's you."

He stepped back, letting the door swing wide. With a slight tilt of his head, he invited me in.

The room was simple but spacious, with a king-sized bed and navy blue accents that matched the upholstery of the small sofa and chairs near the window. The left side of the bed was rumpled, while the right side remained pristine, untouched. A desk to the side of the room was piled with papers and a laptop.

As I took in the details, I felt James's eyes on me. His smirk made it clear he'd caught me inspecting his space.

"So, I presume you came to see me, not to check out the hotel?"

"Yes, sorry to drop by unannounced," I said, perching on the edge of the sofa. "I wasn't sure you'd want to see me."

He frowned. "Why wouldn't I?"

"You seemed annoyed with me last night."

"I'm not annoyed," he said, though his expression hinted otherwise.

"Well, good, because I need your help."

"With what?" He sat on the edge of the bed, leaning forward slightly.

"When Carl and I left here last night, Vinny picked him up for questioning about the attacks."

James's face darkened. "The rapes?" He motioned to the papers on his desk.

"Yes. I think so. Vinny wasn't specific, but I can't think of anything else he'd be referring to."

James leaned back, rubbing his chin thoughtfully. "How well do you know Carl?"

I frowned. "He's Auntie Beryl's nephew. Works as a mechanic. Quiet guy."

James shook his head. "That's not what I asked. How well do you know him?"

The distinction wasn't lost on me. "Not that well," I admitted. "But he's a decent guy. I can't imagine he's capable of something like this."

James's gaze sharpened. "Don't kid yourself, Geraldine. The kind of person who does this? They're calculated, and intelligent. You wouldn't suspect them unless they wanted you to."

"Do you think Carl did it?" I asked, bristling.

"To be honest, no." James exhaled heavily. "The descriptions of the attacker don't fit Carl. He's too short, and the rapist has a limp. Unless Carl's hiding a serious injury, it's not him."

Relief washed over me. "Then why would Vinny take him in?"

James shrugged, getting to his feet and heading for the desk. "Vinny's probably grasping at straws. I told you I've been looking into this, and I'm pretty certain this rapist has been active for years—at least seven. He started small, gaining confidence."

"Carl's only been in the area for a few months. Before that, he was in Australia for three years."

"Then he's not our guy," James said firmly.

"We need to tell Vinny," I insisted.

James sighed. "He won't listen to me. The best thing we can do is wait it out. Vinny doesn't have enough evidence to charge Carl, so he'll have to release him soon."

I nodded, desperate to believe him. "Thanks, James. I owe you."

"Anytime," he said.

Before I left, I leaned up on my toes and kissed his cheek. His expression softened briefly, but he said nothing as I slipped out the door, my mind racing with the possibilities ahead.

Chapter Thirteen

James

JAMES EXHALED SHARPLY, RUNNING a hand through his hair as he stood by the window, staring out at nothing in particular. "Fuck!" The anger bubbling inside him wasn't directed at Geraldine—it was at himself.

"Fuck," he muttered again, shaking his head. He couldn't believe how easily he'd let her get under his skin.

Things had been going so well Saturday night. A dinner that had felt more natural than any date he'd been on in years, laughter over shared stories, even the way her eyes had sparkled when she teased him. But, as was the theme of his life, just as the pages of his personal romance novel seemed ready to turn, a cheeky, grinning mechanic with boyish charm had stepped in to win her over.

"You should be writing bloody romance novels, you pillock," James muttered with a dry laugh. He knew better than to pine after someone who didn't see him the same way, but here he was, staring after her as she walked back to her parents' cottage like some lovesick teenager.

It wasn't as if he had trouble getting women; quite the opposite. Shelly Spears, for instance, had made her interest in him embarrassingly clear. Since her surgery, she was undoubtedly attractive. He had already witnessed her hanging around reception, waiting for him to make a move. But Shelly wasn't who he wanted.

James sighed, his focus remained on Geraldine's retreating figure. She moved as if she were carrying a mountain on her back, her steps heavy with the weight of it. And now, to top it all off, she was asking for his help with Carl, the new bloke who'd apparently swept her off her feet.

Any other man would've told her to piss off. Hell, a more vindictive man might have even help Vinny pin the case on Carl just to keep him out of the picture. But James wasn't that man. He might not like the situation, but Geraldine's desperation was genuine, and he wasn't about to leave her stranded.

Turning back to his desk, he refocused his energy on the case. The stack of files in front of him felt heavier than usual. Five attacks, all vicious, all horrifying.

The fourth attack had been the worst so far—a brutal, frenzied assault that had left the victim clinging to life. Each attack seemed to escalate in violence until that one, but the fifth attack had been different. While still severe, it hadn't reached the same level of brutality. The victim, Samantha Payne, had suffered a traumatic head injury, but it wasn't life-threatening, and she hadn't been raped.

James frowned at the forensic report. There was no doubt in his mind it was the same attacker—the MO, the balaclava, and, most notably, the limp all matched previous reports. But the details were inconsistent. Samantha, heavily intoxicated at the time, had been frustratingly vague in her statement. She'd mentioned the limp but couldn't confirm which leg it affected. In her haze, she'd said, "It looked like both."

The other victims had all reported the limp, too, but no one had pinpointed it to one side. And then there were the boots—size eleven

Caterpillar boots. James held the photo of the sole imprint up to the light, the deep tread unmistakable. The pattern was as distinctive as a fingerprint to someone who knew what to look for.

But Carl didn't fit. Not in height. Not in build. Not even in demeanour. The only physical detail that might connect him was his shoe size. It wasn't enough—at least not to James.

He pushed the papers aside and stared at the wall, frustration building. If Vinny was hell-bent on making Carl the fall guy for these assaults, he might not care about the glaring holes in his theory. James knew that Geraldine was right to worry. Vinny was stubborn to the point of recklessness, and if he was fixated on Carl, proving otherwise wouldn't be easy.

He stood and paced the room. If Vinny didn't have enough evidence, he'd have to release Carl soon. But James couldn't shake the feeling that the real attacker was still out there, watching, waiting.

And if Geraldine stayed tangled up in this mess, she might not see him coming until it was too late.

Chapter Fourteen

Geri

BACK HOME, I BUSIED myself in the kitchen, trying to focus on chopping vegetables rather than the tight knot in my chest.

Mum was still under the weather and had gone upstairs for a lie-down, her pale face etched with exhaustion.

Dad was pottering in the garden, clearing out the flower beds.

The familiar, mundane rhythm of home should have been comforting, but it wasn't enough to drown out the anxiety rattling in my brain.

The doorbell rang, its sharp trill startling me. Wiping my hands on a towel, I hurried to answer it. When I opened the door, relief surged through me.

Carl stood there, looking decidedly worse for wear. His face was pale, his shoulders sagged, and there were dark smudges under his eyes.

"Well, I am glad to see you," I said, stepping aside to let him enter. "Come on in."

He gave me a weak smile as he shuffled into the lounge, collapsing in a heap onto the sofa like a marionette whose strings had been cut.

"You look terrible. Have you been awake all night?" I sat on the edge of the armchair.

He nodded, rubbing a hand over his face. "Yeah, I'm done in. I'll go home to bed soon, but I thought I'd best tell you I was back first. It felt awful getting carted off like that. Must have been the worst date in history." His smile flickered briefly, though it didn't quite reach his eyes.

I laughed. "It was certainly eventful. But I was worried sick about you."

"Yeah, I figured you would be." He sighed.

"I called in to see James. He told me you don't fit the profile *or* match the attacker's description. He said he knew they'd have no choice but to let you go."

"He's right. But..." he hesitated, his expression darkened.

"Something's still bothering you, isn't it?"

"Yeah," he admitted, leaning forward, his elbows resting on his knees. "It's odd. Turns out I've met all the victims at some point without even realising it."

A chill skittered down my spine. "What do you mean?"

"Apparently, the first woman didn't have any recent photos, so the ones plastered all over the news are ten years out of date. I didn't recognise her at first, but the others? Yeah, I've crossed paths with them. Fixed their cars, chatted to one at the bar, met another at a cafe in Kirkby Mayor just last week."

I scratched my head. "Were you even in the area when all the attacks happened?"

"Yes. The first woman was attacked the weekend after I arrived at my aunt's house.

"Carl, this isn't a big place," I said carefully. "It's not unusual to run into the same people, especially if you're working in a customer-facing job."

He nodded but didn't look convinced. "I said the same thing to the cops. But that's not the worst part."

"No?"

He leaned back, his face pale as he looked at me. "They found my plastic cigarette."

My stomach dropped. "The one you said went missing?"

"Yeah." He nodded grimly. "They found it in the house of the fifth victim yesterday."

I stared at him, my thoughts racing. "But how? That doesn't make any sense. When did you last have it?"

"Saturday night in Penrith," he said. "When I woke up Sunday morning, it was gone. She was attacked early Sunday morning. I don't understand how it got there."

Neither did I. The room seemed to tilt slightly as I tried to piece it together. "I remember you had it on Saturday night. You were using it outside the restaurant."

"Exactly." Carl rubbed his face. "It doesn't add up."

I reached over, resting a hand on his arm. "You look shattered. Go home and get some sleep. We'll figure this out when you're feeling better."

He hesitated, his eyes searching mine. "You do believe me, don't you, Geri? I had nothing to do with any of it."

"Of course, I believe you. If the police had any real evidence, you'd still be in custody. They've got nothing."

"Maybe," he said, though he didn't sound convinced. "I'm off to Auntie Beryl's now. I bet she's been worrying herself sick."

I followed him to the front door, only for both of us to jump when someone knocked sharply on it. My heart leapt into my throat.

When I opened it, Vinny leaned casually against the doorframe.

"Geraldine," he said, his voice low and smooth.

"For God's sake, Vinny, give him a bloody break." I stepped protectively in front of Carl. "He's only just got back."

Vinny's eyes narrowed briefly before he glanced past me, spotting Carl. His smirk returned, and the look he gave me made my stomach do an unwelcome flip.

"I'm not here for him." Vinny's gaze locked onto mine. "I'm here for you."

"Me?" My voice came out far too high.

He nodded, his lopsided smile disarming. "Can I come in?"

I stepped aside, my pulse racing.

Carl hesitated, his eyes darting between us. "You want me to stay?"

"No, it's okay." I smiled. "Go get some rest. I'll see you later."

Reluctantly, Carl stepped outside. Vinny's smirk deepened as he watched him leave.

"What can I do for you, Vinny?" I asked, leading him into the lounge.

"Just a few questions about Saturday night," he said, lowering himself onto the sofa. His movements were deliberate, and I couldn't help but notice how his tailored shirt clung to his broad shoulders.

I perched on the armchair, suddenly aware of how small the room felt.

The conversation was routine at first, his questions focused and professional, but there was an undercurrent between us that I couldn't ignore. Every glance, every pause, felt loaded. By the time we reached the front door, I was barely holding myself together.

His hand covered mine as I reached for the lock, his other hand braced against the wall behind me. He leaned in his mouth close to my ear. "Now that's out of the way, how about dinner? Friday night? I'll even stay local."

My breath caught. His proximity was intoxicating, his minty breath brushing my cheek. "Maybe," I whispered.

He smiled, and before I could process what was happening, his lips brushed mine—a featherlight touch that left me reeling.

The creak of the stairs made us spring apart. My mother stood at the top, her disapproving eyes taking in the scene. Vinny didn't flinch, offering her a polite nod before turning back to me.

"I'll pick you up at seven," he said, his voice laced with quiet confidence. Then he was gone, leaving me standing in the hallway, my heart pounding like a drum.

Chapter Fifteen

Geri

MUM DIDN'T HAVE TO say a single word—her eyes did all the talking once Vinny had gone. They were sharp and unforgiving, a judgmental glare that pierced straight through me.

"What?" I snapped, crossing my arms defensively.

"You've been back less than a week," she said, banging plates into the dishwasher like they'd personally offended her. "And I catch you canoodling with man number three. I'm beginning to understand what's wrong with your marriage."

The accusation stung, and I sucked in a sharp breath, trying to push down the hurt. "You know nothing, and it's really sad that my own mum can say such hurtful things."

"I say it as I see it, Geraldine."

Her voice was clipped, final, as though she had declared some universal truth that couldn't be contested.

I shook my head, disbelief and anger twisting in my chest. "Weren't you the one who used to spout all that crap about, 'If you've got nothing kind to say, don't say anything at all?' Maybe you should practice what you preach, Mother."

Without waiting for a reply, I stomped upstairs, the old carpet muffling my steps just enough to keep from slamming them as hard as I wanted to.

***

THE REST OF THE day and half the evening passed in silence. I stayed holed up in my room, staring at the peeling wallpaper and wondering how my life had become such a mess.

At ten o'clock, a soft knock on my door startled me. I was surprised to see Dad standing there when I opened it.

"I wasn't sure if you were home or not," he said. "I've been worrying, what with all the terrible things happening around here lately."

"Yeah, I'm here." I stepped back to let him in. "Nowhere to go."

"Have you eaten anything?" His voice was gentle, but there was an edge of concern that made my chest ache.

"I'll grab something after Mum goes to bed. She's been awful to me again today."

Dad sighed and rubbed the back of his neck. "I'm sorry, lass. She's... she's been getting worse. She went to see Doctor Jessop, and he gave her some medicine, but I don't think it's helping much."

"I noticed that you've been staying out of the way more and more."

He shrugged, a weak smile flickering across his face. "Between you and me, I'm terrified."

"Oh, Dad." I pulled him into a hug, holding him tight. He smelled like stale coffee and fresh air, comforting and familiar.

"She's probably just going through the change or something," I said, though the words felt hollow. I didn't really know much about menopause, but it was the only explanation I could muster, and it could be true—Mum was only fifty-eight—ten years younger than Dad.

"Yeah, maybe you're right." He kissed the top of my head before heading toward the door. "Get yourself something to eat. Mum's already in bed."

"Will do. Thanks, Dad."

I followed him to the landing and watched as he slipped into their bedroom, the door creaking softly behind him.

The kitchen was quiet, save for the hum of the fridge and the occasional creak of the house settling. I filled the kettle and dropped a couple of slices of bread into the toaster. My stomach growled loudly, reminding me I hadn't eaten all day. Between Carl's drama, Vinny's awkward seduction, and Mum's sharp words, my appetite had been non-existent.

As the toast popped, a loud tap on the kitchen window made me jump. My heart thudded in my chest as I pulled the curtain aside. Carl's cheeky grin stared back at me, his face pressed against the glass in a ridiculous, distorted expression that made me laugh despite myself.

I opened the door and motioned for him to come in, placing a finger to my lips. "Hi," I whispered. "I was beginning to think you'd decided not to bother."

"I've been asleep all day. Wasn't sure if it was too late to pop by." He scratched the back of his neck awkwardly. "Didn't want your mum giving me the evil eye again."

"You and me both. She's unbearable lately. I need to get my life together and find somewhere else to live."

He raised an eyebrow. "We could get a place together."

I barked out a laugh, shaking my head. "Yeah, right."

"I mean it." He was serious now. "Auntie Beryl's off on holiday next week. You could come stay with me for a bit. Give it a trial run. No funny business—just flatmates."

I hesitated, buttering the toast slowly. "I've never had a flatmate before."

"Then you've never lived," he said, grinning.

Despite myself, I smiled back. Maybe he was right.

"So, what happened with Vinny?" he asked.

"Nothing much. He just wanted to check your story. See if I had seen you in Penrith on Saturday and if so, what time."

"What did you tell him?"

"The truth, although I wasn't sure of the time."

"Anything else?"

I shook my head, but I was a rubbish liar.

He looked worried. "What else?" he insisted.

"Oh, nothing about you. He asked me out on a date on Friday."

"Talk about kicking a man when he's down," he said, a smile behind his eyes.

"Don't be silly. We're just friends, Carl."

"I know that. But fancy you dating the enemy."

"Vinny's not the enemy. He was just doing his job."

He shrugged one shoulder. "Oh well, I guess you know what you're doing. You've known him long enough."

He pulled a cigarette packet and a lighter from his jacket pocket.

"So, you're smoking again?"

"Yeah. Can't help it. I know that stupid fake ciggie looked ridiculous, but it really worked."

"Why didn't you just buy another?"

"Don't remember where I got it from now. I probably acquired it from someone's car."

"You mean you nicked it?" I shook my head, shocked at his audacity and hard-faced answer. "You could just look on Amazon, like any normal person would do."

"Never thought of that. Coming out while I have a smoke?"

Once I'd finished my toast, I followed him into the garden, the cool night air brushing against my skin, Carl lit a cigarette, and the acrid smell turned my stomach. I stepped back. Threatening to barf all over the marigolds.

"Sorry, Carl. That's making me sick. I'll head back inside."

He quickly stubbed it out, tossing the butt over the fence. "All right, all right. I'm done. Don't start moaning."

I rolled my eyes but laughed. With his boyish charm, I found it impossible to stay mad at him.

"Is it sorted, then?" he asked. "You'll move in next week?"

I hesitated for a moment before nodding. "Why not? We can give it a go. But if I end up doing all the cooking and cleaning, I'm out."

He grinned, his eyes lighting up with excitement. "Deal."

As we headed back inside, I couldn't help but feel a flicker of hope. Maybe this would work. Maybe, just maybe, I could start putting the pieces of my life back together.

Chapter Sixteen

Geri

Friday had arrived before I'd even had a chance to panic about what to wear for my date with Vinny.

If I were back in Manchester, I'd already have been through my usual night-out routine—a leg wax, a manicure, maybe even a Brazilian, given the simmering tension between Vinny and me on Monday. But here in Cumbria, such luxuries weren't as accessible. I'd have to drive miles for an appointment. In the end, I made do with a face mask from the local chemist and a makeshift grooming session in the bathroom.

Carl hadn't mentioned my date with Vinny again, which suited me fine. I was nervous enough without him adding to my stress. He had, however, told Auntie Beryl about me staying at her place while she went away, and she was more than happy with the arrangement. Now, the only hurdle left was telling Mum.

Mum had been distant since our argument on Monday. She'd spent most of the week in her bedroom. While it was a relief not to be walking on eggshells around her sharp tongue, her withdrawal was unsettling in its own way. Tonight, she'd be off to bingo with Beryl, and I needed to speak to her before Beryl spilled the beans.

I made a cup of tea and carried it upstairs. Mum was sitting in the wicker chair by the window, staring out as if she could see a world beyond the rain-dappled glass.

"Cup of tea, Mum?" I set the mug on the windowsill.

"Thanks, love," she said, her voice unusually soft.

So far, so good. She was being civil, at least.

"Looking forward to bingo tonight?" I attempted to coax her into a proper conversation.

"Hmm? Oh, yes," she murmured, her gaze still distant.

I perched on the edge of the bed, admiring the red and cream patchwork bedspread. "Mum, I was thinking," I began cautiously.

She glanced up, a flicker of interest in her eyes.

"You know how Beryl's going away next week?"

"Yes." Her brow furrowed slightly.

"Well, I thought I might stay at hers while she's gone."

"What on earth for?" she asked, though there was no edge to her tone.

"Company for Carl. And I figured you might enjoy a bit of peace and quiet."

She shrugged, her expression unreadable. "Do as you like," she said finally before returning her gaze to the window.

Relief washed over me. That was easier than I'd expected. I stood up and smiled faintly. "I'm going for a bath, Mum. I'm out tonight, too."

"Oh, are you, love? That's nice," she said absently.

I paused in the doorway, stunned by her lack of interrogation. Normally, she'd have had a dozen probing questions ready to fire. Her silence was almost more unsettling than her sharpness.

Locking myself in the bathroom, I applied the face mask and ran a steaming bath. As the tub filled, I exfoliated, shaved, pruned, and plucked, transforming myself into someone who, with any luck, looked date-ready. Vinny hadn't mentioned what we'd be doing, but I assumed dinner was on the cards. Despite that, I couldn't bring myself to eat anything beforehand. My stomach had been in knots all week.

Emerging from the bathroom, I found the house oddly quiet. Mum had already left for bingo, and I could hear the low hum of the television downstairs, where Dad was stationed.

I dressed carefully, opting for black trousers and a coral-coloured blouse. It felt dressy enough without being over the top. A light sweep of mascara, a touch of blusher, and a dab of lip gloss completed the look. With ten minutes to spare, I made my way downstairs.

Dad glanced up from his armchair, his face softening. "You look pretty, lass."

"Thanks, Dad." I perched on the sofa beside him, feeling the nerves fluttering in my chest.

"Where are you off to, then?"

"I've got a date," I admitted, trying to sound casual. "With Vinny."

His eyebrows rose slightly. "I see. Your mum didn't mention it. Does she know?"

"I told her I was going out, but she didn't ask any questions."

He frowned, his lips pulling down at the corners. "Very odd."

"I know," I said with a shrug. "I also told her I'll be staying at Beryl's next week while she's away. She didn't seem to mind that either."

"Well, lass, as long as it makes you happy."

The sound of the doorbell sent a jolt through me. My heart skipped. "That'll be Vinny. See you later, Dad."

"Have a good night, lass." His voice was warm with affection.

"Thanks, Dad." I kissed him on the cheek before heading for the door.

My jaw nearly hit the ground when I saw Vinny. He was dressed to absolute perfection in a tailored navy-blue suit that hugged his frame in all the right places. The matching waistcoat and crisp white shirt made him look every bit the cover model for some upscale men's magazine. His signature hairstyle, just slightly tousled but undoubtedly deliberate, paired with his designer stubble, oozed effortless charm. It was impossible not to notice how even his deep blue eyes seemed to complement the suit like he was custom-built for moments like this.

"Geri, you look beautiful," he said, his voice low and smooth like honey poured over gravel.

"As do you." My voice came out more breathless than I intended, and suddenly, I felt like a scruffy teenager playing dress-up next to him.

"Shall we walk to the restaurant or would you rather I take the car?" he asked, that playful glint in his eye betraying how well he knew me already.

I laughed, hoping to cover how much his presence was affecting me. "It's only a five-minute walk."

"I know, but I wasn't sure what shoes you'd be wearing." He tilted his head as if to examine them. His grin widened, and the twinkle in his eyes made it clear he'd heard all about my high-heel disaster from last week.

"Not too high this time," I replied, sticking out one foot to show him my modest inch-high wedges.

He chuckled and held out his arm. "Then, shall we?"

The short walk to the restaurant felt longer, though not unpleasantly so. The crisp evening air brushed against my cheeks, but all I could focus on was the warmth of Vinny's arm linked with mine and the occasional scent of his aftershave—subtle, woodsy, and intoxicating. As we reached the entrance, he opened the door with an easy confidence, ushering me inside like we were stepping into a movie scene.

"I've made a reservation," he told the waitress, a young woman whose face lit up when she saw him.

"Of course, Mr Martin. Right this way," she chirped, nearly tripping over herself as she led us to a table tucked in the back corner of the room.

Her infatuation was almost comical, but I bit my tongue, suppressing the urge to laugh and tell her to pick her jaw up off the floor. At least I wasn't the only one who found Vinny utterly magnetic, though he appeared oblivious to the attention.

Once we were seated, he poured us each a glass of white wine, swirling and tasting his first sip like a pro. But it almost gave me the ick.

"So, tell me, Geri," he said, leaning slightly forward, his voice lowering just enough to make it feel like a secret. "What's brought you back to this part of the world?"

I took a sip of wine for courage. "Long story short? Simon and I broke up."

His brow lifted slightly, though his expression remained kind. "I was surprised when I heard that."

"So was I." My laugh was short, bitter.

"Not your decision then?"

"Oh, it was." I set the glass down with more force than I'd intended. "The moment I found out he was seeing someone else."

"Ah." He nodded, the understanding in his eyes softening me. "That makes sense."

"What about you?" I was desperate to steer the conversation away from Simon. "Have you always stayed around here?"

"I went away for a bit," he admitted. "But I missed the place. My mum and my sister, Carol, are still here. Carol's got two boys I adore, and I help her out when I can."

"That's nice of you. She's lucky to have you."

He shrugged as though it was nothing. "It's family. You know how it is."

I nodded. "Yeah, I do."

The food arrived before I could delve too deeply into what he'd just said, though his offhand comment about helping Carol stuck with me. There was something comforting about the way he spoke of family, as though it was as natural to him as breathing.

Dinner was exquisite. I devoured my salmon, each bite rich and buttery, while Vinny barely touched his chicken. Instead, he watched me, his eyes glinting with amusement as I raved about the food.

"You enjoyed that, I see," he said, leaning back in his chair with a satisfied smile.

"Can you blame me? This is worlds apart from the pub food I'm used to." I gestured toward his plate. "You didn't like yours?"

He glanced down at his nearly full plate, then back up at me with a look that made my stomach flip. "Oh, I liked it just fine. But I'm not that hungry. Not for food, anyway."

Heat crept up my neck as I broke eye contact, suddenly very interested in my wineglass. Vinny was making his intentions clear—he found me attractive, which was a huge improvement to my last two attempts at a love life.

The evening passed in a blur of laughter and nostalgia, peppered with moments where his gaze lingered on mine just long enough to make my pulse race.

"You know," I said, swirling the last sip of wine in my glass, "even though you've changed a lot since school, I'd have recognised you anywhere. Funny, isn't it?"

"You too," Vinny said, leaning back in his chair. His eyes studied me in a way that made me both self-conscious and flattered. "Although I don't really think people change that much. Their facial features stay the same. We just get older—or fatter—or both." He grinned, the dimple on his left cheek making an unexpected and devastating appearance.

"Or, in your case, thinner," I pointed out, gesturing at his annoyingly trim physique.

His grin turned sheepish. "Yeah, I was a bit of a porker, wasn't I?"

"Compared to now? Yes," I teased, relishing the way his cheeks flushed slightly.

"Compared to anything, Geri," he corrected, laughing. "I was a porker."

"Okay, fine," I relented, holding up my hands. "You were... a little overweight."

He raised an eyebrow. "Little? Be honest, I was one cream bun away from having my own orbit."

I couldn't help but laugh, the warmth between us growing with each banter-filled exchange. "Alright, you win. But I wouldn't say everyone stays the same. Take James Dunn, for example. I was chatting to him for ages and didn't even recognise him. He's changed heaps."

I didn't miss the way Vinny's expression darkened at the mention of James. His jaw tensed almost imperceptibly, but the change was there.

"What?" I asked, leaning forward. "Don't you like him?"

He shrugged. "Not fussed either way."

I gave him a slow, deliberate nod, my eyes fixed on his. "Uh-huh. Sure, Vinny."

His lips twitched, but he held his ground. "Don't look at me like that," he said, his voice a mix of exasperation and amusement.

"Well, you're not the only one who can tell when someone's spinning them a line, you know," I shot back, crossing my arms and raising an eyebrow.

That did it. He laughed, his eyes crinkling in a way that made him look both boyish and ridiculously attractive. "You're relentless," he said, shaking his head.

"Am I wrong?"

His laughter faded into a grin, and then he sighed. "It's stupid. Something that happened years ago, but it really pissed me off."

"So, what was it?"

He hesitated, rolling his glass between his palms. "You promise not to laugh?"

"I promise," I said solemnly, though I already felt my resolve weakening.

He leaned forward, dropping his voice like he was confessing a state secret. "He laughed at me in the showers. Told Suzie Daikin I had a little todger." To illustrate, he wiggled his little finger.

I bit down on my lip so hard it hurt, but it was no use. A laugh exploded out of me, sharp and loud.

"You promised!" he protested, sitting back with an exaggerated huff, his arms crossing over his chest like a petulant child.

"I'm sorry," I gasped, trying to pull myself together. "I'm sorry. It's just..." Another laugh escaped before I could stop it, and soon I was bent over the table, clutching my stomach.

His mouth twitched, fighting his own amusement, but he held on longer than I expected. Finally, my relentless laughter broke him, and his deep chuckle joined mine.

Before I knew it, we were both laughing so hard that tears streamed down my cheeks. The absurdity of the moment—of two grown adults in fits of laughter over a decades-old schoolboy insult—made it impossible to stop.

"God, you're a menace," he said through his laughter, shaking his head.

I wiped at my damp cheeks, trying to catch my breath. "I can't help it. It's just... it's you. I can't believe you've carried that grudge all this time."

He smirked, his eyes twinkling. "It was a matter of principle. My pride was at stake."

"Your pride," I repeated, dissolving into one last burst of giggles. "Alright, alright. I'm done, I promise."

"Fuck, speak of the devil," Vinny muttered, his voice low enough that only I could hear.

Curious, I followed his gaze and felt my stomach plummet when I saw James striding into the restaurant with Shelly-Pigface-Spears clinging to his arm. Her laugh was loud and fake, the kind that grated on your nerves and made you want to claw at your ears.

I blinked a few times, then quickly grabbed a napkin to dab at my tear-streaked face, trying to compose myself. The universe clearly had a twisted sense of humour. James—my utterly disastrous, kind-of ex—showing up on a date while I was here with Vinny? What were the odds?

Still, I couldn't deny the twinge of jealousy in my chest, which irritated me to no end. What right did I have to feel like this? It wasn't like James and I were anything more than mates—he made that blatantly clear. Besides, I was on my third date of the week. How could I possibly comment?

"Thank you for not laughing, by the way," Vinny said, snapping me out of my thoughts.

I glanced at him, and the amusement bubbled up in my chest made me chuckle again.

"What?" he asked, his brow furrowing.

I shook my head, smiling at the ridiculousness of it all. "Oh, my God, Vinny—just look at yourself. You've got to be the most handsome man I've ever set eyes on, and you're worried about a comment made years ago by nerdy James Dunn." I cast a quick glance toward James and Shelly, making sure they weren't within earshot. They were still at the bar, waiting for drinks.

Vinny tilted his head, a slow grin spreading across his face. "Since you put it that way, it does sound rather pathetic, doesn't it?"

"Totally." I nodded, smirking.

His grin widened, his eyes dancing with mischief. "Alright, then. Let's go back to your last comment—do you really think I'm handsome?"

Heat rose in my cheeks. "Shut up."

"Let me think," he said, tapping his chin theatrically. "What was it you said again? Ah, yes, 'the most handsome man I've ever set eyes on.'" His deep, teasing voice mimicked mine perfectly, and I couldn't help but laugh, even as my face turned crimson.

I shook my head and bit my bottom lip to keep from grinning like an idiot. "You're impossible."

Before he could respond, James and Shelly were being led to the table directly next to ours. Of all the places in the room, of course, they had to sit there.

"Geri. Vinny." James gave us a nod of acknowledgement, his expression unreadable.

"Hi, James," I said, trying to sound as civil as possible. "How are you?"

"I'm well, thanks," he replied, his tone just as neutral.

How very polite we were being. A full-fledged war could have been simmering under the surface, but here we were, exchanging pleasantries like grown-ups.

"Shelly, you look lovely," I said, flashing her a smile that I hoped didn't look too forced. "I like your dress."

Her smile wavered just slightly before she responded, "Thanks, Geraldine. So do you."

The awkwardness in the air was thick enough to cut with a knife, and I was already plotting my escape. But first, there was the matter of the waitress buzzing around their table, delivering menus and water.

"I recommend the salmon," I said with a bright, overly cheerful tone. "It was divine."

James's head snapped up, his eyes locking with mine briefly. "Thanks," he said curtly before returning his attention to the menu.

There was something unreadable in his gaze, and for one insane moment, I wondered if he felt it too—this strange, unfinished business between us. But he'd made his thoughts perfectly clear. And I'd wasted enough of my life on someone who couldn't decide what they wanted—I was damned if I'd do it again.

I turned back to Vinny, widening my eyes and smiling a little too brightly. He raised a brow, clearly catching on to my growing discomfort.

"Do you want dessert?" he asked, his voice gentle but knowing.

I shook my head rapidly, my silent get me out of here plea received loud and clear.

"Can I have the bill, please?" Vinny asked the waitress as she passed by.

A few minutes later, we were stepping out into the cool night air, the tension of the restaurant finally fading away.

"Gosh, that was awkward," I muttered, glancing back toward the glowing windows. "Especially since we were just talking about him."

Vinny laughed, shoving his hands into his pockets. "I wouldn't worry about it. I don't think they noticed much. They only had eyes for each other."

That stung more than I wanted to admit. What the hell did Shelly Spears have that I didn't?

"So, what now?" I asked, desperate to shake the lingering bitterness from my thoughts.

"I hadn't planned to leave the restaurant so early." He shrugged, the corner of his mouth quirking up. "I thought you had something in mind."

"And you're stuck in the village?"

He nodded. "I'm on call." He kicked at the grass with the tip of his shoe, his gaze lifting to meet mine. There was something impossibly cheeky in his expression, something that made my stomach clench, and my pulse quicken.

I'd never felt this kind of carnal pull before. It was the kind of thing I'd read about in romance novels, the kind of connection I'd always assumed was more fantasy than reality. But now, standing there with Vinny, I knew it was real.

"You could always show me your house," I ventured, my voice softer than I'd intended.

He tilted his head, one eyebrow lifting in a way that was both devastatingly sexy and utterly teasing. "I've got a bottle of wine," he said, holding out his hand.

I didn't hesitate. I slipped my hand into his, the warmth of his skin sending sparks up my arm.

"Lead the way, kind sir," I said, smiling as he laced his fingers with mine and led me toward the unknown.

Chapter Seventeen

Geri

AFTER A QUICK DETOUR back to my parent's cottage to pick up Vinny's car, we headed to Vinny's home.

"Okay, now you can't accuse me of being presumptuous," Vinny said, flashing that easy, devil-may-care grin he seemed to carry everywhere. "I didn't expect you to come back with me tonight, so you've got to promise me something first."

"Oka-ay."

"Count to one hundred—slowly—before you follow me in."

I tilted my head, narrowing my eyes at him. "Are you serious?"

"Deadly. Now promise me."

"Alright, alright, I promise," I said with a laugh, stepping out of the car.

He darted up the path to the tiny stone cottage, his long coat flaring behind him like he was part of some grand heist. With one quick movement, he unlocked the door, pushed it open, and disappeared inside. Over his shoulder, he called out, "Count!"

Shaking my head, I started to count aloud, feeling slightly ridiculous. I glanced around the modest front garden—if you could even call it that. Two tiny patches of earth flanked the stone path, the plants inside sparse and desperate for a bit of TLC. The stone wall hugging the garden was low enough to step over, giving the space a humble, almost vulnerable charm.

By the time I reached seventy, I could hear muffled bangs and thuds coming from inside. I imagined him stumbling over shoes or a stack of magazines. For someone as meticulously dressed as Vinny, the idea of his house being chaotic didn't fit. But if it was a mess, how much could a hundred seconds do to fix it?

"Ninety-nine... one hundred." I pushed the door open, grinning. "Coming, ready or not!"

The hallway was as compact as the cottage itself but warm and inviting. To my right, a few more clattering noises drew my attention. Vinny suddenly appeared in the doorway, leaning casually against the jamb. His dishevelled hair and half-unbuttoned shirt made him look like he'd been waiting for hours. The smouldering expression on his face was nothing short of cinematic.

I burst out laughing. "What are you doing?"

"Come on in," he said, his voice low, rough-edged in a way that made my stomach flip. He reached for my hand, lifting it to his lips. The kiss he planted there wasn't chaste—it lingered, deliberate. My pulse quickened, and I knew he felt it.

The lounge was small but impeccably tidy. A two-seater sofa sat neatly along the back wall, flanked by a coffee table and a modern armchair in muted grey. Above the sofa, a large flat-screen TV was mounted on the wall, incongruous against the duck-egg blue walls and the black accents scattered throughout the room. It was a strange mix—modern sophistication meeting rural charm—but somehow, it worked. Goodness knows what he'd needed to tidy up, as I could see no evidence of clutter or mess.

I perched on the edge of the sofa, trying to play it cool. Vinny, meanwhile, picked up a remote and clicked a few buttons. The room filled with the smooth rhythm of Motown, a melody so soulful it seemed to settle into my chest, nudging my heartbeat to its tempo.

He shrugged off his jacket and laid it over the armchair, then undid his waistcoat with infuriating precision. My mouth went dry as I watched. He knew what he was doing, the way his fingers moved slowly, unhurried, teasing. His eyes never left mine, and in them, I saw something electric. Dangerous.

He produced a condom from somewhere and placed it on the coffee table—this was really happening.

By the time he sat down beside me, my breathing was shallow. He tucked one leg underneath him, the proximity too close, too far. Every nerve in my body screamed at me to close the gap, to do something, but he didn't move. He just stared, letting the silence and the music stretch between us, pulling the tension taut. I'd never experienced anything like this with Simon—with anyone.

When he finally kissed me, it wasn't rushed. It wasn't even hurried. It was deliberate, like everything else about him, every touch a calculated invasion. His lips explored mine, and his hands, warm and firm, found their way to my waist, my back, and the hollow at the base of my neck.

The world outside ceased to exist.

Somewhere between his lips and his hands, my clothes vanished. I didn't even notice when his followed. The passion within me that had been compressed for years roared to life, consuming me. His touch wasn't rushed, but it wasn't hesitant, either. It was confident, claiming, leaving no part of me untouched, unexplored. Every nerve in my body lit up, his mouth igniting something primal in me, something I hadn't known I possessed.

My breath hitched as his lips trailed down my neck, his teeth grazing my skin with just enough pressure to make my pulse race. Shivers cascaded through me, electrifying every nerve. Every sound he made—each inhale, each exhale—seemed to echo louder, amplifying my own sensations. His scent, a heady mix of cedarwood and something darker, muskier, filled my senses, clouding my thoughts.

But when I did manage to piece my thoughts together, it wasn't Vinny's face I saw. No matter how hard I tried to focus, it was James's rugged, intoxicating face that kept surfacing in my mind. His deep, soulful eyes, the way his lips curved when he smiled—it all came rushing back, unbidden and unwelcome.

I clenched my eyes shut, trying to block him out. James doesn't want you, I reminded myself, a bitter mantra that repeated like a broken record. He'd already moved on, hadn't he? Shelly was his next conquest. Shelly with her brand new button nose, her perfect smile and endless charm. He probably wasn't even thinking about me, not after that night.

But Vinny wanted me.

It was flattering in a way that I hadn't expected. He looked at me like I was the only woman in the world. He touched me with a hunger that made me feel desired and craved. And yet...

The thought gnawed at me. What did James see in Shelly? Had I imagined the connection we'd shared the other night? Had I read too much into his words, his glances? Had it all been in my head?

I shouldn't be here. Not with Vinny. Not like this.

But things had already gone too far. Every touch, every kiss, every whispered breath between us felt like its own eternity. A part of me wanted to pull away, to end this before it could go any further. But another part of me—a darker, lonelier part—held on and allowed it to continue.

When it was over, I lay still, staring at the ceiling, my emotions a tangled, unrecognisable mess. I'd let Vinny consume me, not because I wanted him, but because he wanted me. Because he didn't reject me. Because, in that moment, being wanted felt like it might heal the cracks Simon, and more recently, James had left behind.

But it didn't

A wave of emotion crashed over me, sudden and all-encompassing. My chest tightened, and before I could stop it, the tears came. Hot and fast, spilling down my cheeks as if a dam had burst inside me.

Vinny noticed immediately. He didn't say a word, just pulled me into his arms, holding me close. His body was warm and solid, grounding me in a way that I hadn't expected. I clung to him, burying my face in his chest. He stroked my back, his movements slow and steady, offering comfort in silence.

But even as I leaned into him, I couldn't escape the gnawing ache. This wasn't right. No amount of tenderness from Vinny could change the fact that I'd come here to fill a void that he was never meant to fill.

"I need a new sofa," he murmured suddenly, his voice light but edged with something I couldn't quite place.

I choked out a laugh through the tears, wiping at my face with trembling hands. "What's wrong with this one?"

"It's too short, or I'm too long," he said, smirking in that crooked, devilish way that made it hard to tell if he was joking or serious.

He groaned, sitting up, and then he kissed me on the nose. The small gesture felt disarmingly intimate. "How about that wine?" he asked softly, as if nothing monumental had just happened.

I nodded, smiling faintly despite the storm brewing within.

Vinny rose to his feet, entirely unselfconscious in his nakedness. His body was lithe, every muscle defined and effortless. He moved with the kind of ease that came from knowing exactly how good he looked.

I felt raw, vulnerable.

Scrambling, I searched the floor for my clothes, grabbing at anything within reach. By the time he returned, two glasses of red wine in hand, I was mostly dressed, my top clinging awkwardly to my still-flushed skin.

"What's the hurry?" he asked, his voice smooth, teasing, as he set the glasses down on the coffee table.

I shrugged, avoiding his eyes. "I'm not as confident as you," I mumbled, slipping the top over my head.

Vinny sat beside me, leaning in close, his eyes fixed on mine. There was something unreadable in his expression, a flicker of hesitation that didn't match his usual air of control.

"I've got some bad news," he said, his tone measured.

My heart dropped. "What?"

"The condom... it broke."

His words landed like a punch to the chest. I stared at him, frozen. The room suddenly felt too small, the air too thin.

"When were you last tested for anything... you know, nasty?" he asked, his voice calm, almost clinical.

The question caught me off guard, my mind racing. "I—never. I mean, I've had routine smears, but I don't really know what they test for. I've only ever been with Simon..." My voice trailed off, the weight of what I'd just admitted hanging heavy between us. What I didn't say—couldn't say—was that Simon hadn't exactly been faithful. Or straight.

Vinny raised an eyebrow, his lips pressing into a thin line.

"How about you?" I asked.

"I'm careful," he replied. "This is the first time something like this has ever happened. You are on the pill, right?"

I shook my head, and just like that, the tenuous hold I had on my composure snapped. My chest tightened as realisation struck. My stomach churned, a queasiness I'd been dismissing for days now demanding my full attention.

Simon had mentioned it just last week and I had dismissed it. But now, in the glaring light of this moment, it all made sense.

Fuck.

"I need to go home," I said abruptly, standing.

Vinny blinked, startled. "Hold on—don't you want to drink your wine first?"

"I can't." I shook my head, fumbling to gather my things. "I'm sorry, Vinny, I just—I need to go."

He frowned, getting to his feet. For once, his easy confidence seemed shaken. He pulled on his trousers and buttoned his shirt halfway, his smooth chest still on display as though tempting me, daring me to stay. But I couldn't. Not now.

"Are you sure you're alright?" he asked, his voice softer now, almost hesitant.

"I'm fine," I lied, offering him a tight smile. "I just need to go."

The drive home was silent, the tension thick between us. When he pulled up outside my parents' cottage, I turned to him, forcing a smile. "Thanks for... tonight," I said, leaning in to kiss his cheek.

"You're welcome," he replied, his voice low. "I'm sorry if I frightened you off. That's honestly never happened before."

"It's not you," I said quickly, the words tumbling out. "I swear."

"I'll call you," he said, though his tone betrayed a hint of doubt.

I nodded, slipping out of the car. Standing by the gate, I watched as he drove away, the tail lights fading into the night.

The lights were still on in the lounge, and as I stepped inside, my mother glanced up from the sofa. "Didn't expect you home so early," she said, her brow furrowing. "Are you alright?"

I managed a weak smile. "I'm tired. How was your night?"

"So-so. Couldn't wait to get home, if I'm honest."

I sank onto the sofa, the events of the evening crashing down on me. Tears burned at the back of my eyes, and before I could stop them, they spilled over.

Mum's face tightened with concern. "Geri, what's wrong?"

I shook my head, but the words slipped out before I could stop them. "It's all such a mess, Mum."

"What is?" she pressed, leaning closer. "Tell me."

I met her eyes, my lips trembling. "I think... I think I might be pregnant."

The silence that followed was deafening, my confession hanging heavy in the air.

Chapter Eighteen

Geri

I BARELY SLEPT A wink. How could I have been so stupid? So reckless?

I'd planned this—every part of it. I'd decided to have a baby, made a conscious effort to get pregnant, and then, after learning of Simon's betrayal, I'd just forgotten.

How do you forget something like that?

Even after Simon brought it up the other day, it still hadn't registered.

And now, to top it all, I'd slept with Vinny. What a mess.

My stomach clenched, this time not from nausea but from the memory of the night before. I'd enjoyed the date with Vinny—we'd had a good laugh. But if James hadn't arrived with Shelly, I probably wouldn't have taken it any further—but he did, and I had.

It didn't mean anything to either of us. It had just been sex—pure, unadulterated sex. And the worst of it was, I'd imagined James in place of Vinny. What was wrong with me?

And all the while, I was pregnant.

I hadn't bought a test yet, but I didn't need to. Every fibre of my being was certain. My body felt different, my emotions raw. It didn't matter how much I tried to rationalise it—something deep inside told me there was a tiny life growing within me.

And that changed everything.

I felt dirty, tainted somehow. I would never have slept with Vinny if I'd known. Christ knows what diseases or infections I might have picked up—what I might have passed on to this fragile life forming inside me. Not a baby yet, Just a cluster of cells. But that didn't matter. To me, it was a baby. It was my baby. And as much as I'd doubted myself in the past, now I knew. I wanted this baby. And if I had to do it alone, I would.

Mum had been wonderful after I'd blurted it all out the night before. She hadn't said much, She just listened, held me, and reassured me. That was her way, always steady when I needed her most. She'd gone into Kirkby Mayor this morning to run some errands and promised to grab a pregnancy test for me.

Dad had left for his weekly game of golf and, for once, I had the house to myself.

I rang Lucy, hoping to talk things over, but the call went to voicemail. I left a quick message—leaving out the most recent discovery, of course. That wasn't something you left on an answering machine.

Carl was working until two, and we'd planned to catch up later. So, with nothing else to do, I curled up on the sofa, the TV droning on in the background. Some light-hearted cookery programme filled the silence, but I wasn't paying attention. My mind was far away, running through the same cycle of questions, doubts, and what-ifs.

When lunchtime came and went, and there was still no sign of Mum, I started to worry.

Dad came home just after one. I made him a sandwich and tried to act normal, pushing my growing anxiety down as far as it would go.

No point in us both spinning out. He finished eating and went into the garden, humming to himself, blissfully unaware.

I couldn't take it anymore. I dialled Mum's mobile on the off chance she had it with her, but it went straight to voicemail.

Where the hell was she?

I grabbed my keys off the table, just as a sharp knock sounded at the door. My heart lurched in my chest.

When I opened it, I froze. Vinny was leaning casually against the stone wall, his hands stuffed into his pockets. His dark blue eyes locked onto mine, and for a moment, I thought I might be sick.

"Oh... hi, Vinny," I said, the words tumbling out awkwardly. "I can't stop. I have to find my mum." I strode past him, clicking the key fob to unlock the car.

"Geri," he called after me.

"What?" I snapped, spinning around.

"This isn't a social call," he said, his voice calm but firm.

A chill ran through me. My stomach dropped like a stone. "Is it Mum?" I asked, my voice barely more than a whisper.

"Calm down." He held his hands out as if trying to steady me from a distance. "She's alright, but... you need to come with me."

"What's happened, Vinny? Tell me, please." My voice cracked.

His expression softened, but the hesitation in his eyes only made the dread in my chest worse.

"Your mum's been arrested."

Chapter Nineteen

Grace

GRACE STOOD IN THE police cell, her back to the door, staring at the dull grey wall. The air felt stale and heavy. She knew she'd done it now—crossed some invisible line she hadn't even seen coming. What the hell was she supposed to tell them? She didn't even know what was happening.

She closed her eyes, the reality crashing over her like a wave. How could she have been so stupid? So careless? A jar of olives. It sounded ridiculous. She wanted to laugh and cry all at once.

The sound of muffled voices in the corridor made her stomach lurch. She turned just as the door creaked open, and Geraldine stepped inside, her face a mix of confusion and concern.

"Mum! What's happened?" Geri asked her voice tight with worry.

"Nothing, Geri," Grace replied quickly, too quickly. She straightened her shoulders, trying to sound casual, as though she wasn't standing in a holding cell. "It was just a silly mistake. I didn't want Officer Martin to bother anyone, but he insisted. And I couldn't very well call your father, now, could I? He'd have kittens!"

Geraldine's frown deepened. "Mum..."

"It's fine," Grace cut her off, her tone clipped. She didn't need a lecture—not now.

Geri turned to Vinny, who stood in the doorway, his expression professional but sympathetic. "Is she free to go home now?" she asked.

Vinny nodded. "She is, for the time being. I don't know if the shopkeeper plans to press charges, but we'll be in touch."

Grace avoided Geri's eyes as her daughter gently draped an arm around her shoulders, guiding her out of the station. The silence between them on the drive home was oppressive. Grace stared out the window, her thoughts racing, trying to piece together how it had come to this.

She replayed the scene in the shop over and over. Ian had been there. He was an old friend of Max's, and he was standing near the canned goods aisle, waving like they were old friends. They were, but she hadn't wanted to talk to him. Not because she disliked him, but because her head had been too full, too foggy. So, she'd turned away, shoved the jar of olives into her handbag without thinking, and walked out.

She hadn't even realised what she'd done until the shopkeeper came running after her, his voice sharp and accusing. Then came the police car, the stares from strangers, the endless, humiliating questions. Grace clenched her fists, her cheeks burning at the memory. She'd never live this down.

When they pulled into the driveway, Grace felt like her nerves were frayed to breaking point.

Geri turned off the engine and turned to her, her gaze heavy with unspoken questions. "What do you want to tell Dad?"

"The truth," Grace snapped, her voice sharper than she intended. "Jesus, you'd think I was guilty of murder or something. I forgot to pay for a jar of bloody olives. What's the problem? Have you never made a mistake?"

Geri's face fell, her breath hitching as she stared at her mother. "Okay, okay, Mum. Keep your hair on. I was just checking." She threw open the door and stormed into the house, leaving Grace to follow behind.

Inside, Max was sitting in his usual chair, a crossword in his lap. He looked up when they entered, his brow furrowing. "Grace, where have you been?"

Grace sighed, dropping her bag onto the table. "The cop shop," she said bluntly.

Max's jaw fell open, the shock evident in his expression.

Grace rolled her eyes, regretting her tone instantly. "Oh, don't look at me like that. It's all Ian's fault." But before she could say any more, the floodgates opened. Her body heaved with sobs so violent they left her gasping for air.

Max was on his feet in an instant, his arms wrapping around her. "Oh, my darling." He stroked her hair. "Don't cry. Everything will be alright. Let me make you a nice cup of tea, and you can tell me all about it."

Later that evening, after several cups of tea and a long cuddle on the sofa, Grace felt a little steadier. Max and Geri had made a pan of soup for dinner, and while she appreciated the gesture, she couldn't help but notice the way they kept glancing at her when they thought she wasn't looking.

They were worried. She could see it in their faces, in the way Max's hand lingered on hers when he passed her a bowl, in the way Geri kept darting nervous glances at her from across the room.

But for now, at least, the house was quiet. Max had settled into his chair to watch a documentary, and Geri had gone out with Carl, leaving Grace alone with her thoughts.

She stared into the flickering glow of the fireplace, her hands wrapped around a mug of tea. The truth was, she didn't know what was happening to her. The forgetfulness, the mood swings, the sharp edges of anger that had started to creep into her words.

It wasn't just the olives. It was everything.

And deep down, Grace knew it wasn't going to go away.

***

IT HAD STARTED A few weeks ago—small things at first—blurred vision and headaches that came and went without warning. Grace had chalked it up to her reading glasses. They were overdue for an update, after all.

When she finally made an appointment with the optician, she was almost certain it would be a quick fix—a stronger prescription, maybe some new frames. But when the optician told her that her prescription hadn't changed and her glasses were perfectly fine, she felt a flicker of unease.

Still, she brushed it off. She was probably just overdoing it. Let's face it—she wasn't a spring chicken anymore. She'd been burning the candle at both ends for months now, with her charity work, keeping the house running, and the extra classes she'd taken on. Then Geraldine had turned up, adding to the pressure. She now found herself fretting over Geri's situation on top of everything else. It was bound to catch up with her sooner or later.

At first, she cancelled her lunch dates, skipped her volunteer shifts, and spent the week pottering around the house in an attempt to unwind. But despite the restful days, nothing changed. The headaches persisted, and her vision remained stubbornly blurry.

By the end of the week, she couldn't ignore it anymore, so she reluctantly made an appointment with the doctor.

He also suggested her glasses, until she told him the optician's findings. That seemed to give him pause. "Alright," he said, reaching for his notepad. "Let's run a few tests. Just to rule anything out."

It had sounded simple enough at the time. Routine. Nothing to worry about. But when the surgery called a week later, asking her to come in for the results, Grace felt her stomach drop.

She hadn't told anyone—not Max, not Geri, not even her friends. What was the point in worrying them if it turned out to be nothing? So, she decided to keep it to herself for now.

The morning of her appointment, Max had taken the car to Penrith for his weekly shift at the charity shop, Grace planned to catch the bus into Kirkby Mayor. While standing at the bus stop, staring absently at the clouds rolling across the sky, a familiar car pulled up beside her.

"Grace!" Beryl called through the open window, her face beaming. "Where are you off to?"

"Just into Kirkby Mayor," Grace replied, forcing a smile. "I've got a routine doctor's appointment."

Beryl, always eager for company, offered her a lift. Grace climbed in, grateful for the distraction. However, Beryl was so busy chattering about her grandson and the price of petrol that she didn't seem to notice Grace's strained expressions or the nervous way she clutched her handbag.

When they reached Kirkby Mayor, Beryl insisted on waiting for her. Grace protested, telling her she planned to browse the shops afterwards, knowing full well that Beryl wouldn't want to hang around. Reluctantly, Beryl left, and Grace was finally alone with her thoughts.

The surgery was unusually quiet, the faint hum of a radiator filling the silence. Grace barely had time to sit down before her name was called.

She followed Doctor Jessop into his office, her heart pounding in her chest. He'd been their family doctor for thirty years, and she'd always trusted him. He was the one who'd delivered Geri, for heaven's sake. But today, as he gestured for her to sit, his expression was different. Reserved.

"Okay, Grace," he began, his tone professional, measured. "We've had some of the results back, and the blood test has shown an abnormality."

Her stomach dropped. She gripped the edge of the chair, her knuckles white. "What... what does that mean? What kind of abnormality?" she stammered, her voice barely above a whisper.

Doctor Jessop leaned forward, his expression softening. "It's probably nothing serious," he said, though his eyes betrayed a flicker of something else—concern, perhaps. "But we'd like to run some further tests, just to be on the safe side. I've requested an urgent appointment at Carlisle Hospital. You should receive a letter in the next few days."

The words washed over her like static, and she stopped hearing him altogether. Her mind spiralled, latching onto the word "abnormality" like a thorn she couldn't dislodge. It's bad, she thought, her chest tightening. I know it's bad.

The rest of the conversation passed in a blur. She nodded at the appropriate moments, thanked him, and walked out of the surgery in a daze.

By the time she got home, her head was pounding. She went straight to bed, telling Max she had another headache. He'd offered to bring her tea, his brow furrowed with concern, but she waved him off. She couldn't face him. She couldn't face anyone.

That was last week.

Since then, she'd been in a fog. She knew she was acting strange—snapping at Max over trivial things, forgetting where she'd put her keys, staring into space for hours on end. But how could she explain it when she didn't even fully understand it herself?

She couldn't tell them. Not yet. Geri had enough on her plate, dealing with the fallout from her marriage. And Max... well, Max didn't need to know until there was something concrete to tell.

For now, she'd keep it locked away. Whatever it was, she'd deal with it on her own.

But deep down, in the quiet hours of the night, a small voice whispered the truth she wasn't ready to face. This wasn't nothing. It wasn't something that would simply pass.

Something was very wrong.

And it was only a matter of time before she wouldn't be able to hide it anymore.

Chapter Twenty

Grace

"MUM, I'VE BEEN THINKING," Geri said hesitantly the following day, She was standing by the window, her arms crossed as though braced for battle. "I might look for a place of my own once Beryl gets back."

Grace gripped the back of the chair for support. "Whatever for?" She lowered herself into the chair as though her legs might give way.

"I just feel like I'm getting in the way. You've not been yourself lately, and my situation can't be helping."

"Me not being myself has nothing to do with you being here," Grace retorted, the words sharp and defensive. She knew she'd been horrible to Geri lately, snapping over the smallest things, but she couldn't help it. She needed her daughter now more than ever, and the thought of her leaving made her chest tighten. "I want you here. I need you here."

"I know, Mum. But if Carl and I get along alright, we've been talking about finding a place together. I can't stay here forever," Geri's tone was gentle but firm. "I need to get my life into some sort of order. Especially now, if there's a baby on the way."

The words felt like a slap. Grace stared at her, horrified. "You can't move in with him. You've only known him five minutes!" Her voice was louder than she intended, the words tumbling out in a rush. "What will people think?"

"It's nothing like that, Mum," Geri said, exhaling slowly. "We're just friends."

Grace narrowed her eyes. "I've heard that before." Her voice dripped with scepticism.

Geri raised her eyes to the ceiling, clearly trying to keep her patience. "I don't want to fight with you, Mum."

"I don't want you to move out." Grace's voice softened. She could feel her defences crumbling. "Why won't you listen to me?"

"It's for the best." Geri stood up and grabbed her bag. "I'm going into Penrith to look for a job. I'll see you later."

Grace watched her daughter head for the door, her heart heavy with dread. How could Geri even think of moving in with Carl when she was carrying Simon's baby? It was wrong—wrong in every possible way. And Carl. There was something about him that didn't sit right with her, though she couldn't quite put her finger on what it was. He was too flighty.

"Don't worry, Mum," Geri said as she leaned down to kiss her on the cheek. "It'll be fine, you'll see."

The door clicked shut behind her, and Grace was left alone with her thoughts, spiralling into the past.

Geri had been a good daughter. Grace knew she was lucky, especially compared to some of her friends, whose children had caused no end of trouble. Geri had been easy, a dream to raise, and Simon... well, Simon had seemed perfect for her. They'd been inseparable since they were teenagers. So, what had gone so wrong?

Grace and Max had longed for Geri to start a family. But not like this—not apart, not like a broken puzzle. Children needed both parents, Grace thought firmly. That was how they grew into balanced, well-rounded adults. Maybe her view was old-fashioned, but that didn't make it wrong.

She thought of her own marriage to Max and how it had weathered its fair share of storms. Their relationship now was solid and loving. They adored each other. But it hadn't always been easy. No marriage was. There had been moments—years, even—when it felt like they were teetering on the edge of collapse.

The memories came rushing back with startling clarity, like a film reel unspooling in her mind.

It was when Geri was three, the light of Grace's life, a constant source of joy she hadn't realised she'd needed so badly... *Max had been working away during the week, driving long-haul lorries between Manchester and London, only coming home on weekends. At first, the arrangement worked. They missed each other, sure, but it felt manageable.*

Then it wasn't.

Since giving birth, Grace had changed. She loved Max, but she didn't want him anymore. Her libido had vanished, replaced by an exhaustion so deep it seemed to settle into her bones. She dreaded his touch, the way he'd slide into bed beside her on a Friday night, full of longing and expectation.

One Friday, she made sure she was already tucked up in bed, pretending to snore before he even walked through the door. She heard him come in, the disappointment in his sigh as he climbed into bed. When he reached out to hold her, her body stiffened, and he felt it. She knew he did. His hand fell away, and he turned his back to her.

The pattern repeated. Eventually, Max stopped coming home every weekend. He claimed it was overtime and that they needed the money. They didn't, but Grace didn't argue. She relished the space, the absence of guilt. But deep down, she knew their marriage was falling apart.

By the time Geri started school, Max was practically a stranger. He came home sporadically, his visits short and stilted. Grace pretended not to notice. She thought if she ignored it, it might go away.

But it didn't.

The day he came home unexpectedly, her heart nearly stopped. She could see the resolve in his face, the sadness in his eyes. "We need to talk, love," he said, his voice soft but firm.

The words she'd been dreading. She tried to deflect and busy herself with tea and scones, but Max wasn't having it. When he told her he wanted to separate, she felt the ground crumble beneath her feet.

"Please, Max," she sobbed, clinging to him as though her life depended on it. "Don't go. I'll change. I'll fix it. I promise."

And she had. That night, she'd realised how much she loved him, how much she couldn't bear to lose him. They'd talked until dawn, unpacking years of resentment and miscommunication. It hadn't been easy, and the revelation of his brief affair had nearly broken her. But they'd rebuilt their marriage, piece by piece, finding their way back to each other.

... Now, as Grace sat alone, she couldn't help but wonder if Geri and Simon needed their own wake-up call. Maybe they could find their way back to each other too—if it wasn't already too late.

Chapter Twenty-One

Grace

THE NEXT MORNING, GERALDINE packed up her things and moved in with Carl. She'd promised it was temporary at first—just to see how things went. Grace hadn't been too concerned at the time, assuming Geri would quickly tire of living with someone new, someone who wasn't Simon.

But now it was clear this wasn't temporary. They intended to make it permanent if they got along.

It upset Grace no end.

She'd tried again to talk Geri out of it, using every excuse she could think of. She pleaded that Geri would regret it and that she should take more time to think things through. But Geraldine had dismissed her worries, convinced her mother would feel better if the house returned to "normal."

Normal. Grace wanted to laugh at the word. Nothing in her life felt normal anymore. She wanted to shake Geri, scream that she needed her to stay. But doing so would mean telling her the truth. And she couldn't—not yet. Not when everything still felt so precarious.

Max wandered into the lounge, pulling on his jacket. "I'm off to the chemist to get my blood pressure tablets, lass. Do you need anything while I'm out?"

Grace shook her head, her mind elsewhere. "No, I'm fine, love."

He gave her a quick peck on the cheek before heading out. She watched from the window as he walked down the path, waiting until he turned the corner and was out of sight. Then she picked up the phone, her hands trembling slightly as she dialled a number she hadn't called in months.

The line rang four times before an unfamiliar male voice answered. "Hello-o," he said brightly, his tone catching Grace off guard.

"I'm sorry," she stammered. "I think I must have dialled the wrong number."

"Are you looking for Simon?"

Her heart skipped a beat. "Y-yes. Is he there?"

"He certainly is. Who shall I say is calling?"

"It's Grace—Grace Eve."

There was a muffled exchange on the other end of the line before Simon came on. "Grace?" His voice was cautious, tinged with worry. "What's wrong?"

"Oh, hi, Simon." Grace felt suddenly self-conscious. "I'm sorry to bother you, but I was wondering if you have a few minutes to chat?"

"Of course I do. What's wrong? Is it Geri?"

"Yes and no, really," Grace replied, her voice faltering. She hesitated, knowing how angry Geri would be if she found out. But there was no turning back now. "She'll kill me if she finds out I called, but I need to talk to you. In person. Do you think you could meet me somewhere soon?"

Simon was quiet for a moment. "I'm really busy at work this week, but leave it with me. I'll call you back later to sort something out."

"No!" Grace said sharply, then softened her tone. "Don't call me. I'll call you tomorrow. And please, Simon, keep this to yourself."

He gave her his office number, which she jotted down on the back page of her address book. As she hung up, a wave of guilt washed over her. She hated meddling in Geri's life like this, but she was sure she was doing the right thing.

At least, she hoped she was.

At 8:30 the next morning, Grace rang Simon again. This time, he told her he'd managed to rearrange some of his appointments and could meet her that afternoon. They decided on a small coffee shop in Kendal at 2:30 pm.

But the logistics of living in a sleepy country village made things complicated. With only one bus before 3 p.m., Grace would have to leave at 10:30 am to make it on time. She sighed, cursing the unreliable bus service and her reliance on sharing a car. But there was no other option.

As the clock ticked closer to 10:30, she found herself pacing the lounge, her nerves fraying. She hadn't seen Simon since Geri had moved back home. Would he think she was overstepping? Would he even take her seriously?

Grace grabbed her bag and slipped out of the house, glancing around to make sure no one saw her. The last thing she needed was Max asking questions. This was something she needed to do alone.

The bus was late, of course, rattling up to the stop nearly fifteen minutes behind schedule. By the time Grace climbed aboard and found a seat, she was already regretting the whole thing. But it was too late to back out now.

As the bus wound its way through the countryside, Grace stared out at the passing fields, her mind racing. She kept thinking of Geraldine, of how determined she was to forge ahead with Carl. Grace had tried to be supportive, but the more she thought about it, the more convinced she became that Geri was making a mistake.

And Simon—sweet, steady Simon—deserved to know.

Grace arrived in Kendal with two hours to spare. The morning had been uneventful, save for the nerves gnawing at her stomach, so she wandered aimlessly around the shops. She stopped to browse at a small boutique, letting her fingers trail over the soft fabrics of a display. But nothing held her attention. She glanced at her watch—it was still too early. With a sigh, she headed to the coffee shop, hoping the steady hum of background chatter and the comfort of tea might calm her nerves.

By the time Simon hurried in, Grace was on her third pot.

He looked thinner, she noticed. His cheeks were a little hollow, and his shirt hung slightly loose on his frame. His hair, which was usually neatly trimmed, had grown longer, curling slightly at the ends. Despite the changes, he still looked like Simon—familiar and steady in a way that brought a small flicker of comfort.

"Grace," he said warmly, sliding into the seat across from her. "Sorry I'm late. Traffic was a nightmare."

"It's alright," she replied, pouring him a cup of tea from the pot she'd ordered for them. "I've been keeping myself busy."

After a bit of small talk, Grace set her cup down and leaned forward, her expression serious. "Simon, I need to ask you something. And I need you to be honest with me."

He tilted his head, watching her warily. "This is why you asked me here, isn't it?"

"Partly. There's more, but... I need to know what happened between you and Geri."

Simon shifted in his seat, his hands curling around the teacup. "And what has she told you?"

"Nothing," Grace admitted. "That's why I'm asking you. Is there any chance of you making up?"

He shook his head, his lips pressing into a firm line. "No. I'm sorry, Grace. It's gone too far for that."

"But why not? You two have been best friends—inseparable since you were nippers. Please, Simon, just tell me. I need to know that you tried your best."

Simon opened his mouth as if to speak but hesitated. He swallowed hard, his hand rubbing his jaw. Finally, with a deep breath, he blurted it out.

"I've been having an affair."

Grace froze her teacup halfway to her lips. Of all the things she'd expected, this hadn't even crossed her mind. "An affair?" she echoed, her voice barely above a whisper. "And... are you still seeing her?"

"Yes." He sighed heavily. "But it's not what you think, Grace. It's not as straightforward as that."

"Oh, I get it," she said, her voice rising. "She's pregnant too, isn't she?"

The words left her mouth before she could stop them, and as soon as she saw the shocked look on Simon's face, she realised her mistake.

"You said 'too,'" Simon said slowly, his eyes narrowing. "Is Geri... you mean, is she...?"

"Pregnant?" Grace sighed, slumping back in her chair. "Yes. And she's making bad choices, though it all makes sense now. You have another woman, and poor Geri has to go through this alone."

Simon flinched at her words but shook his head. "It's not a woman," he said softly.

Grace blinked, uncomprehending. "Pardon?"

"It's a man," Simon said, his voice firmer this time. "I'm seeing a man, Grace."

The air seemed to leave the room. Grace sat back, staring at him as if he'd just spoken in a foreign language. She tried to process what he'd said, but the words didn't make sense.

"It's not what I planned," Simon said, breaking the silence. "I never meant to hurt Geri. I love her. I always will. But... Kevin is my true love. It just happened. I know that doesn't make it right, but it's the truth."

Grace felt as if the ground had shifted beneath her feet. This wasn't at all what she'd expected. She'd thought that once Simon knew about the baby, he would rush back to Geri's side, ready to make things right. But this? This would never be right. Poor Geri. No wonder she hadn't told anyone.

"I'm sorry, Grace." Simon's voice filled with regret.

Grace still hadn't spoken. She felt her chest tighten, a mix of anger, sadness, and confusion swirling inside her.

Simon glanced at his watch, then stood, grabbing her coat from the back of her chair. "Come on. I'll drive you home."

He helped her into her coat and opened the car door for her, his movements slow, almost hesitant. Once they were inside, Grace reached over and placed her hand on his.

"Don't go yet, Simon," she said quietly. "I appreciate how hard that must have been to tell me. And... since we're getting things out in the open, there's something I need to tell you, too." She paused, taking a deep breath. "But you have to promise me, Simon. You can't tell anyone—not Geri, not Max. No one."

"I promise," Simon said without hesitation.

Grace told him everything—about the headaches, the blurred vision, the doctor's visit, and the letter from the hospital. Simon listened, his face sombre, his hand never leaving hers.

"Right," he said when she finished. "When are you going to the hospital?"

Grace fished the crumpled letter from her handbag and smoothed it out. "Next Tuesday. Ten o'clock. Carlisle Hospital."

"Right then," Simon said, starting the car.

"What do you mean?" she asked, puzzled.

"I'll pick you up at nine."

"Simon, I can't ask you to do that."

"You didn't ask," he said, glancing at her. "I offered. You've been like a mother to me, Grace. You were there for me when my own parents didn't want to know. I'm not about to let you deal with this alone now."

For the first time in weeks, Grace felt a glimmer of relief. She didn't argue. She couldn't. Instead, she squeezed his hand, grateful beyond words that she'd finally confided in someone.

Simon dropped her off in Kirkby Mayor as she'd insisted. The thought of him pulling up outside her house was too risky—too many watchful eyes in their small village. If anyone saw them together, questions would be asked, and Grace wasn't ready to answer them.

"You'll think things through before you talk to Geri?" she asked as she climbed out of the car, clutching her bag tightly.

Simon nodded, his expression serious. "I promise. No knee-jerk reactions. I'll give it some time."

"Thank you."

He hesitated, as though he wanted to say something more, but then gave her a small, tight smile. "Take care, Grace. I'll see you next week."

She watched him drive away, her emotions tangled. Simon's confession had blindsided her, and her heart ached for Geri. But sharing her own burden with him had been a relief she hadn't realised she needed.

Grace decided to call into the mini-mart before heading home, picking up a few essentials for dinner. The shopkeeper, a sour-faced man in his late fifties, gave her a look that lingered too long.

She met his gaze head-on, daring him to say something, but he didn't. Of course, he hadn't pressed charges after the olive fiasco. She supposed she should feel grateful for that, but instead, the urge to stick two fingers up at him bubbled inside her.

She grabbed her shopping and left without a word.

When Grace arrived home, the familiar scent of peeled potatoes and cooking oil greeted her. She stepped into the kitchen, and the sight before her stopped her in her tracks.

Max stood at the counter, a potato in one hand and a knife in the other. His brow was furrowed in concentration as he meticulously whittled the spud into a series of perfect square shapes.

"Goodness, Maxwell Eve," she said, her voice filled with mock astonishment. "Did those potatoes start out round? I've never seen square spuds before in all my life!"

Max glanced over his shoulder, a sheepish grin spreading across his face. "They make better-shaped chips this way."

Grace laughed, a real laugh that rose from somewhere deep inside her. She set her shopping bag on the counter, feeling lighter than she had in weeks. "Since when have you cooked dinner?"

"I've been thinking about that," Max said, turning back to his work. "And I've decided it's time I started helping out a bit more around here. Especially now that Geri's gone again. I know she's been a big help to you."

Grace's chest tightened at his words. She hadn't realised how much Max had noticed—the strain she'd been under, the way Geri had stepped in to shoulder some of the load. She walked over to him, wrapping her arms around his waist from behind and resting her cheek against his shoulder.

Max stilled, then turned his head slightly. "What's that for?"

"For being you," she said softly. "For loving me when I don't deserve it."

Max set down the knife and turned to face her, his hands finding her waist. "You daft woman," he said with a grin. "I've been the lucky one. Always have been."

Grace leaned in and kissed him, a gentle press of her lips that felt like a thank-you for all the years they'd shared, the good and the bad.

"Well," she said, stepping back and brushing a tear from her cheek before he could notice. "What are we having with those chips?"

Max chuckled. "I thought maybe an omelette. Or beans, if I can't figure out the omelette."

Grace laughed again, shaking her head as she opened the fridge. "You're a good man, Maxwell Eve. Square spuds and all."

And for the first time in what felt like forever, Grace felt a little lighter.

Chapter Twenty-Two

Grace

THE FOLLOWING WEEK CAME around much too quickly for Grace's liking. She'd felt calmer since confiding in Simon, but as Tuesday approached, the nervous energy began to creep back in. Still, she was determined to face whatever came next with dignity.

She told Max she was heading into Carlisle for a manicure and a spot of shopping. He hadn't questioned it, though she felt a pang of guilt as he waved her off cheerfully.

Simon was already waiting at the bus stop when she arrived, parked just out of sight from the village. She glanced around to make sure no one was watching before climbing into the car.

"Good morning, Simon," she said, leaning over to peck him on the cheek.

"Well, you seem brighter today," he replied, his expression lightening. "I'm glad."

"I decided I couldn't mope around forever," she said, buckling her seatbelt. "It still might be nothing, eh?"

The journey started smoothly enough, but as they neared Carlisle, traffic ground to a halt. The roadworks on the M6 had created a backlog, and Grace could feel her patience unravelling with every passing minute.

"Hurry up, Simon," she said sharply, gripping the edge of her seat.

"Hey, calm down," he said, glancing at her. "We won't get there any quicker by snapping at each other."

"Yeah, right. Why don't you just shut the fuck up?" The words came out before she could stop them. Her cheeks burned as she realised what she'd said. "I'm sorry. I didn't mean that. Please ignore me. I can't seem to help it." She touched his arm apologetically as they finally pulled into the hospital car park.

"It's okay, Grace," Simon said with a reassuring smile. "I've got thick skin."

As it turned out, the traffic delays had affected everyone, and they weren't the only ones running late. Grace and Simon still had to sit in the waiting room for nearly an hour before her name was called.

The nurse led them to a small, sterile room at the end of the corridor, and Simon held Grace's hand tightly as they waited. Her heart pounded in her chest, and the silence felt oppressive.

A few minutes later, a woman in a white coat entered, introducing herself as Dr. Kate Price. She had a kind face, but Grace didn't miss the serious tone in her voice as she began speaking.

"Mrs Eve, your blood tests showed some abnormalities that we need to investigate further," the doctor explained. "It may be nothing sinister, but we'd like to run a series of tests to make sure."

The next few hours were a blur—eye tests, blood tests, question after question, followed by an MRI and a CT scan. Grace felt like she was being passed from one machine to the next, her nerves fraying with every moment. Simon stayed by her side through it all, his presence steadying her even as her thoughts raced.

After the tests were finished, they were told the results would be ready soon. This worried Grace more than anything—never had she heard of anybody getting their results so fast, especially with the current length of waiting lists. She concluded they must be worried if they were rushing the tests through the same day.

Simon left his mobile number with the receptionist.

The hospital canteen was crowded, the air filled with the hum of conversation and the clatter of trays. Grace felt detached from it all, as though she were watching everything through a thick pane of glass.

"I could do with a brandy," she joked weakly as they sat down.

"Just the one?" Simon quipped. "I could do with a whole bottle."

"Tea then?" she asked.

"Don't mind if I do. I'll get them."

As Simon headed to the counter, Grace found a table at the back of the room, away from the noise. Her thoughts swirled, her anxiety ebbing and flowing like a tide. She was certain the news wouldn't be good—she could feel it in her bones. But what troubled her most was how she would break it to Max. And what about Geri? The baby? Who would be there for her if Grace wasn't?

When Simon returned, he carried a tray laden with sandwiches, cakes, and tea.

"Oh good, I'm famished," she said, trying to sound cheerful.

"I thought you might be. I couldn't eat a thing this morning, but I had a feeling you'd be starving."

The sandwiches tasted like cardboard, and the tea was watery, but Grace ate quickly, grateful for something to do with her hands.

"How's Geri?" Simon asked, his voice careful but eager.

Grace hesitated. She knew he'd been holding back all day, desperate for news. She cursed herself for not preparing better for this question.

"She's fine, I think. To be honest, I haven't seen much of her the past few days."

Simon's eyes narrowed. "Why, Grace? What haven't you told me?"

"She's looking after my friend's house while she's on holiday," Grace said quickly, but she could see Simon wasn't convinced.

"And?" he pressed, pouring another cup of tea.

Grace sighed. "She's got a boyfriend staying there too."

Simon's face darkened, his hand clenching the edge of the tray. "What? What about the baby? My baby? She can't go shacking up with some random guy while she's carrying my child!"

"Calm down," Grace said firmly, though she could feel her own irritation rising. "She's not thinking straight at the moment, but I'm sure she'll come to her senses. Carl's a nice lad but not her type. You'll see."

Simon exhaled sharply, rubbing his temples. "I'm sorry, Grace. I shouldn't have brought it up. Today is supposed to be about you, but it's driving me mad not being able to talk to her."

Grace reached across the table and patted his hand. "It's alright. Honestly, I'd rather have a distraction."

Simon's eyes softened, tears brimming as he nodded. "Okay."

"Tell me about Kevin," Grace said suddenly, surprising even herself. "It'll help take my mind off everything."

Simon hesitated, then began to talk. The more he said, the more Grace wished she hadn't asked. She listened in silence, her stomach twisting as he confessed to orchestrating Geri's pregnancy to make peace with his guilt.

"Simon!" she gasped, horrified.

"I know," he said quietly. "I'm ashamed of myself. I never meant for things to spiral like this."

Before Grace could respond, Simon's phone buzzed loudly on the table. He glanced at the screen and then met her eyes.

"They've got the results," he said, his voice steady but tense. "They're waiting for us."

Grace's hands trembled as she stood. "Let's go."

Together, they headed back down the long corridor, the weight of what was to come pressing heavily on them both.

Doctor Price was standing at the reception desk when they returned, her face calm but serious. She smiled—a sad, practised smile that didn't reach her eyes—and gestured for them to follow her into her office.

Grace felt like she was walking underwater, her legs heavy, her breath shallow. Simon was at her side, his hand hovering near hers as though ready to steady her if she faltered.

"Please, take a seat," Doctor Price said, her tone kind but professional as they entered.

Grace sank into the chair, gripping her handbag tightly in her lap. Simon sat beside her, his knee brushing against hers, grounding her.

"Okay, we have the results, Mrs. Eve," the doctor began, sitting opposite them. She paused, her hands clasped on the desk. "It's not good news, I'm afraid."

Grace nodded, her throat tightening as the words sank in. She felt Simon stiffen beside her, and she reached for his hand, finding comfort in his steady grip.

"You have a brain tumour," the doctor continued. "A glioma, which is one of the more common types of brain tumour." She paused again, her eyes flicking between Grace and Simon. "At this stage, we can't determine the grade—whether it's malignant or benign. However, it's quite large and will need to be removed as soon as possible."

Grace's voice sounded alien to her own ears when she finally spoke. "So, I'll need an operation?"

Doctor Price nodded. "I'm afraid so. The tumour is pressing against your optic nerve, which is likely causing the blurred vision and headaches. If you'd like, I can show you the scans."

Grace nodded numbly, and the doctor stood, placing a brain scan onto the back-lit clip on the wall. She pointed to a white mass near the centre. "As you can see, the tumour is relatively large. Based on its location and appearance, it shouldn't be too difficult to remove, but of course, we won't know for certain until we're in there."

Grace stared at the image, her hands trembling. The stark whiteness of the tumour stood out like a foreign invader in her brain. She glanced at Simon, who smiled at her tentatively and squeezed her hand.

"Do you think you can get it all?" Simon asked, his voice steady but firm.

"I'll certainly do my best," Doctor Price said, her tone measured. "But there are no guarantees, I'm afraid."

"And if you can't get it all?" Simon pressed.

"We'll remove as much as we can and then discuss the next course of action, which could include chemotherapy or radiotherapy, depending on the tumour's nature."

Grace's voice was barely a whisper. "What if I don't have the operation? Could I just have the chemo?"

Doctor Price shook her head gently. "Unfortunately, there's no way of knowing if the tumour is cancerous without surgery. But even if it's benign, it's growing rapidly. If left untreated, it could cause severe complications—or even become life-threatening."

"So even if it's non-cancerous," Grace said slowly, "it could still kill me?"

"Yes," the doctor replied, her voice soft. "In fact, I'm surprised you haven't experienced more severe symptoms already. Tumours of this size in similar locations often cause seizures and significant vision problems."

Grace swallowed hard. "When would you want to do the surgery?"

"We'd like to admit you on Sunday afternoon, with surgery scheduled for early Monday morning."

"This coming Sunday?" Grace's voice wavered, panic creeping in.

"Would that be a problem?"

She thought about it, the weight of the situation pressing down on her. Then she shook her head. "No, it's just... I haven't told my family yet."

Doctor Price smiled kindly. "That's understandable. But if I may offer my opinion, I'd suggest moving forward as soon as possible."

Grace looked at Simon, who nodded encouragingly. "We'll tell them together, Grace. You're not alone in this."

And just like that, it was decided. Admission on Sunday. Surgery on Monday. It sounded simple when you said it quickly.

They sat in the car park in silence, the weight of the news settling between them. Grace stared out the window, watching the clouds drift across the sky. "Now what?" Simon finally asked, his voice breaking the quiet.

"I don't know," Grace mumbled, her hands fiddling with the strap of her handbag.

Simon reached over and took her hand. "I'll come home with you. Shall I call Geri and ask her to meet us there?"

"No, Simon," Grace said, shaking her head. "You've done enough for me today. I'll be fine, honestly." Despite her words, she felt a pang of gratitude for his unwavering support.

I insist, Grace." He squeezed her hand. "We're in this together, okay?"

Grace sighed, the corners of her lips tugging into a small smile. "Okay. But God only knows what Geraldine will say when we show up together."

Simon called Geri using the car's hands-free system, but the call went straight to voicemail. "Geri, it's Simon," he said, his voice calm but firm. "I need to speak to you urgently. I'll be at your mum's house in about an hour. You need to be there." He ended the message and glanced at Grace.

His phone buzzed almost immediately. "It's Geri," he whispered before answering. "Hi, Geri."

"Simon, can't you just leave me alone? I've told you there's nothing more to say, I—"

"Geri, this is not about us," he interrupted sharply. "Just be there. Please." He hung up before she could argue further.

Grace chuckled softly, imagining Geri's reaction. "Oh, she won't like that. She's probably turning every shade of beetroot right now."

Simon smirked. "Better her be mad at me than not show up."

"She'll be there," Grace said confidently. "If only to string you up by your nether regions."

Simon laughed, and for a moment, the tension eased. But as they pulled out of the car park and began the drive home, the weight of what lay ahead returned, heavy and unyielding.

Chapter Twenty-Three

Geri

I'D SPENT THE DAY with Carl, and honestly, it had been great. We got on like a house on fire. He reminded me so much of Simon that I couldn't help teasing him about it. On more than one occasion, I'd accused him of being gay. He'd always laughed it off, never denying it, which somehow only made the comparison more amusing.

As we drove back into the village, my phone rang. Of course, it was buried at the very bottom of my handbag, and by the time I fished it out, the call had stopped. A voicemail notification beeped, and I sighed, dialling it back.

Simon's voice cut through the line, crisp and direct: "Geri, I need to see you at your mum's in an hour. Be there."

I gawked at the phone. "The bloody cheek of him!"

"Who?" Carl asked, glancing at me as he navigated the narrow country road.

"Simon! The cheeky bastard's demanding to see me at my mum's in an hour."

Without thinking, I hit redial, ready to give him a piece of my mind. The call connected, but before I could unleash, Simon cut me off.

"Geri, just be there. Please," he said firmly, then hung up before I could even form a proper sentence.

I stared at the screen in disbelief. "The cheeky...!"

Carl chuckled beside me. "What's he done now?"

"It's not funny," I snapped, my voice rising a few octaves. "He hangs up on me! As if I'm the one in the wrong. He ruined everything, and now he thinks he can just demand when and where I see him?"

"Calm down, Geri. Simple solution—don't go. That'll teach him."

"Yeah, you're right. The obnoxious prick can just fuck off!"

"That's my girl." Carl grinned, holding up his hand for a high-five.

But by the time we pulled up outside Auntie Beryl's house, my resolve had crumbled.

"I'm gonna have to go, Carl," I said reluctantly, unbuckling my seatbelt.

"You're joking."

"No." I sighed, gripping the door handle. "I can't leave Mum alone with him. She'll only go and blab about... you know." I touched my stomach meaningfully.

Carl's expression softened, and he gave me a knowing nod. "Yeah, I get it. May as well get it over with. I'll be here when you get back. You can chew my ear off then."

"Gosh, how have I ever lived without you?" I teased, leaning over to hug him before heading toward my parents' cottage.

Dad was alone when I walked in. I splurted it out about Simon coming before I realised. "Where's Mum?"

"She went to Carlisle this morning," he said, pouring himself a cup of tea. "I thought she'd be back by now."

"Has she taken her mobile?"

"No." He nodded to the side table, and the phone there charging. "You know your mum. She either forgets to take it or forgets to turn it on. You youngsters can use them with your eyes closed, but we just get panicky around the things."

I half-smiled, but before I could respond, a car pulled up outside. I craned my neck, catching sight of Simon through the window.

"Okay, Dad—it's him—he's here" I said, my stomach knotting. "Just act normal."

"You ready?" Simon asked, his voice low but steady.

"As I'll ever be. Come on, let's get this over with."

Dad and I were mid-sentence, chatting about nonsense to fill the silence, when we heard the sound of the front door opening. I frowned. Simon didn't have a key—at least, I didn't think he did.

When Mum walked in behind him, my stomach dropped.

Oh fuck! She's done it. She's only gone and done it. She's told him!

My mind raced, my fury drowning out whatever Simon was saying until I caught the tail end of his sentence.

"... she's had more tests today, and it's not good news. Grace, do you want to tell them?"

Mum shook her head, her gaze fixed on the carpet.

Simon exhaled and pressed on. "Don't panic, but... they think they've caught it in time. Still, it's serious."

"What is it? Spit it out, for God's sake, Simon!" My voice came out sharp, cutting through the tension.

He glanced between Dad and me, his hands wringing together. "She has a brain tumour."

My world tilted. Simon kept talking, his words measured and calm, but they didn't register. His voice became a dull hum in the background as the weight of his words hit me like a blow to the chest.

Mum sat quietly on the sofa, her head bowed as though she were ashamed. Ashamed. My heart twisted. I'd spent the past hour cursing her in my head for betraying me, for siding with Simon, for putting him ahead of me.

And now this. My mum. My wonderful, strong, infuriating mum. A fucking brain tumour.

I couldn't move. Couldn't speak. I wanted to scream at how unfair it all was, but the words wouldn't come.

Dad asked questions—calm, measured, as though he were absorbing everything with stoic resolve. I couldn't focus on his words or Simon's answers.

"She's only fifty-eight," I mumbled under my breath.

I needed to get out. My body couldn't stay in that room a second longer.

"I need some air," I muttered, standing abruptly. Without waiting for a response, I stepped outside, the cool evening air hitting me like a slap.

The cottage lights glowed behind me, but I couldn't bring myself to turn back.

This wasn't happening. It couldn't be.

And yet, it was.

Chapter Twenty-Four

Grace

MAX AND GERALDINE WERE sitting on the sofa when Grace walked in with Simon. Their jaws dropped in unison, a moment so perfectly synchronized it would have been comical—if it weren't so tragic.

Grace froze, unable to speak. Her carefully rehearsed words vanished, replaced by an overwhelming tide of fear and guilt.

Simon stepped in seamlessly, sensing her paralysis. He explained everything with a calmness that seemed impossible, considering the gravity of the news. He answered their questions with steady resolve, his voice unwavering as he navigated their devastation.

Grace sat there, silent and numb, as though she were watching someone else's life unfold on a television screen.

Max was in shock. His wide eyes darted between her and Simon, his hands trembling in his lap. His mouth opened and closed several times, but no sound came out. It was as if he couldn't find the words—or perhaps the words wouldn't come.

The colour had drained from Geraldine's face. Her fists clenched in her lap, her lips pressed into a thin, rigid line. She asked questions, though her voice trembled with barely restrained panic.

Grace drifted in and out of their conversation, her mind retreating to a distant corner where she didn't have to process their reactions. When she finally blinked back to the present, she realised they had all stood up.

Max shook Simon's hand, pulling him into a brief, awkward man hug. Geraldine lingered by the door, her arms crossed protectively over her chest as if shielding herself from the weight of the moment. Then, to Grace's surprise, Simon and Geraldine left together.

Grace couldn't face Max. She slipped into the kitchen, her hands automatically reaching for a tea towel as she busied herself without any real purpose. She scrubbed at an already clean counter and rinsed a mug that didn't need rinsing. Her mind buzzed with the echoes of Simon's voice, replaying the devastating words over and over again.

Then she heard it.

A sound so pained and raw it stopped her in her tracks. It was coming from the lounge.

Quickly wiping her hands on the tea towel, she hurried to see what was happening.

Max was on his knees in front of the fireplace, his shoulders heaving as a terrible wail escaped him. Tears streamed down his face, his expression one of utter devastation.

"Max!" she gasped, rushing to him with her arms outstretched.

He turned to her, burying his face in her chest like a lost child. "Grace... Grace, my Grace..." he sobbed, his voice breaking on her name.

She held him tightly, her own tears falling freely now. They stayed like that for what felt like an eternity, clinging to each other as the weight of the truth bore down on them.

Eventually, Max's sobs quieted, and he pulled himself to his feet. He helped her to the sofa and sat down beside her, wrapping his arms around her as though afraid she might disappear if he let go.

"I'm sorry, Max," Grace whispered, her voice trembling.

"You have nothing to be sorry for, my love," he replied, his voice thick with emotion. "I should have known something was wrong. You haven't been yourself for weeks. I just..." His voice broke again. "I just wish you'd told me sooner. You must have been going out of your mind. And Simon? How did he get involved in all this?"

Grace hesitated, unsure how much to reveal. "I needed to talk to someone," she admitted. "I didn't want to worry you or Geri. And Simon's been like a son to us for years. Just because things aren't good between him and Geri right now doesn't mean we have to shut him out of our lives, too."

Max sighed, his grip on her tightening. "I suppose you're right. But, Grace..." He tilted her chin up, so she was looking at him. "Do you have any other secrets I should know about?"

She froze, the weight of Simon's confession pressing down on her. "Eerrmm... no... er... do you want a cup of tea?"

Max's expression darkened. "Grace? What is it?"

The panic in his eyes was unmistakable. He was going to fill in the blanks himself if she didn't tell him, and that would only make things worse. Taking a deep breath, she decided to lay it all out.

She told him everything—about Geri's pregnancy, about Simon's sexuality, about his relationship with Kevin.

To her relief, Max took it in his stride. Though he was visibly shocked, he nodded slowly as he absorbed each piece of information.

"Well," he said finally, his voice steady. "That explains a lot. Poor Simon... and Geri. I don't even know what to say."

"They'll figure it out," Grace said, though her voice lacked conviction. "But now we have more pressing things to deal with."

He nodded again, his focus shifting back to her. "What did the doctor say about the tumour? What are we dealing with here, Grace?"

I don't remember much, to be honest," she admitted, tears welling up again. "There was so much information, and it's all a blur. We'll know more after the surgery."

He took her hands in his, his gaze steady and unwavering. "Then we'll wait together. Whatever happens, Grace, we'll get through this. You're not facing anything alone."

She leaned into him, letting his words wrap around her like a warm blanket. For the first time since the diagnosis, she felt a flicker of hope. Maybe, just maybe, they'd come out the other side of this together.

Chapter Twenty-Five

Geri

SIMON CAUGHT UP TO me at the gate, his voice calm but insistent. "Geri, wait!"

"Just leave me alone, Simon. I can't take it all in. I need to walk for a bit."

"It's okay. I'll walk with you," he said softly. "We don't have to talk if you don't want to."

I hesitated, my emotions swirling too wildly to make sense of. He ran back to his car and returned with two jackets. I hadn't even realised how cold it was until he draped one around my shoulders. His movements were careful, almost parental, and I stood there, letting him do it, feeling strangely like a child being dressed against the cold.

We walked in silence, leaving the village behind. The stars were out in full force, scattered across the black sky like shards of broken glass. When we reached the edge of the village, Simon pulled a torch from his pocket, its beam cutting through the darkness.

At first, neither of us spoke. But then Simon slipped his arm through mine, and something in his familiar face—the gentleness in his expression, the unwavering presence—triggered a release I couldn't hold back.

I started crying.

Not the silent, dignified kind of crying, but deep, heaving sobs that shook my entire body. Tears poured down my face, and I didn't think I would ever stop. Simon pulled me into his arms, holding me tightly as I cried into his chest. All the while, he whispered calming words into my hair, his voice steady and soothing.

When the tears finally ran dry, I pulled back, wiping my face with my sleeve. My voice was hoarse when I finally managed to speak. "Will she die?"

"Stop that!" Simon scolded, his tone sharper than I expected. "Of course she won't die."

"But what if she does, Simon?" I whispered. "What will I do? I've been an awful daughter. I even moved out when she obviously needed me. She couldn't tell me what was happening because I've been too wrapped up in my own problems." I paused, swallowing hard. "I knew something was wrong. She's been acting so strange lately. She even got arrested for shoplifting."

"You're joking," Simon said, his eyebrows shooting up in disbelief.

"I wish I was." My voice cracked. "If I'd known what was happening, I would've never moved out."

Simon gripped my shoulders, his voice firm but kind. "Hey. I know you wouldn't. And so does she. Don't beat yourself up about the past, Geri. You know about it now and you can be there for her moving forward. Things will be rough for a while, but we'll get through it."

"We?" I asked, looking up at him.

"Pardon?"

"You said we'll get through it."

Simon hesitated, then gave me a small smile. "I'm not going to leave you to deal with this alone. Unless you want me to, that is."

I shook my head quickly.

"Listen," he continued, his tone earnest. "We've been married for years. You were my girl long before that. And your parents—they've been there for me through everything. I'm part of this, too."

I felt a lump rise in my throat. "Promise?"

"I promise."

We continued walking into Kirkby Mayor, our breath visible in the chilly night air. The village was quiet, the stillness only a countryside town could muster.

"Let's go into the pub to warm up," Simon suggested.

The Speckled Hen had been our second home once we were old enough to drink. Simon and his family had moved to this village when he was fourteen, and his connection to the place was as strong as mine.

We settled into a table near the roaring fire, the warmth seeping into my bones almost immediately.

"Can I get you something to eat?" Simon asked.

I wasn't hungry, but I knew I needed to eat for the baby. "Yeah," I said. "Just get me what you're having."

He nodded and headed to the bar, leaving me alone with my thoughts.

When Simon returned with two huge plates filled with burger and chips, we began to eat, and the conversation flowed more easily. We talked about mundane things, skimming over heavier topics. For a moment, it felt almost normal—almost like old times.

After we finished, we left the pub, planning to walk back. But the air outside had turned icy, and we had no phone signal.

"Let's walk to my parent's house and call a taxi." Simon tucked my arm in his.

As we walked, our steps, crunching on the frosty ground, sounded totally in sync.

Suddenly, a screeching sound shattered the stillness. A police car skidded to a halt beside us, its blue lights flashing.

Simon grabbed me, pulling me back dramatically, though the car wasn't close enough to hit us.

"What the—" I began, but my words died in my throat when the car door flew open, and Vinny jumped out.

"Watch out, mate. You almost knocked us flying," Simon shouted as Vinny strode up, his steps sharp and purposeful.

"Oh, I get it now," Vinny sneered, his eyes darting between Simon and me. "Simon McIntyre's back on the scene. Explains why you've been giving me the cold shoulder, Geraldine."

"What the fuck do you want, Vinny?" Simon asked, his tone sharp.

Vinny's expression darkened. "Watch your mouth, boy." His voice low and threatening.

Simon let out a derisive laugh, shaking his head. "Boy? We're the same bloody age." He squared his shoulders, stepping closer, his eyes locking onto Vinny's in a challenge. "Don't try to pull that macho crap with me, mate."

Vinny mirrored Simon's movements, squaring up with an equally defiant glare. The tension between them was electric, crackling in the chilly night air.

"Hey—hey, enough of that," I said, forcing myself between them. I planted a hand on Simon's chest, pushing him back slightly while casting a warning look at Vinny. "Did you want something, Vinny? Or are you just here to puff out your chest?"

Vinny smirked, but it didn't reach his eyes. "Just thought you'd like to know your other boyfriend's being taken in for questioning again."

I followed the direction of his nod and froze. Sitting in the back of a police car, looking uncharacteristically sheepish, was Carl.

"Carl!" I cried, stepping toward the car.

Carl gave me a half-hearted smile, shrugging his shoulders as though to say what can you do?

"What for this time, Vinny?" I asked, my voice sharper than I intended.

"Same as before," Vinny said, crossing his arms. "We've got further evidence."

For the first time, I noticed the uglier side of Vinny, the one James had warned me about. The boyish charm and easy grin that had once drawn me in were gone, replaced by something hard and unkind. His eyes glinted with something close to malice, and his lips curled in a smug, self-satisfied smile.

"So, you two are back on then?" he asked, his tone dripping with contempt.

"And what's it to you, Vinny?" Simon cut in before I could respond. "It's none of your fucking business."

"I've already told you," Vinny said, his voice deadly calm. "Watch your mouth when you speak to me."

I could see where this was going, and it wasn't anywhere good. "Enough!" I snapped, grabbing Simon's arm. "Come on, let's go."

As we passed the car, I leaned down to the window where Carl was sitting. "Can I do anything?" I asked, my voice softening.

Carl shook his head, his expression resigned.

"You'll be okay," I said, trying to sound reassuring.

He smiled faintly and nodded as the car pulled away with a screech of tyres, leaving the faint smell of burnt rubber in its wake.

"Fucking prick," Simon muttered, watching the red tail lights disappear into the distance. "What the hell's wrong with him?"

"I think he might be jealous," I said, linking my arm through Simon's as we continued up the street.

"Jealous? Of me?" Simon asked, incredulous.

I nodded. "I went out with him Friday night, and now he clearly thinks he owns me."

Simon stopped in his tracks, turning to face me. "Oh, my God, Geri! You went out with Vinny? What's wrong with you? He's always been a narcissistic prick."

"I don't know what that means," I said with a shrug. "But yeah, you're right—it was a mistake."

Simon raised an eyebrow, his tone laced with disbelief. "You don't know what 'narcissistic' means? Geri, come on."

I waved him off. "Doesn't matter. What's important is you were right. But seriously—how gay are you?"

Simon blinked, taken aback. "What the hell is that supposed to mean?"

I rolled my eyes. "Did you not notice how effing hot he is? I mean, objectively speaking?"

Simon opened his mouth, then closed it again as though he couldn't quite process what I'd just said. Finally, he smirked, shaking his head. "You know what, Geri? I think your taste in men might be well and truly broken. I can't believe I'm saying this, but you really need to stop picking men based on how 'hot' they are."

"Oh, shut up," I said, elbowing him playfully. "Like you've never made bad decisions."

Simon chuckled, his laughter easing the lingering tension. "Touché."

As we walked further into the night, I couldn't help but replay Vinny's words in my mind. Carl being questioned again? Further evidence? And that nasty edge to Vinny. I couldn't shake the feeling that there was more to this story than I realised.

And whatever it was, it wasn't going to end here.

"So why was it a mistake then?" Simon asked as we walked, his tone curious but laced with concern. "Your date with Vinny?"

"It just was," I said, tugging my cardigan tighter around me. "And now he's going to take it out on Carl."

"Who is this Carl anyway?" Simon's voice carried a hint of suspicion.

"He's just a friend—Auntie Beryl's nephew. I'm staying with him at her house while she's away."

"Oh." Simon nodded, his expression unreadable.

"You don't seem surprised," I said, narrowing my eyes. "Did Mum tell you?"

"She... mentioned it," he admitted, shifting uncomfortably.

I wondered what else Mum might have "mentioned." Then, the thought of her tumour rushed back, and my chest constricted painfully. I held onto Simon's arm a little tighter as we turned into his parents' street. There were no streetlights here, just the dim glow of the stars above, and the shadows felt heavier than usual.

"You didn't say why Vinny arrested Carl," Simon pressed.

"There have been a number of rapes in the area, and Vinny's got it in his head that it's Carl."

Simon stopped abruptly, turning to face me. "Geri! I've been following that case on the news. That guy's a monster. You need to stay away from him."

"From who? Carl?" I scoffed. "For God's sake, Simon. Are you not listening? It isn't him."

"You don't know that, Geri," Simon said, his voice firm. "You've only just met him."

"I do know it. Trust me."

Simon sighed, pulling a bunch of keys from his pocket. "Let's just call that taxi and get you home."

"Keys!" I groaned, smacking my forehead with the heel of my hand. "I don't have a key to Auntie Beryl's, and I can't go back to Mum's tonight—they'll be in bed now."

"Stay here, then," Simon said simply, holding the door open.

"With you?" I asked, hesitating.

"Of course, with me."

I stepped inside. It was dark and cold, the kind of chill that clung to the walls of a house left empty too long.

"I'll put some lamps on and light the fire," Simon said, reading my mind like he always used to.

The house felt strange. As kids, we'd never been allowed to hang out here—Paul and Agnes, as Simon called his parents, weren't exactly the warm and welcoming type. Instead, Simon had practically lived at my house, growing up as an unofficial member of the family.

Paul and Agnes weren't bad people, just different. They were happy in their own company, which explained their frequent escapes to their villa in the South of France or wherever else they galivanted off to. Simon's brother, Peter, was much the same—reclusive, distant, and rarely in touch.

Simon, I realised, had been the only normal one. And that was probably because of us—my parents and me.

I thought of Mum again, and my stomach twisted.

"Have you spoken to your parents lately?" I asked as Simon set a match to the fire.

"No—not for a while. The last time was when you were there."

"Gosh, Simon. You need to call them."

"I will, I will," he said, rolling his eyes dramatically and lifting his hands to his ears like he always did when he thought I was nagging.

"I'm not nagging," I said, exasperated. "But if you want to keep up the pretence, I suggest you pick up the phone."

"I'll call them," he promised. "First chance I get." He straightened up with a groan. "Now, do you want a cuppa?"

"Yes, please." I sank into the cold leather sofa, tucking my legs beneath me. "Do you have milk?"

"Yes, I brought some with me last night. Got in late but thought it was easier to stay here just in case the traffic was bad. I didn't want to make your mum late for her appointment."

I smiled at him. Grateful he had been there for my mum. I owed him for that, at least.

By the time Simon came back with the tea, my eyelids were already drooping. He turned on the TV and settled into the armchair opposite me, but I was out before I even finished my tea.

I woke to find Simon standing over me, the main light on and the TV off.

"Oh, I'm sorry," I mumbled, rubbing my eyes. "I must have nodded off."

"You don't say," he teased, his grin warm and familiar.

"Was I snoring?" I asked, chuckling.

"Just the usual piggy grunts."

"Piss off," I said, shoving him playfully.

"Come on," he said, helping me to my feet. "Let's go up."

I hesitated, unsure of how this was going to work. The most natural thing would have been to share a bed—we'd done it before without any issue—but I wasn't about to suggest it.

To my surprise, Simon led me to his parents' room.

"Oh, gosh, Simon, I can't sleep in here," I protested. "Can't I have your room?"

"It's much nicer in here," he said with a shrug. "But yeah, if you want to swap, we can."

"Please. If you're sure you don't mind."

Simon's bedroom looked exactly as it had years ago. The navy blue duvet and fleecy black throw on the single bed were inviting, and I couldn't wait to climb in.

Simon rummaged in his bag and handed me a white T-shirt. "Here. In case you need something to sleep in."

"Thanks," I said.

"Can I get you anything else?"

I shook my head. "No. I should be fine."

"Goodnight, Geri," he said, pausing in the doorway for a moment before backing out and closing the door behind him.

I crept to the bathroom later, and on the landing, I heard Simon's voice. He was on the phone, and though I couldn't make out the entire conversation, it was clear he was talking to Kevin.

A fresh wave of anger and jealousy surged through me. It wasn't Kevin's fault, not really. If it hadn't been him, it would have been someone else. Simon was gay—end of story.

Back in the room, I snuggled into the squeaky old bed, trying to focus on Mum, the baby, and everything that mattered now.

But my dreams were wild—Mum and Dad salsa dancing, Carl behind bars, Vinny's evil laughter. And then there was Vinny again, his hands on me, his lips scorching mine.

Three light knocks on the door startled me awake, and Simon poked his head in.

"Are you okay, Geri? I could hear you crying—are you worrying about your mum?"

I nodded. I couldn't tell him the cries he'd heard were from something far less innocent.

"Do you want me to stay for a while?" he asked softly.

I nodded again, scooting over to make space. Simon climbed in beside me, his warmth and steady breathing comforting. I fell asleep with my head on his chest, his heartbeat strong beneath my ear.

***

Waking up in Simon's arms, for a fleeting second, I thought everything was back to how it used to be. The weight of the last few weeks felt like nothing more than a nasty dream. But then I rubbed my eyes, saw the familiar navy blue walls and the Manchester City memorabilia scattered around the room, and reality came crashing back.

"You okay?" Simon's voice broke through my thoughts.

I hadn't noticed he was awake. "Wha—oh, yeah, fine," I said quickly, sitting up. "I'd best get going, though."

I climbed over him, careful to keep my back to him as I began to dress. The room felt charged with unspoken words, the awkwardness of shared intimacy that didn't belong to us anymore.

Simon cleared his throat and slipped out of the room, giving me space to finish getting ready.

When I came downstairs, Simon was waiting by the front door, his overnight bag at his feet.

"I've called a taxi," he said, his voice neutral.

I nodded, my cheeks burning with a mix of embarrassment and gratitude after last night. I mumbled a quick thanks before practically sprinting down the path as the taxi pulled up.

Dad was watching from the window when the taxi arrived, and he opened the door before I'd even stepped out.

"Good morning," he greeted me, though his usual cheer seemed dampened.

"Hi, Dad." I kissed his cheek. "How's Mum?"

"She's upstairs," he said. "Didn't sleep well last night, so I convinced her to take a nap."

Simon stepped out of the cab behind me, and Dad's smile grew slightly.

"How are you, Max?" Simon asked, slapping him lightly on the back in a manly display of affection.

"Coping... just about." Dad gave him with a wry grin.

"I saw both your cars were still parked." Dad's voice was curious. "Is everything alright?"

"Yeah," Simon said.

"We ran into Vinny in Kirkby Mayor last night. He's arrested Carl again," I added.

Dad raised an eyebrow. "And?"

"I didn't have a key to Beryl's house," I explained, "so we ended up staying at Paul and Agnes' place."

Dad nodded thoughtfully. "And how are they doing?"

"Mum and Dad?" Simon shrugged. "They're in Portugal... I think."

"I thought I hadn't seen them around recently," Dad said.

"They're rarely here anymore," Simon replied. "I keep telling them they should sell up and enjoy the money, but they don't listen."

"They're probably worried about what might happen if they get sick in their old age," Dad said. "It's all well and good gallivanting around the globe, but when it comes to medical attention, you're better off in your own country."

"I guess I never thought of it like that," Simon admitted.

Simon glanced at his watch. "Okay, I'd better scoot. I'll be here Sunday to take you out to dinner before Grace has to be at the hospital."

"You don't need to do that," Dad said, though his smile showed he appreciated the gesture.

"I want to," Simon said firmly. "That is if you don't mind me being there."

"Of course, we don't mind," Dad replied, looking at me for confirmation.

"No, I don't mind," I said softly.

"Great," Simon said with a smile. "If you need me before then, you know where to find me."

He reached into his jacket pocket and pulled out a brown envelope, holding it out to me.

"What's this?" I asked, frowning.

"I noticed you haven't been using much from the joint account," he said.

"I didn't know if I should," I admitted. "I haven't worked in ages."

Simon's smile was gentle. "It's our money, Geri. Also, I'm getting the house valued. Whatever it comes in at, I'll pay you your share."

"Really?"

"You didn't think I'd rip you off, did you?" He sounded almost offended.

"To be honest, I haven't given it much thought," I said truthfully.

"Well, rest assured, I won't. And with a bit of luck, I might have an idea of the value by Sunday."

I nodded, overwhelmed by his fairness.

"One last thing," Simon added. "It'll be easier to transfer large amounts directly, so if you get the chance, maybe you could set up a new account."

"I'll do it this week. Thanks, Simon."

He leaned in to kiss my cheek, shook Dad's hand, and let himself out.

"He's a great guy, you know?" Dad said as we watched Simon walk down the path.

"I know, Dad, but..."

"Your mum told me," Dad said gently. "It's a crying shame, though. He obviously still thinks the world of you."

"I know." My voice cracked slightly. "But sadly, that's not enough."

Dad gripped my hand with both of his, his eyes warm and steady. "At least it seems like he's going to do right by you, and that goes a long way in my eyes. Divorce is hard enough, but divorced and penniless? That must be bloody terrible."

"Dad, I have something else..."

"Mum told me about the baby, too," he said, cutting me off.

I stared at him, my mouth falling open.

"Don't worry, I won't say a word," he promised. "But I think it's lovely. You'll be a fantastic mum."

"I hope so, Dad."

"I know so." He squeezed my hand.

His words settled something inside me. Maybe I couldn't fix everything, but with Dad's unwavering support, I knew I could face whatever was coming next.

Chapter Twenty-Six

Geri

THE REST OF THE day had been a blur of activity, though none of it managed to distract me completely. I cleaned, cooked, and prepared vegetables for dinner, trying to ignore the gnawing anxiety in my chest. Mum hadn't come downstairs, though I could hear her pottering about upstairs. I took her a cup of tea, but she was in the bathroom, so I left it on her sideboard and decided not to press her.

Dad was out in his shed, doing whatever it was he did out there to keep himself busy. I hadn't had the heart to ask, and honestly, it was probably better for both of us to have some space.

I'd gone to Auntie Beryl's house a couple of times to check on Carl, but there was no sign of him. His phone went straight to voicemail every time I called. It left me feeling helpless. All I could do now was wait.

A light knock at the door jolted me from my thoughts. Wiping my hands on a tea towel, I hurried to open it.

Standing there was James Dunn, his large frame hunched slightly as he stared down at his feet. His hands were shoved deep into his jeans pockets, and his dishevelled hair and unshaven face gave him the air of someone who had just rolled out of bed, though it was already late afternoon.

"Hi, James," I said, surprised to see him.

"Geri," he said, glancing up at me. "I hear Vinny's arrested Carl again."

"Yeah, last night," I said cautiously, my stomach tightening. "Why?"

James' lips twitched in a wry half-smile. "I've just had a tip-off from a friend of mine at the Kirkby Mayor station. Looks like they're planning to charge him with the rapes."

"What?" I gasped, gripping the edge of the door. "That's ridiculous. Carl's no more capable of that than I am."

James raised an eyebrow, his lips curling slightly. "Well, I'd say Carl's slightly better equipped than you for the job, but I take your point."

"You know what I mean," I snapped, annoyed at his attempt at humour.

"For the record, yeah, I do," he said, his voice softening. "I don't believe for a second that Carl's the rapist. But the police must think they have something solid to pin on him."

"I can't imagine what," I said, shaking my head. "Do you want to come in?"

"I was actually heading for a pint. Do you want to join me? Thought we could put our heads together and see if we can figure out a way to help your mate."

"Alright," I said, grabbing my coat. "Let me leave a note for Dad."

We walked toward the pub in silence for a while, the cool air biting at my cheeks.

"How have you been?" James asked, breaking the quiet.

"Not too bad," I said, though my voice lacked conviction. "We had some awful news yesterday. Mum's got a brain tumour."

James stopped in his tracks, his Adam's apple bobbing as he swallowed hard. "Grace?"

I nodded, my throat tightening.

"Shit," he said, running a hand through his messy hair. "Is there anything they can do?"

"She's having surgery on Monday," I said.

He let out a low whistle. "I'm really sorry to hear that, Geri. And I'm sorry to bother you with all this—sounds like you've got enough on your plate."

"No," I said quickly. "I need a distraction. And I need to know what's happening with Carl. Please, let's keep going."

"You're sure?"

I nodded, and we continued toward the pub.

The main bar was almost empty when we arrived. A couple of old men were playing dominoes in the corner, but otherwise, the place was quiet.

We ordered drinks—an orange juice for me and a bottle of lager for James—and took a seat in one of the booths.

"So, tell me what you know about Carl and Vinny," James said, leaning forward.

I sighed, running a hand through my hair. "There's really not much to tell. Carl and I are just friends. I moved into Auntie Beryl's place with him because I needed space. Mum's been acting so strange lately."

"And Vinny?"

I shrugged. "I had one date with him. It was a mistake. Now I think he's taking it out on Carl."

James nodded, his expression thoughtful. "I suspected as much. But Vinny couldn't arrest Carl without evidence. There has to be something tying him to the case."

"Like what?" I asked, leaning forward.

"Let's start with what we know about the rapist," James said, pulling a notepad from his pocket. "He's tall—at least six foot. How tall is Carl?"

"Five-seven, maybe five-eight," I said.

"Not six foot, then."

"Definitely not."

James nodded, flipping a page. "The rapist has a noticeable limp. He shuffles when he walks."

"Carl's like a whippet," I said. "He never sits still, and he moves fast."

"Exactly," James said. "That's why this doesn't add up. But here's the kicker—size eleven feet."

"Carl does have big feet," I admitted. "But that doesn't make him a rapist."

"No, it doesn't," James said. "But it's enough for someone like Vinny to build a flimsy case around if he's motivated enough."

"There is something else." I sipped at my drink.

"Go on."

"They apparently found Carl's stupid plastic cigarette at Samantha's house."

"Fuck."

By the time we left the pub, the sky was growing darker, and a chill had settled over the village.

As we crossed the green, James suddenly stopped, pointing toward Auntie Beryl's house.

"What's going on there?"

Three police cars were parked in the road, and an officer stood in the gateway.

My heart sank as I set off at a trot, James close behind me.

"What's happening?" I asked the officer at the gate.

"I'm sorry, miss," he said, holding up a hand. "We have a warrant to search the property. Everything is above board."

"But I live here!"

The officer shook his head. "You'll have to wait until we're done."

"Let's go," James said gently, steering me away.

We hadn't gone far when Vinny emerged from the house, dangling a key in his hand.

"You really spread yourself around, don't you, Geraldine?" he sneered.

"Excuse me?" I snapped, turning to face him.

"One boyfriend in the slammer, another fawning over you on the street. And where's your husband? Nowhere, as usual."

"You're disgusting," I hissed. "I don't know what I ever saw in you."

Vinny laughed, tossing the key to me. "Thought you'd need this. Oh, and by the way..." He leaned closer, his voice dripping with malice. "We just found the rapist's clothes in darling Carl's bedroom."

My hand flew to my throat, and I stared at him in disbelief.

Vinny smirked, turning on his heel. "Give the officers time to finish up before you go back in."

James was at my side in an instant, his hand on my shoulder.

"Did you hear that?" I asked, my voice barely above a whisper.

"Every last unbelievable word," he said grimly.

Chapter
Twenty-Seven

Grace

GRACE SPENT MOST OF Sunday morning flitting around the house, trying to keep herself occupied. She couldn't sit still for long, even though Max and Geri had both encouraged her to rest. The truth was, resting gave her too much time to think, and thinking was the last thing she wanted to do right now.

She had spent the better part of the week distracting herself. On Thursday, she and Geri went to Carlisle, where she bought a couple of new nightdresses for the hospital and a smart toiletry bag. On Friday, Max had driven them to visit her mum at the nursing home.

That visit had been both heartwarming and heart-wrenching. The entertainer had everyone in the communal lounge singing along to old tunes, and for the first time in months, Grace saw her mum genuinely happy. But as she hugged her goodbye, she felt an ache deep in her chest, the kind that whispered, *What if this is the last time?*

It had hit her then—she was quietly saying her goodbyes. Not just to her mum, but in small ways, to everyone around her. She didn't want to, didn't intend to, but her mind wouldn't let her avoid the possibility.

Still, she had chosen not to tell her siblings about the tumour. What would be the point? They all had their own lives, their own families. She'd decided to wait until *after* the surgery. There was nothing they could do now except worry, and Grace didn't want to be the reason for more sleepless nights in anyone's household.

By Sunday, the house felt unusually full of life. Simon had arrived to take them out for dinner, and Grace was touched by how insistent he'd been. She tried to get out of it—there were still a hundred things she felt she needed to do—but he wouldn't take no for an answer.

"Come on, Grace," Simon said, his tone light but firm. "You can't spend your last night before the hospital running around like a headless chicken. Let someone else fuss over you for a change."

It wasn't the worst idea. Seeing Simon and Geri laugh and joke together, like they used to, filled her heart with a bittersweet joy. For a few fleeting hours, it was as though the world hadn't fallen apart.

Back home later that evening, Grace wandered through the house, checking and re-checking everything. She'd prepared meals for the freezer, even though Geri had protested.

"You really don't need to do this, Mum," Geri had said, her voice tinged with frustration. "I'll take care of Dad. You just need to focus on getting through this."

But Grace couldn't help herself. Geri had been looking pale and tired lately, and though she hadn't said anything, Grace knew. She could see it in the slight curve of her daughter's stomach, the fullness in her face and hips. Geri *was* pregnant. Grace was going to be a grandmother—a role she had longed for.

Grace smiled to herself, thinking of how beautiful Geri looked with the extra weight. She seemed softer, more at peace in her body, even if she didn't realise it. Girls these days, with their obsession over being thin, didn't understand how lovely curves could be. In Grace's day, curves were celebrated. A girl wasn't ashamed of a bit of flesh—she flaunted it.

As she stood in the living room, giving it one final glance, she noticed a thin layer of dust on the mantle and a few crumbs under the dining table.

"It could do with a quick vacuum," she murmured, but there was no time now. It would have to do.

Max came in from the shed, wiping his hands on a rag. "Everything alright, love?" he asked, his voice gentle.

"Yes," she said, smiling at him. "Everything's fine."

He walked over, pulling her into a warm hug. For a moment, she let herself sink into him, finding solace in his steady presence.

"We're going to get through this, Grace," he said quietly, as if reading her mind.

"I know," she replied, her voice softer than she intended.

It was strange. She had spent so much of the past few weeks pretending to be strong, putting on a brave face for everyone else, but here, in Max's arms, she allowed herself a moment of vulnerability.

Tomorrow, everything would change. But tonight, in their home filled with love and laughter lingering in the air, she let herself believe that maybe—just maybe—it would all be okay.

Chapter Twenty-Eight

Geri

THE FAMILY ROOM WAS cold and sterile, and I felt its grey walls closing in on me. The ticking of the clock on the wall seemed louder with every passing second, each tick a reminder of how much time had gone by without news.

Dad was sitting across from me, his face buried in his hands, shoulders shaking with sobs he couldn't control. I wanted to reach out, to comfort him, but I couldn't. I was too numb. My hands rested limply in my lap, my fingers occasionally twitching as though they didn't know what to do.

The image of Mum being wheeled into the operating theatre kept replaying in my mind. Her brave smile, the way she held our hands tightly and told us not to fret. It felt like she was comforting us when it should have been the other way around.

Her eyes had flashed with panic just before they pushed her through the double doors. That look would haunt me forever.

Simon came through the door, balancing three paper cups of tea. He placed them on the table, then did something I never expected—he wrapped his arms around Dad, pulling him close like it was the most natural thing in the world.

Dad clung to him, sobbing into Simon's shoulder.

And that's when I finally broke.

The tears came fast and hard, and I couldn't stop them. My chest heaved with sobs, and I felt like I was splintering apart from the inside out.

Simon released Dad and turned to me, sitting down beside me on the uncomfortable plastic chairs. He didn't say anything. He just placed an arm around my shoulders and pulled me close.

Mum had been so strong—how could she be so strong? That thought gnawed at me, over and over, as we waited.

The surgeon, Doctor Price, had been honest with us that morning. She said she would try to remove the entire tumour, but there were risks. The tumour was close to the optic nerve, and there was a chance it could affect Mum's vision or her personality.

But the worst case was that they wouldn't be able to remove it all.

That possibility hung over us like a dark cloud, suffocating every thought. None of us dared to say it aloud, but it was there, unspoken, in every glance we exchanged.

By 5 pm, I was shaking uncontrollably in Dad's arms, certain something had gone terribly wrong.

"What's taking so long?" Dad whispered for the hundredth time, his voice trembling.

"I'll go see if I can find anyone." Simon rose quickly.

When he returned a few minutes later, there was a small, hesitant smile on his face.

"They've brought her up to recovery," he said.

"Oh, thank God," I gasped, my hands flying to my mouth. "Is she okay?"

"They said she's still asleep, but we'll be able to see her soon. The surgeon will be out to talk to us shortly."

Simon sat down between us, his arm around me and his hand resting on Dad's arm. The warmth of his presence was reassuring, even though my mind refused to stop racing.

It was another twenty agonising minutes before Doctor Price entered the room. She looked tired, her shoulders slightly hunched. She sat down across from us, so close her knees nearly brushed ours.

Her expression was unreadable, and I realised I was holding my breath.

Simon, Dad, and I huddled together, our hands forming a tight, desperate knot.

She placed her hand over ours, her touch warm but heavy with meaning.

"How is my wife?" Dad asked, his voice cracking.

"She's holding her own at the moment," she began, her tone cautious. "We removed as much of the tumour as we could, but unfortunately, we weren't able to get it all."

We all gasped, a mix of relief and fear.

"The mass has been sent to the lab," she continued. "We won't know if it's malignant until we get the results back."

Dad's tears began again, rolling silently down his face. And then I realised the sobbing I heard wasn't coming from him—it was coming from me.

I grabbed a crumpled paper towel from the table and wiped my face, willing myself to stay calm. "What does it mean? Will she die?"

Doctor Price sighed, her expression softening. "It's very early days. The tumour had progressed further than we initially thought, and there were complications during the surgery."

"What complications?" My voice rose with panic.

She hesitated. "I'm sorry to have to tell you this, but your mum suffered a stroke during the procedure."

The room fell silent as her words sank in.

"She had to be resuscitated," she continued. "She's stable now, but she's still unconscious. We won't know the extent of the damage until she wakes up and we can run further tests."

Her words hit me like a physical blow. "You told us she was okay," I said, my voice trembling. "And now you're telling us she had a stroke? That she stopped breathing?"

Simon tried to pull me close, to calm me, but I shoved him away. "No, Simon. Leave me alone!"

I turned back to the doctor, my voice breaking. "So now what? Is she going to be a... a cabbage? Is that what you're telling us?"

Doctor Price's expression didn't waver. "I understand your fear, but let's not jump to conclusions. We need to wait for her to wake up and assess her condition. I know this isn't the news you wanted, but your mum *is* holding her own right now."

Her words were meant to reassure, but they didn't. They couldn't.

My body was racked with sobs, the emptiness inside me almost too much to bear. I slid from my chair to my knees at Dad's feet, burying my face against him as we cried together.

When I finally looked up, Doctor Price was gone, and Simon was standing by the window, his back to us. His shoulders shook, and I realised he was crying too.

It was unbearable. The waiting. The not knowing. The gnawing fear of what might come next.

God, this was awful. Absolutely awful.

Chapter Twenty-Nine

Grace

THERE WAS NOISE ALL around her—muffled voices, a persistent beeping, the faint shuffle of feet on tile. Everything felt distant as if it was happening on the other side of a thick pane of glass.

Where the heck am I?

Grace's thoughts felt foggy, slipping through her mind like sand through her fingers. Her throat was so dry it hurt like she'd swallowed shards of glass.

She could feel someone holding her left hand, gently stroking it. The touch was warm and familiar, but she couldn't place it. Her body felt unbearably heavy, each of her limbs weighed down as though she were made of stone.

She tried to open her eyes, but they wouldn't budge. Exhaustion washed over her, and she drifted into the warm, fuzzy haze again.

When she stirred again, it felt darker somehow, like the world around her had dimmed. She couldn't see—her eyelids stubbornly refused to lift—but she knew it was night.

Somewhere in the darkness, a voice whispered.

"Mum? Mum, can you hear me?"

It was Geri. Grace wanted to answer her and tell her she could hear her, but the words wouldn't come. She tried to lift her hand, just the smallest of movements, but her arm might as well have been made of lead.

The whispering continued, softer now, and Grace caught snippets of other voices mingling with her daughter's—low, soothing tones that were impossible to make out.

What's happening?

She tried again to fight through the fog, to make her body respond, but the effort left her exhausted. She sank back into the hazy warmth. There was something she needed to do—something important. But what was it?

The thought slipped away as sleep claimed her once more.

A sharp, scratchy sensation dragged her back. Someone was tickling the bottom of her left foot. The sensation annoyed her, and she tried to kick out instinctively, but her leg remained unresponsive.

She wanted to shout at whoever it was to stop, but her throat burned at the mere thought of speaking. Her sore throat was unbearable as if something was stuck there.

In the background, she could hear Max's voice. He was talking to another man, but the words were muffled and unclear.

Her head ached, a dull, throbbing pain that made it hard to focus. She felt confused and tired. Why couldn't she move? The question echoed in her mind, unanswered, as frustration bubbled beneath the surface.

Then Max's voice grew louder, closer. She felt him kiss her cheek, his lips soft against her skin.

"I love you," he whispered over and over. His voice trembled slightly, and Grace felt her heart ache for him.

He began to talk, his words wrapping around her like a comfort blanket.

"Do you remember our wedding day?" he asked softly. "You were so beautiful. You still are. The envy of all my pals. I couldn't believe my luck—I kept thinking you'd wake up one morning and realise you'd made a mistake."

Grace wanted to reach for him, to tell him how wrong he was. She'd loved him from the moment they'd met. He was older, yes—ten years her senior—but he'd been so sophisticated, so handsome.

Memories floated to the surface, vivid despite the fog. They had been introduced by mutual friends at a wedding anniversary party. She could still see him standing across the room, blatantly staring at her until his friend finally introduced them.

She'd thought he was the most charming man she'd ever met, and he'd swept her off her feet. They were married within four months, and though the early years hadn't been without their challenges, they'd built a good life together.

She remembered the heartbreak of trying for a baby and the years of disappointment until, when they had almost given up hope, Geraldine came along. Their miracle baby. And now, their baby was having a baby of her own.

The memory brought a flicker of warmth to Grace's chest, even as her body remained still.

That beeping again.

It was incessant and rhythmic, cutting through the haze. The sound tugged at her memory, pulling fragments of understanding together. A hospital. I'm in a hospital.

The fog in her mind began to clear slightly, and she remembered. The operation.

She wasn't dead. That was something.

But why couldn't she move? Why couldn't she open her eyes? Something wasn't right.

There had been commotion earlier—she vaguely recalled hearing Geri crying. Why had she been crying? Grace's thoughts raced, trying to piece together what she knew, but her head throbbed with the effort.

She tried to focus on her breathing, on the steady rhythm of the beeping beside her. One thing at a time, she told herself.

She could feel Max's presence again. He was there, holding her hand, his voice a soothing balm against the rising panic in her chest.

"Grace," he murmured, "you're going to get through this. I know you will. You're the strongest woman I've ever known. We've been through too much together for it to end now."

His words gave her something to hold onto, a lifeline in the darkness.

She wasn't sure how long she stayed like that, drifting in and out of awareness, but she began to focus on one thought that burned brighter than the rest:

She had to wake up. For Max. For Geri. For the baby.

No matter how heavy her body felt or how thick the fog in her mind, she would find a way.

She just had to.

Chapter Thirty

Geri

IT HAD BEEN THREE days since Mum's surgery, and the silence surrounding her condition was unbearable.

The doctors avoided us as much as possible, their polite, clipped updates offering no comfort. There's no medical explanation for why she hasn't woken up, they said. She's not in a coma, they insisted. But that only made it worse. If they didn't know what was wrong, how were we supposed to believe she'd ever open her eyes again?

Dad was a wreck. He refused to leave her side, mumbling to her endlessly about everything and nothing, as if his words alone could will her back to consciousness. He wouldn't eat, and the only way we got him to drink was by standing over him like he was a stubborn child. He hadn't gone home once—not even for a shower—and now his clothes hung on him like they belonged to someone else, his shirt wrinkled and stained, his face unshaven and pale.

Simon, as always, was the calm one. He'd taken over everything—calling family, dealing with the flood of well-wishers, and keeping the endless chaos at bay. Without him, I didn't know how we would've managed. He'd stepped in as if no time had passed like the wounds of our breakup hadn't happened. And for once, I didn't care about Kevin or what had gone before. I was just grateful for him.

Simon walked back into the room, balancing three steaming cups of tea. He set them down on the table, glanced at Dad, and, without hesitation, wrapped an arm around him. The sight of it—Simon comforting my father like they were still family—broke me. Tears spilled over, the weight of everything finally hitting me.

***

SIMON POPPED OUT INTO the corridor to call Kevin to give him an update. It was funny, but I no longer cared about Kevin and all that had gone before. I was just relieved that Simon and I were mates again. I don't know what I'd have done without him. I watched him through the glass chatting animatedly. *"I love you too,"* he mouthed into the phone before ending the call. It was strange how okay I was with this situation. But I was.

He walked back into the room.

Dad was talking quietly to Mum. On and on he went. All we could hear was a steady, mumbling drone, but it seemed to make him feel better, so we left him to it.

Simon stood behind my chair and began rubbing my shoulders.

"Is Kevin coping without you?" I asked.

"Seems to be. He sends his best wishes to you."

"That's nice," I said absently.

"There's something we need to talk about, Geri. Shall we go for a coffee?"

That had my attention. "What is it?" I asked, snapping my head around to look at him.

"Come on." He held his hand out towards me. "We'll bring your dad a sandwich back. Is that okay, Max? We're just going to the canteen."

"Wha ... yes, fine, whatever," Dad said impatiently, annoyed to have been disturbed.

We held hands in silence all the way to the canteen, my mind racing. Was he planning to go back home and leave me again? I didn't want to know.

We ordered coffee and a couple of tasteless sandwiches.

"I still haven't heard any more from James about Carl. I know Vinny's charged him, and he's been refused bail, but I wanted to go to see him." I was talking ten to the dozen just to avoid what I thought was coming. James had been calling every day for updates on my mum, but there had been no more attacks or information.

"Best you just focus on your mum for now. You'll make yourself ill at this rate," he said.

"I'm fine. Besides, I need to get out of here for a while."

"What about the baby?

I froze. "What baby?"

"Your mum told me about the baby."

Simon's words stunned me as I sat across from him in the hospital canteen. My mind raced. Of all the conversations I'd imagined having with him, this wasn't one of them.

The canteen was dimly lit, filled with the faint hum of conversation and the clatter of cutlery. The coffee in front of me was lukewarm, and the sandwich I'd picked at was tasteless, but none of that mattered now. All I could think about was that my secret—the one thing I hadn't been ready to share—was out.

I stared down at my hands, twisting a napkin between my fingers. "She told you?"

Simon nodded, his expression unreadable. "She wanted me to know. I think she was worried you wouldn't tell me, and she thought I needed to hear it."

A pang of frustration shot through me, but it was quickly swallowed by guilt. Mum had always known me better than I knew myself. If she'd told Simon, it was because she thought it was what I needed. And maybe, just maybe, she'd been right.

"I was going to tell you," I admitted, my voice barely above a whisper. "But with everything going on, I didn't know how. And honestly, I wasn't ready."

"I get that," he said softly. "I wasn't trying to push you. I wanted to give you the time and space to tell me yourself. But Geri, I'm worried about you. You're running yourself ragged between your mum and everything else. Have you been to see a doctor? Checked in on how things are progressing?"

I shook my head, tears stinging my eyes. "No. I just... I've been so scared, Simon. Scared about Mum, about the baby. About doing this without her."

He reached across the table, his hand warm and steady as it covered mine. "You're not alone, Geri. I know things between us haven't been easy, but I'm here for you. I'll be here for you, for the baby. Whatever you need, you've got it."

I looked up at him, the sincerity in his blue eyes undoing me. The man who had broken my heart was sitting here now, offering me a lifeline when I needed it most.

"I don't hate you," I said finally, my voice trembling. "I thought I did, but I don't. You're right—we've always been best friends. That's who we're meant to be. And I think, deep down, I've always known that."

Simon's grip on my hand tightened, his gaze never leaving mine. "I don't regret marrying you, Geri. I only regret that I couldn't be the husband you deserved. But I'm so glad we can still be this—whatever this is. And I'm so glad about the baby. This baby is going to be the best thing that's ever happened to us."

I let out a shaky laugh, the tears finally spilling over. "I'm scared, Simon. I honestly don't know how to do this without her. I need her to wake up."

Simon didn't say anything. He just stood, came around the table, and pulled me into his arms. His embrace was warm and familiar, and for the first time in days, I let myself cry—really cry. Every ounce of anger, fear, and sadness poured out of me, each sob pulling something heavy from my chest.

When the tears finally slowed, I pulled back, wiping my face with my sleeve. "I feel like such a mess."

"You're allowed to be a mess," Simon said gently. "But you're not in this alone, Geri. I'm not going anywhere."

For the first time in days, I felt a glimmer of hope. Maybe we could do this. Maybe everything wasn't as broken as it had seemed.

***

As we approached Mum's ward, the sound of alarms pierced the air, followed by hurried voices and the shuffle of feet. My heart plummeted, the chill of dread wrapping itself around me like an icy grip.

"Dad!" I called out, spotting him in the corridor outside Mum's room. He looked like a ghost of himself—pale, vacant, his hands wringing as if he could twist the worry out of them. His shoulders were slumped, and his eyes stared at something I couldn't see.

"Dad!" I shouted again, my voice trembling with panic. I grabbed his arms, shaking him slightly. "Dad, what happened?"

He turned his haunted eyes to me, his mouth opening and closing, but no words came. It was like he couldn't bring himself to say it, couldn't make the nightmare real by giving it form.

A nurse hurried out of the room, her face tight with focus. "Please, you'll need to wait in the family room," she said, gestured the room down the hall.

"No! Tell me what's going on! Is she okay? What happened?" My words tumbled out in a rush, but she was already moving away, her attention consumed by the commotion in Mum's room.

"Doctor Price will speak to you as soon as she's able," she called over her shoulder before disappearing back inside.

The world tilted. My legs felt like jelly, and I leaned against the wall for support. Simon was beside me in an instant, his hand on my back, grounding me. "Come on," he said gently. "Let's go to the family room."

The waiting room was quiet except for the faint hum of a vending machine in the corner. It felt too calm, too still, in stark contrast to the chaos unfolding down the hall.

Dad sat by the window, staring out at nothing. His hands gripped the arms of the chair so tightly that his knuckles were white.

"Dad," I said softly, kneeling in front of him. "Look at me."

He didn't move, his gaze fixed on something beyond the glass.

"Dad!" I repeated, louder this time. I reached out, gripping his arms to anchor him. "Tell me what happened."

His eyes finally focused on me, and the grief there nearly broke me. "She woke up," he said, his voice hoarse. "She woke up, and she was... fine. She smiled at me, Geri. She smiled. And then... then the alarms started. They told me to get out of the room. They pushed me out."

He broke off, his voice cracking. "Oh, Geri, what if she doesn't make it? What if—"

"Don't say that," I cut in, my voice shaking but firm. "She'll make it, Dad. She's stronger than this."

I glanced at Simon, desperate for reassurance. He stepped closer, placing a steadying hand on Dad's shoulder. "Geri's right," he said, though his eyes betrayed his own fear. "Grace is a fighter. She's going to pull through."

The minutes dragged like hours, the tension so thick it was suffocating. Finally, the nurse returned, her expression unreadable.

"You can come through now," she said, her voice clipped but not unkind.

We followed her down the hall, moving quickly despite the weight of our fear. My heart hammered in my chest as we entered the room.

And there she was—awake.

Mum," I breathed, my hand flying to my mouth. Relief and disbelief washed over me in equal measure. She looked frail, her skin pale against the stark white of the hospital linens, but her eyes—those beautiful, kind eyes—were open and filled with tears.

Dad was at her side in an instant, his trembling hand reaching to stroke her face. "Grace," he whispered, his voice breaking. "Oh, my Grace."

Tears streamed down his cheeks, falling onto her blanket as he leaned over to kiss her forehead. I could see his shoulders shaking, the weight of days of worry finally spilling out.

I stepped closer, brushing my fingers against her arm. "Hey, you," I whispered, my voice thick with emotion. "You gave us a scare, you know."

Mum's lips twitched into the faintest of smiles, her eyelids fluttering as if the effort was too much. Her gaze lingered on me for a moment before she closed her eyes again, her body sinking back into the bed as if the act of waking had drained all her strength.

Doctor Price stepped forward, her tone firm but compassionate. "She needs to rest now. I know it's hard, but you'll need to keep your visit brief."

I glanced at Dad, who was still holding her hand like a lifeline. "She's right, Dad. Let's go home for a bit. You need to rest too."

For a moment, he didn't move, his gaze fixed on Mum's peaceful face. Then he nodded, reluctantly releasing her hand. "Okay," he murmured. "But just for a couple of hours."

While Dad gathered his things, I pulled Doctor Price aside in the corridor.

"What happened in there?" I asked, my voice low but urgent.

She sighed, her professional composure slipping for just a moment. "We believe she forced herself out of her state, and her system went into shock as a result. It's not uncommon in cases like this. But she stabilized quickly, and I'm confident she's on the right track now."

"She'll be okay?"

"She'll need rest, but yes, I believe she'll be fine. When you come back later, you should see a real improvement."

Her words were like a balm to my frayed nerves. "Thank you," I whispered.

Dad and Simon joined us in the hallway, and I was struck by the change in Dad's expression. The despair that had haunted him for days was gone, replaced by a cautious hope.

"Come on," Simon said, his voice warm and steady. "Let's get you home, Max. Grace is going to need you well-rested when she wakes up again."

And for the first time in days, Dad smiled. It was small and tentative, but it was there. And that alone was enough to give me hope.

Chapter Thirty-One

Geri

"You missed a bit," Mum said, pointing to the corner of the window I'd already cleaned three times this morning.

"Thanks, Mum," I muttered, trying to keep my irritation in check.

Since returning home from the hospital, she'd transformed into a relentless supervisor, micromanaging every little thing I did. I knew she was desperate to get up and do it herself—she hated being idle—but strict doctor's orders confined her to rest. Dad and I had made it our mission to enforce them. It wasn't too difficult most of the time. The chemoradiotherapy was doing that job for us, draining her of the energy she once had in abundance.

The last five days had been brutal. Each morning, Dad had driven her back to the hospital for her radiation treatments. The mask terrified her—she'd cried after the first fitting and every session since. I could still hear her muffled sobs in my head whenever I thought about it. She wasn't usually one to complain, but her eyes told the story of her exhaustion and fear.

I straightened up from where I'd been crouched near the window, wiping my hands on a rag. "Oki-doki, Mother. What would you like for lunch?"

"Nothing for me, thanks. I'm not hungry."

She'd said the same thing at every mealtime for the past eight days.

I let out an exaggerated huff. "Soup it is, then. You're not skipping meals on my watch."

I went to the kitchen and warmed up some leftover vegetable soup, ladling it into two bowls. By the time I brought it to the table, she hadn't moved from her chair in the lounge, staring absently at the garden through the window.

After lunch, I was scrubbing dishes in the kitchen when I heard her moving upstairs. I figured she'd gone to the bathroom. I didn't think much of it at first—she'd been restless all morning, her anxiety bubbling just under the surface.

But after a while, the silence grew heavy. Uneasy, I dried my hands and headed upstairs. The bathroom door was closed, the faint sound of muffled movement coming from within.

"Mum?" I called, tapping lightly on the door. "You alright in there?"

No response.

I knocked louder. "Mum, come on. Are you okay?"

Still nothing. My stomach twisted, my mind leaping to the worst.

"Mum, I'm serious. Open the door. You're freaking me out." My voice wavered, panic creeping in. "If you don't open this door right now, I'm calling Dad."

I heard the faintest shuffle behind the door, followed by the click of the lock. Slowly, it creaked open.

I wasn't prepared for what I saw.

Mum stood in the doorway, scissors dangling from her hand. Her hair—her beautiful, thick chestnut hair—was gone. Clumps of it stuck out at odd angles, some areas shaved down to the skin, others unevenly chopped. It was a jagged, raw mess.

Her shoulders sagged, and the scissors slipped from her hand, clattering to the floor. She let out a low, keening sob that cut through me like a knife.

"Oh, Mum," I whispered, stepping forward. Tears blurred my vision as I wrapped her frail body in my arms and guided her to the bed.

We sat there, side by side, on the edge of the mattress, her sobs shaking her small frame.

"Why, Mum?" My voice broke as I spoke, brushing a hand against her cheek.

She couldn't meet my eyes. "It was falling out," she whispered, her voice raw.

I blinked, trying to process her words. We'd been warned this would happen, but there hadn't been any sign—no strands left on her pillow, no clumps in the brush. It felt too soon, too sudden.

"I couldn't bear it," she said, finally looking at me. Her tear-filled eyes were pools of anguish. "Every time I touched it, more would come out. It felt like... like I was losing myself piece by piece."

I swallowed hard, tears slipping down my own cheeks. "It's okay, Mum," I murmured, stroking her arm. "It's only hair. It'll grow back. And until it does, we'll figure something out. We'll get you scarves, hats—anything you want."

She nodded weakly, but the defeat in her posture remained. "I look hideous."

"No, you don't," I said fiercely. "You look like my beautiful Mum. You always will."

Her lips quivered, fresh tears spilling over. I stood and went to retrieve the scissors from the bathroom. As I swept the pile of her hair into a corner with my foot, I caught my reflection in the mirror. My curly locks framed my face.

And in that moment, something shifted inside me.

I picked up the scissors, my fingers gripping the handles tightly. Without hesitating, I pulled a handful of my curls forward and began cutting. The first snip felt jarring, but I didn't stop. Over and over, I hacked at my hair until it was short, uneven, and scattered around my feet.

I stared at my reflection, my chest heaving. I didn't feel regret or sadness. Just a strange sense of solidarity, of closeness.

"Mum?" I said softly, stepping back into her room.

She gasped when she saw me, her hands flying to her mouth. "Oh, Geri," she whispered, tears spilling anew.

She held her arms out to me, and I walked into them, climbing onto the bed like I'd done as a child. We clung to each other, our heads pressed together. I felt her fingers run gently over the jagged ends of my hair, her touch tender.

"You didn't have to do that," she murmured.

"I know," I said, my voice thick with emotion. "But I wanted to."

For the first time in days, I felt like I'd done something right—something that truly mattered. And as we sat there, holding each other, I realised we didn't need words to bridge the chasm this illness had created.

We had each other, and that was enough.

***

THE TIMER BEEPED AGAIN, snapping me out of my thoughts. I pulled the pie from the oven, the warm scent of golden pastry and bubbling filling wafting into the air. The cauliflower on the stove was ready, too, the creamy white florets perfectly tender. I drained it, scooped everything onto serving dishes, and arranged the plates neatly on a tray.

As I carried the food through to the dining room, the laughter and voices coming from the lounge softened my mood.

Dad had finally got over the shock—or at least, he was trying to. When I entered, he was seated at the table, still looking a little bewildered, but there was a small, amused smile tugging at his lips. Mum had taken her usual spot opposite him, her chin propped in her hand as she toyed with a stray jigsaw piece, the picture on the table half-formed but already colourful and bright.

"Dinner's served," I said, forcing cheer into my voice as I set the dishes down.

"Smells amazing, love," Dad said, but his eyes flicked back to me, lingering on my freshly shorn hair. He opened his mouth to say something, then seemed to think better of it and closed it again.

Mum reached out and patted his hand. "Stop staring, Max. It's only hair."

Dad let out a soft chuckle, shaking his head. "I wasn't staring," he protested half-heartedly. "I just... wasn't expecting it. That's all."

I slid into my seat, pouring gravy over the pie and vegetables. "It's a fresh start for both of us," I said lightly, although my heart still ached when I glanced at Mum's head. The hair we'd carefully trimmed into something tidy only accentuated the fragility of her face, the way her illness had thinned her cheeks and dulled the warmth in her skin.

Mum reached for her fork, taking her first bite with a little hum of appreciation. "This is lovely, Geri. You've outdone yourself."

"Glad you like it," I said, my tone casual, but the knot in my chest loosened. Getting her to eat was still a battle most days, but for once, she seemed genuinely hungry.

Dad dug in, too, the clink of utensils filling the space between us. For a moment, it was almost like any other family dinner—a pocket of normalcy amidst the chaos of the last few weeks.

But when I glanced up, I caught Dad looking at me again. This time, his expression wasn't shocked or amused. It was something else entirely—sadness, maybe, or worry. It was hard to tell.

"You okay, Dad?" I asked softly.

He nodded quickly like he didn't want me to dwell on it. "Just proud of you, that's all," he said, his voice thick with emotion. "Both of you."

I felt the sting of tears and quickly looked down at my plate, pretending to fuss with my food.

Mum reached for his hand again. "Oh, Max, stop being so sentimental. You'll set us all off." But her teasing was gentle, and there was a glimmer of amusement in her tired eyes.

Dinner passed in a mix of quiet chatter and comfortable silences. By the time we'd cleared the plates, and I was standing in the kitchen again, scrubbing at the dishes, I felt the weight of the day settle on me. My reflection in the window caught my eye once more. The sharpness of my new haircut still startled me, the way it framed my face so differently from the wild curls I'd had my whole life.

I ran my fingers over the prickly edges. It wasn't just hair; it was a part of who I'd been. Now it was gone.

But when I thought about Mum sitting at the table, smiling through the exhaustion, her laughter filling the room even for just a few fleeting moments, I knew I'd do it all over again.

It wasn't about the hair. It was about standing with her, showing her she wasn't alone. It was about reminding her that she was still beautiful, still strong, no matter what the cancer tried to take from her.

I took a deep breath, shaking the stray tears from my lashes. This is a new chapter, I told myself. For both of us.

Chapter Thirty-Two

Geri

IT'S SHOCKING, ISN'T IT? The way people stare, unashamedly, at anything or anyone slightly out of the ordinary. A blatant curiosity tinged with pity. I'd always been fortunate to blend in before, to move through the world unnoticed. But lately, I couldn't even bear to meet someone's eyes for fear of seeing that dreaded mix of morbid interest and thinly veiled sympathy. If it made me squirm, I couldn't imagine how Mum must have felt. After all, while I only looked the part—with my buzz-cut and brightly patterned bandana—she was the one actually fighting the battle.

My fingers smoothed the soft fabric wrapped around my head, the scarf that Mum insisted on calling a "head covering," as though it was something dignified and elegant. Simon had sent a whole boxful—rainbow-bright and cheerful—as soon as he'd heard about our new 'dos.' He said they'd help us "embrace our inner warriors." I wasn't feeling much like a warrior as I finally nosed my car into an empty parking space after twenty minutes of aimless circling. Mum would think I'd got lost.

I'd dropped her off at the hospital entrance earlier; there was no way she could have made the long walk from the car park. Still, guilt prickled at me as I hurried across the street. The January air bit at my face, cutting through my jacket as I spotted her sitting awkwardly on the bench near the doors.

"Mum, I'm so sorry," I called as I jogged over. She looked up, her pale face lifting into a wan smile that didn't quite mask her exhaustion.

"I couldn't face going in alone," she said softly. "My legs felt wobbly, so I thought I'd wait."

I noticed a man at the far end of the bench, blatantly staring at us. His gaze lingered too long, his eyes darting between Mum's hollowed cheeks and my vibrant pink bandana. I shot him a pointed glare, poking out my tongue at him for good measure. Mum chuckled faintly, her voice lighter for a moment.

"Come on, Mum. Think you can manage, or should I grab a wheelchair?"

"You won't catch me in one of those," she snapped, the spark of defiance flashing briefly in her tired eyes. Then, almost as quickly, she softened. "Sorry, love. I'll be fine to walk."

But she wasn't. Her shoulders sagged as if she bore the burden, and her frailty seemed more pronounced today. This was week three of chemoradiotherapy, and no matter how stoic she tried to be, the treatment was clearly wearing her down. I made the decision for her, darting inside and returning moments later with a wheelchair.

"Mum," I said gently, "do it. For me."

She sighed heavily but settled into the chair without further protest, and though she didn't say it, I could see the relief on her face.

Inside the oncology ward, the reception area was set up like a strange parody of a living room—worn armchairs circled around a low coffee table piled with old magazines. A boy, no older than seven, sat on a red plastic fire truck. A tangle of tubes ran from his arm to a rolling

IV stand, but his big hazel eyes shone with the boundless curiosity of childhood. My chest tightened at the sight of him.

"Hello," I said softly, sitting nearby.

"Hi." He sounded shy, but his smile was pure sunshine.

His mother slumped in the chair beside him, stirred awake and offered me a tired, apologetic smile. Her face was a map of sleepless nights and unseen battles. I nodded in return, my hand instinctively resting on the small bump of my belly.

"Have you got some cancer?" the boy blurted suddenly, his small face tilting in innocent curiosity.

"Toby!" his mother scolded, horror flashing across her features. "You can't just ask people things like that."

But I was already laughing, the sound spilling out despite myself. "It's okay," I assured her. "No, I don't have cancer, but my mum does."

Toby's eyes widened as he considered this, his gaze flicking to the bandana tied snugly around my head. "Then why don't you have hair?"

"Toby!" His mum buried her face in her hands, mortified.

"Because I think it's a cool look," I said, grinning. "Don't you?"

Toby giggled, and I felt a little lighter. There was something healing about his unfiltered honesty.

When Mum returned from the bathroom, the boy had opened up about his dream of becoming a firefighter. His enthusiasm was contagious, and I leaned in, captivated by his stories.

"I've got a fire truck at home, too," Toby said proudly, gesturing to the red plastic one he was perched on. "But when I grow up, I'm going to drive a real one. With a siren!"

"That sounds amazing," I said. "You'll save lots of people, I bet."

His mother stirred beside him, her expression softening as she watched him. I could see the pride mingling with something deeper—an ache that couldn't be masked. She nodded when he turned to her for confirmation.

"You'll be the best fireman," she said, her voice tender but thick with the effort of holding it together.

Mum was standing by the front desk now, quietly letting the nurse know we'd arrived. I waved her over, eager to introduce her.

"Mum, this is Toby. He's going to be a firefighter when he grows up."

"Well, hello, Toby," Mum said, crouching slightly to shake his tiny hand. "That's a very brave job. You must be strong."

He puffed out his chest, delighted. "I am. And your bandana's cool," he added, eyeing the deep blue scarf wrapped neatly around her head.

Mum smiled, her hand instinctively brushing the fabric. "Why, thank you. I think you would look great in blue, don't you?"

Toby's eyes lit up. "Can I try it?"

"Of course." Without hesitation, Mum untied the scarf and handed it to him. The moment was so natural and selfless that it nearly broke me. She didn't seem to mind at all as her bare scalp was exposed under the bright hospital lights.

Toby beamed, trying clumsily to tie the scarf around his head. His mum reached over to help, her hands trembling slightly as she adjusted it. When he looked up, his grin stretched ear to ear.

"Look, Mummy! I'm like Grace!"

Mum chuckled. "You wear it better than I ever could. I think you just might have to keep it."

Susan smiled at her son, though her eyes shimmered with unshed tears. "You're too kind," she murmured, almost as if to herself.

A while later, I followed Susan outside for a breather while Mum chatted with Toby. She led me through a maze of sterile corridors and out to a small courtyard lined with benches. A large ashtray, sand-filled and overflowing with cigarette butts, stood between the benches like a silent monument to the stress of illness.

Susan lit a cigarette, her hands shaking as she inhaled deeply. "You don't mind, do you?"

"No, of course not." I shook my head.

She exhaled a plume of smoke. "Toby had an aggressive brain tumour." Her voice was flat, as though she'd repeated the words too many times to count. "It was rare, and it only affects kids his age. They've managed to remove it, so that's good news for now, but if it comes back..." She shrugged one shoulder and took another drag of her cigarette. "The specialists have warned me it is likely to return."

My chest tightened as her words sank in. "I'm so sorry," I whispered. "But there must be a small chance it won't—surely?"

She nodded. "I pray for that every day. Miracles happen all the time, so I'm told. But if it comes back, I don't know what they'll do. His little body can't take any more chemo or radiation."

Tears pricked my eyes, and I turned my face away, ashamed to let her see my grief when she was the one living this nightmare. "Let's hope it won't come to that. He's fighting it for now—and they managed to remove it all. I know it's easy for me to say but maybe try to focus on the positives."

Susan nodded, her gaze distant. "Yeah. You're right. It's just hard, you know?" She took a last drag on the cigarette and stubbed it out in the ashtray.

I nodded and stroked her arm, wishing I could offer some comfort or words of wisdom, but I was helpless.

We stood in silence for a moment. When we finally made our way back to the ward, Toby was curled up in his chair, his energy visibly waning. But his face lit up when he began telling us about his trip to

Disneyland. Mum listened intently, smiling as though his words were the most important thing she'd ever heard.

When it was time for Toby to leave, he wrapped his little arms around Mum and me, his hug fierce and unrestrained. "Will you be here tomorrow?" he asked, his voice tinged with hope.

"Every day for a few weeks," Mum said. "How about you?"

He nodded. "Me too."

As they walked away, hand in hand, I felt the tears spill over. Mum reached for my hand, her own trembling as much as mine.

"What a special little boy," she said, her voice breaking. "It certainly puts what I'm going through into perspective. I've lived my life. His has barely begun."

I nodded, unable to speak. In that moment, all the frustrations, fears, and bitterness I'd felt over the past few weeks seemed to dissolve. Toby and his mum had shown us what true courage looked like.

Later, as we sat in the car, Mum reached up to touch the pink bandana I'd tied around her head.

"Thank you, Geri," she said softly. "For everything. But most of all, for just being here."

I held her hand tightly. "No, Mum. Thank you—for being you."

Chapter Thirty-Three

Geri

I DIDN'T TELL MUM what Susan had confided about Toby. There was no need—she already sensed how ill the boy was. She'd commented several times how unfair it all seemed, how it was different for her because, in her words, she was "old." It broke my heart to hear her rationalising her illness like that, trying to make it somehow less cruel, less tragic.

I couldn't imagine how she'd take the full truth—that the doctors had told Susan that Toby would need a miracle to save him—and miracles, it seemed, were in short supply.

The mood in the house was heavy when we got home. The air seemed to cling to us, weighted with unspoken fears. Dad was sitting in his usual armchair, but he looked up sharply when we walked in, his body tensed as if bracing for a blow.

"What's happened?" His voice was tight, his eyes darting between Mum and me. "What did they say?"

"Nothing, Dad. It's okay," I said quickly, forcing a reassuring smile. "Mum didn't even see the specialist today—just had her treatment. Didn't you, Mum?"

Mum nodded, shrugging off her jacket with trembling hands. She hung it on the bannister—a small act of rebellion that was so out of character, it startled me. I took the jacket quietly and placed it in the cupboard, the familiarity of the action grounding me.

"Are you sure?" Dad pressed. His eyes searched my face for any sign of deceit.

"Yes," Mum said softly. She placed a hand on his back, rubbing in slow, soothing circles. He visibly relaxed under her touch, the tension draining from his shoulders. But as I watched him, I noticed the deep lines etched into his face, the hollows under his eyes. His fair hair, once peppered with grey, seemed to have turned entirely silver overnight.

"Are you all right, Dad?" I asked gently once Mum had gone upstairs.

"Of course I am, lass," he said, but his voice wavered slightly. "Don't you go worrying about me."

I followed him into the kitchen, the warm light spilling over the cluttered countertops. "Are you sleeping at night?" I asked, leaning against the counter.

"Are you?" he shot back, his tone sharper than intended. He sighed, running a hand through his hair. "I'm sorry, love. I know you mean well. Truth is, I can't seem to get more than an hour or two at a time."

"That's no good, Dad. You'll make yourself ill. Maybe you should see Doctor Jessop. He could give you something to help you sleep."

He shook his head, his jaw tightening. "I'm not taking any of that stuff. I need to keep my wits about me while your mum's ill."

"But you'll be no use to anyone—least of all Mum—if you make yourself sick." I hesitated, then added, "You've lost weight, Dad. Honestly, you look worse than Mum does right now."

He flinched at that, his face softening. "I'll mention it to the doc next week. I've got an appointment booked. Will that do you?"

"If that's all you'll agree to, it'll have to," I said, though my worry lingered. "But promise me—if he suggests something to help you cope, you'll take it."

He nodded reluctantly. "I'll think about it. I promise."

I smiled faintly and patted his hand. "Good."

When he asked about the hospital visit, I told him only part of the truth. "Mum met a little boy who also has a brain tumour. It upset her, that's all." I didn't have the heart to tell him more. The weight of Susan's confession felt like a burden I hadn't asked for but now couldn't shake. Toby's bright smile and fragile body haunted me, and I couldn't reconcile the cruelty of it. But there *was* a chance—there *was* still hope.

Later, after checking on Mum and finding her fast asleep, I decided to call James. His familiar voice was a balm to my frayed nerves.

"Any news?" I asked.

"Not a sausage," he replied. His tone was light, but there was an undercurrent of frustration. "And no more attacks."

"That's something, at least," I said. "Do you fancy meeting up? I could use some company."

After some playful negotiation about food—James boasting about his toasted sandwich maker and me insisting on proper fish and chips—we agreed I'd head to his place for a gourmet toastie.

When I left the house, the sky was ink-black, and the sharp winter air cut through my coat. As I stepped off the kerb outside the village hotel, the heel of my boot snapped clean off.

"Bugger," I muttered, trying to keep my balance.

"Trouble there, Geri?" a familiar voice drawled.

I turned to see Vinny striding toward me, his smirk already in place. "I'm fine, thanks," I said coldly, hobbling toward the side entrance of the hotel.

"James in for a treat, is he?" he sneered.

"Fuck off, Vinny."

His laugh was low and mocking.

"What did I ever see in you?" I muttered, shaking my head.

"Oh, I can remind you," he said, his grin widening. "You told me I was the most handsome man you'd ever set eyes on."

I snorted. "Must've been drunk. Oh, and Vinny... James was right." I raised my little finger and wiggled it before disappearing into the hotel.

The reception area was nearly empty, save for a woman I didn't recognise behind the desk. She glanced up from her phone and offered a smile that felt forced.

"Good evening," she said, dragging out the syllables like she was reading off a script.

"Hi. James Dunn is expecting me," I replied, shifting my weight to my unbroken boot.

She nodded and waved me through with minimal enthusiasm.

I headed straight for the lift. The idea of hobbling up the stairs with a broken heel was laughable at best, humiliating at worst. The lift doors opened with a low chime, and I stepped inside.

When James opened the door, his grin was immediate, almost boyish. "What happened to you?" he asked, the chuckle escaping before I could answer.

"My bloody stupid heel broke," I grumbled, slipping the offending boots off and kicking them to the side.

"You don't have much luck with shoes, do you?"

I snorted, brushing past him. "Tell me about it. And to top it off, I just ran into Vinny. He drives me absolutely wild!"

James shook his head. "He has the same effect on me."

"Can't just be us," I said, glancing around the room. "He must do it to everyone."

True to his word, James had gone all out. The table was set with a couple of mismatched plates and a pile of toasted sandwiches in the middle piled onto a piece of kitchen roll.

"Are you actually allowed to do this in here?" I teased, gesturing to the teeny countertop cluttered with the toastie maker and utensils.

He shrugged, unbothered. "Don't care. I'm sick of the restaurant food downstairs. Fish and chips gets boring after a while."

"Fair point. And you really can't beat a cheese and ham toastie," I said with a grin.

"My sentiments exactly." He laughed, pouring two glasses of fizzy drink. As he carried them to the table, I couldn't help but notice how his shoulders stretched his plain white T-shirt. I quickly looked away before he turned back and caught me staring.

After we'd eaten far more than we should have, I joined him in the cramped bathroom to wash the dishes. I scrubbed a plate under the tap and grimaced. "I'm not sure this is very hygienic, James."

"Probably not." He laughed again, drying a mug with a tea towel. "Anyway—what did you want to talk to me about?"

"I just needed to get out," I admitted. "It's been a tough day at the hospital."

He paused, tilting his head. "Is it the chemotherapy?"

I shook my head. "No. Actually, it's nothing to do with Mum this time."

We moved back to the table, and I told him about Toby and Susan. His face darkened as he listened.

"That's terrible. Poor woman."

"I know. It's just so sad. Mum guessed something was wrong, even though Susan didn't tell her. She took it really hard."

"She would. She's a mother herself."

As if on instinct, my hand drifted to my stomach. The movement didn't go unnoticed. James, always sharper than he let on, raised an eyebrow. "Do you have something to tell me?" he asked, nodding at my stomach.

I hesitated, then smiled. "How did you guess?"

"I'm a good guesser," he said with a laugh. "Congratulations."

"Thanks. It's not exactly public knowledge yet."

He mimed zipping his lips and throwing away the key. "So, you and Simon?"

"Yeah, we're going to have a baby," I said softly.

"It's all back on with you two, then?"

"Not exactly. But we're in this together."

James leaned back, studying me. "Anyway, you didn't tell me what Vinny did to upset you."

"Oh, just his usual smart mouth. You know how he is."

"Unfortunately, yes. I've spoken to a few cops from Kirkby Mayor. He's not popular—he's like that with everyone."

"He can be nice when he wants to be," I said, recalling the charm he'd turned on during our date.

James raised an eyebrow. "Anyone can fake it for a short time."

"Maybe," I admitted. "It's a shame, though."

"His own sister has even washed her hands of him."

I frowned. "Are you sure? He told me he helps her with the kids because she's sick."

"She's sick, alright," James said. "But she won't let him near her or the kids."

"That's odd. He said he was only staying in the area to help her."

"More lies. They haven't been on speaking terms for years. Even his mum has barely any contact with him."

I shook my head, shocked. "He's a liar, then—not a great quality for the village's only policeman."

"Not great at all," James agreed.

When it was time to leave, I grabbed my broken boot and laughed. "Guess I'm walking barefoot."

"You're joking. It's freezing out there!" James grabbed a pair of trainers and handed them to me.

"They're massive," I said, slipping them on.

"You'll survive," he said with a grin.

As I shuffled to the door, laughing at my awkward gait, James stopped mid-motion, his coat halfway on.

"What?" I asked.

"That's it!" His eyes lit up, and before I could react, he scooped me up and spun me around, laughing like a madman.

"James! What the hell?" I shrieked, but his laughter was contagious.

"You've just solved the puzzle," he said, setting me down and planting a kiss on my lips, leaving me speechless.

James paced the small room like a caged tiger, his excitement palpable. "It's been staring us in the face all along!" he said, his hands gesturing wildly. "The footprints! We've been searching for a man with size eleven feet, but the rapist's wearing shoes that are too big to throw us off!"

I leaned against the table, still wearing his oversized trainers, and watched him work through the revelation. "So, you think the real rapist has smaller feet—like, what, size eight or nine?"

"Exactly." He stopped pacing, gripping the back of a chair. "Think about it, Geri. It's brilliant in a sick way. The only thing he couldn't avoid leaving behind at the scene were footprints. By wearing oversized shoes, he completely misled the investigation from the start. Every detail we've built around his physical profile is wrong—his shoe size, his gait, everything."

"But why would the rapist frame Carl specifically?" I asked. "Was it just convenient, or is there something else?"

James frowned, his expression darkening. "I don't think it's random. Vinny was awfully quick to arrest Carl and close the case, wasn't he? And Vinny supposedly found the rapist's clothes in Carl's wardrobe—but the shoes? Conveniently missing."

My stomach turned. "You think Vinny planted evidence?"

James nodded grimly. "I wouldn't put it past him. He's got a reputation for cutting corners, and he clearly has a grudge against Carl. But we need proof before we accuse him of something that serious."

"Do you have any contacts who'd listen to this theory?" I asked. "Vinny certainly won't."

"I've got a few people in Kirkby Mayor who might help," James said, pulling his notebook from his jacket pocket. "But before we approach them, I want to refine the profile. I've got notes on nearly every man in the village—height, build, even shoe sizes. If we can identify someone who matches the new profile, we might get somewhere."

I watched as he spread his notes across the small table, pages of meticulous handwriting detailing the characteristics of various men in the village. It was a puzzle, and James was determined to solve it.

"Let's start with the basics," I said, leaning over the table. "We're looking for someone with a medium build, tall, and size eight or nine shoes. Someone who lives locally and had access to Carl's place to plant the clothes."

"Maybe—if *he* actually planted the clothes."

I nodded.

"And someone the victims wouldn't immediately see as a threat," James added. "He's been described as having a limp—but that's likely fake, part of the oversized shoes."

"Do you think he'll strike again?" I asked, the thought sending a chill down my spine.

James hesitated, his jaw tightening. "I hope not. He'll be keeping a low profile while Carl is in the frame. But if he thinks the heat's off, he might."

His words settled heavily between us. The rapist was still out there—still walking the same streets we did—biding his time. It was a terrifying prospect. But for the first time, I felt like we were finally getting closer to the truth. And I knew James wouldn't stop until he uncovered it.

"Does this mean you're not going home after all?" I asked, thrilled.

"You bet it does."

Chapter Thirty-Four

Geri

MY STOMACH CHURNED WITH nerves as James and I shuffled forward in the queue toward the visitors' centre of Durham Prison. The cold, institutional smell of disinfectant hit my nose, a sharp reminder of where we were. I wrapped my coat tighter around me, wishing I could swallow the lump in my throat.

"You did bring your ID, didn't you?" James asked, for what felt like the third time that morning.

"For the last time, yes. I've got my driver's license." I sounded more irritable than I meant to.

"Sorry," he muttered, stuffing his hands into his jacket pockets. "These places unnerve me. I don't know why. It's not as if they'll lock me up and throw away the key if I look too shifty or don't avoid the guards' eyes." He forced a laugh, trying to lighten the mood.

"I know what you mean," I said, distracted by the large woman in front of us who had just let the heavy door swing shut in our faces.

James lunged forward, catching it before it could slam. "Charming," he muttered under his breath.

The woman turned sharply, sucking her teeth loudly in disdain. Her glare lingered far too long, her eyes narrowing like she was daring us to say something. My stomach flipped uneasily as I instinctively reached for James's arm, patting it for reassurance.

James offered her a tight smile, but his hand hovered protectively near mine. The woman finally turned back around, her broad shoulders blocking the view ahead.

I whispered, "I really don't want to end up in a fight here."

James squeezed my hand briefly. "You won't. Just stick with me."

I nodded, though my heart continued to race. Glancing around, I couldn't help but notice the assortment of people in the queue. A few looked normal enough—a well-dressed elderly couple, a man with the harried air of a solicitor—but the rest made my skin crawl. Hardened faces, loud conversations filled with curses, and the kind of body language that screamed they weren't strangers to confrontation.

My teeth chattered as we approached the metal detectors. "We have to go through separately," James murmured, motioning for me to take the line to the right while he went left.

I stepped forward hesitantly, eyes darting to the two dogs weaving through the visitors. One of them, a sleek brown spaniel, stopped suddenly next to the woman in front of me and sat down, tail wagging expectantly.

The guards moved in almost instantly, leading the woman to a side room without a word. The door clicked shut behind her, leaving the rest of us to gape.

I found James on the other side. "Did you see that?" I whispered.

He frowned, looking around. "See what?"

"The dogs sniffed something on that woman. They whisked her away." I nodded toward the door.

James raised an eyebrow. "Couldn't have happened to a nicer person." He smirked.

When we reached the reception desk, a grim-faced clerk asked for our names and IDs. After that, we were told to sit in a small waiting area until we were called. The grey plastic chairs were uncomfortable, and the stark fluorescent lighting made the space feel even colder.

It wasn't long before a female guard called our names and led us to the visiting room. The air was thick with tension as we entered, the low murmur of voices punctuated by the occasional outburst of laughter or tears.

James guided me to one of the plastic tables. My knees felt weak, and I was sure I was about to faint.

"You alright?" he asked, concern etched across his face.

I nodded, though my shaking hands betrayed me. James didn't hesitate—he steadied me around the waist and eased me into the chair. "Stay here. I'll get you some water."

He returned moments later with a plastic beaker. I took it gratefully, sipping slowly to calm my racing heart.

The side door opened, and prisoners began filing in. I watched, tears prickling my eyes, as families embraced their loved ones. The raw emotion in the room was almost too much to bear.

When Carl appeared, my stomach lurched. His once-floppy quiff was now shaved into a rough crew cut, and the lines on his face made him look years older.

I jumped up, throwing my arms around him. He stiffened, clearly uncomfortable, and gently pushed me away. "Hey, Carl." I forced a smile.

He nodded at James, shaking his hand. "Good to see you, mate."

We all sat down, the awkwardness hanging thick in the air.

"How are you?" I asked.

"Peachy," he said with a wry smile. "Love the new look". He nodded toward my bandana.

I laughed nervously, touching my head. "Thanks. Could say the same to you. Did you get my letter?"

"I did. Sorry, I didn't write back—I'm not much of a letter writer. How's your mum?"

"She's doing okay," I said. "We wanted to bring you cigarettes and toiletries, but when James rang yesterday, they said it wasn't allowed."

Carl shrugged. "I'm trying to quit anyway. Place like this gives you plenty of reasons to stop."

James cleared his throat. "Anyone want a drink?"

We both nodded, and he got up to head for the vending machines.

"I'm sorry it's taken so long for me to visit," I said quietly.

Carl shrugged again. "Can't say I blame you. With everything pointing my way... It's not like I've made it easy for anyone to believe me."

"I believe you. I don't think you're the rapist for one minute—neither does James," I said firmly, my gaze locked on Carl.

His eyebrows shot up in surprise. "Really?" For a fleeting moment, his face lit up, but the hope faded almost immediately. "Auntie Beryl does, though. I can tell."

"I don't think she does," I said, shaking my head. "She's just struggling to understand how those clothes ended up in your wardrobe. It doesn't make sense to her—or to me."

James returned to the table, carefully balancing three cups of tea. The liquid sloshed precariously with every step. I jumped up to help him, taking two cups and placing one in front of Carl.

"Thanks, James," I said as he fished sachets of sugar and a couple of stirrers out of his pocket, scattering them across the table.

"Yeah, thanks, mate," Carl said, dumping three sugars into his tea before giving it a half-hearted stir.

"We were just talking about Auntie Beryl," I said to James, lowering myself back into my seat. "Carl thinks she believes he's guilty."

James frowned. "That's tough."

"It's not just tough—it's wrong," I interjected, glancing at Carl. "Who could have put those clothes there?" I scratched my head in frustration, wishing for an answer to appear out of thin air.

Carl shook his head slowly. "I've no idea. No one came to the house except me, you—and Auntie Beryl, of course. I've gone over and over it, and nothing adds up."

James leaned forward, his brow furrowed. "Did anyone else have access to your keys? Someone at work, maybe?"

Carl seemed to consider this for a moment before shaking his head. "I don't think so. My house key was always on my car keyring. The only time I took it off was that night we saw you and Simon in Kirkby Mayor."

I froze, the memory of that night flashing vividly in my mind. "Hold on a minute—you gave Vinny the key for me that night?"

Carl nodded. "Yeah. That's why we stopped."

"He didn't give it to me," I said, my voice hardening. "I didn't get it from him until after they'd searched the house—late the day after."

"Really?" Carl's eyebrows furrowed, confusion clouding his face.

"I can confirm that," James said, his tone grim.

Carl sighed, running a hand over his face. "No matter. It's just Vinny flaunting his power, as usual. But it's bloody frustrating."

"Vinny being a bastard—surprise, surprise," I muttered, rolling my eyes.

James cleared his throat, drawing our attention back to him. "Anyway, we think we've come up with some evidence of our own. Don't we?"

I turned to James expectantly, feeling a flicker of hope.

James hesitated before speaking, his voice measured. "Yeah. We think the rapist wore boots that were too big for him—probably two sizes or more. It explains the shuffling limp witnesses described. But the problem is, I don't know how we can prove it yet."

Carl sat up straighter, his shoulders squaring as though he'd finally found a lifeline. "That's great! At least you've got something to go on."

I shrugged, unwilling to let hope take root just yet. "It's something, but it's not enough. James thinks he might be able to convince one of his cop mates in Kirkby Mayor to re-examine the case. But he wants to go through all his notes first—at least then he can put forward some potential suspects instead of just a theory."

"That's a good idea," Carl said, nodding firmly. "At least someone's on my side."

I reached across the table, placing my hand lightly over his. "It might take some time, Carl, but we won't give up on you. I promise."

His expression softened, his eyes glistening with unshed tears. "Thanks, Geri. That means everything."

James gave a small, encouraging smile. "We'll get there. We just have to be smart about it."

As the conversation shifted to lighter topics, the heaviness in the air eased slightly, though the weight of what lay ahead still lingered in the back of my mind. There was no denying the uphill battle we faced, but as I glanced between James and Carl, I knew one thing for certain—we wouldn't stop until we uncovered the truth.

***

"Penny for them?" James asked, breaking the silence as he manoeuvred the car onto the motorway. The hum of the engine filled the space between us, but it didn't drown out the unease twisting in my chest.

"Oh, you know—I feel terrible leaving him in that awful place," I admitted, staring out of the window as fields blurred into patches of grey sky.

"He seems to be coping alright, though," James offered, his voice steady, though I caught the flicker of doubt beneath it.

I shook my head. "That was just an act. He's not, not really. I could see it in his eyes."

James sighed, gripping the steering wheel tighter. "I don't know how we're gonna get him out, Geri. We have to play this safe. If Vinny gets even a whiff of what we're up to, he'll make our lives hell—and Carl's."

"I know," I said softly. "Don't worry. I won't say a thing."

The rest of the drive passed in heavy silence, my mind swirling with the weight of it all. When James finally turned onto the gravel path leading to the cottage, I let out a sigh of relief, ready to be home. But the sight that greeted us made my stomach drop.

The front door was wide open.

James cursed under his breath, his hands tightening on the wheel as he brought the car to an abrupt stop. My pulse quickened, panic spreading through me like wildfire.

"Stay here," he said sharply, but before he could even undo his seatbelt, Beryl appeared in the doorway, her face ashen. Her dishevelled hair and the way her hands clutched the doorframe sent a cold wave of dread through me.

My heart plummeted to the stone floor as I scrambled out of the car, my legs shaking so badly I could barely stand. "Beryl, what's wrong? What happened?" My voice came out higher than I intended, a tremble betraying the fear I was trying to suppress.

She didn't answer immediately. Her lips parted, but no sound came out at first. Then, finally, she found her voice, though it was thick with emotion. "Geri—it's your mum."

Chapter Thirty-Five

Geri

"HEY, YOU," SIMON CALLED as he stepped out of his car, his smile lighting up his face despite the tension I knew he must have felt.

I hurried toward him, relief flooding through me at the sight of his familiar face. "I'm so glad you're here." I leaned up to kiss his cheek, barely holding back the tears that had been threatening to spill all morning. Mum was in the lounge, and the last thing I wanted was for her to see me upset.

"How is she?" he asked, glancing past me toward the cottage.

"No more seizures, touch wood." I tapped my temple. "Let's get your stuff inside, then we can go for a walk. I don't want her overhearing anything."

"Of course." He moved to the boot of his car and pulled out a white Adidas sports bag.

"New bag?" I asked, eyeing it curiously.

"A gift," he replied, his voice tight as he avoided my gaze.

Mum's face lit up as Simon entered the cottage. She held onto him tightly when he bent to hug her, her frail arms wrapped around him as though he were a lifeline. I bit my lip, fighting back a fresh wave of emotion as Simon clapped shoulders with Dad.

"Put your bag in my room, Si," I told him, gesturing upstairs.

"Are you sure you don't mind me staying here? I could just as easily go to Kirkby Mayor later on."

"Course we don't mind," Mum said, her voice soft but firm.

Dad reached for Simon's bag. "I'll take that up for you."

"Nonsense, Max," Simon protested, reaching to take it back. "You sit yourself down. You've had a long day as well. Geri, are you putting the kettle on?"

I smiled faintly. "Can do. Tea all round?"

Everyone nodded, and I escaped to the kitchen, grateful for a moment to collect myself.

When I returned with the tray of tea, Mum was talking animatedly to Simon, her hands fluttering as she described her last dash to the hospital.

"... I decided to quit the treatment," she said, her voice firm despite the exhaustion etched on her face. "I was feeling terrible, and I don't want to spend whatever time I have left in the hospital dealing with seizures and other things caused by the poisons they were pumping into me."

"And how do you feel now?" Simon asked, his brow furrowed with concern.

"Still incredibly tired. This is the first time I've been out of bed all week. I've been sleeping most of the day and all night, but I'm hoping I'll start to feel a little better soon."

Dad and Simon exchanged a quick glance, one of those silent conversations I wasn't supposed to notice. I pretended not to, pouring the tea and handing out cups.

"And the seizures?" Simon pressed gently.

"I've had three small ones since I've been home. They've put me on medication, but they haven't got the dosage right yet."

Dad asked Simon if he was staying for the weekend, and Simon assured him he could stay longer if needed. Mum waved him off, insisting they didn't need him to do anything. I noticed the flicker of something unspoken in Dad's eyes again.

"Finish your tea, and we'll go for a walk," I suggested, anxious to talk to Simon alone.

"He's only just got here, Geri. Leave the poor boy alone," Mum grumbled.

"I'm fine, Grace," Simon said, standing up and stretching. "I could do with stretching my legs, actually."

I put on my coat and new boots, and we headed outside. The cold air bit my cheeks.

"She's lost so much weight since I was last here," Simon said quietly as we strolled across the green.

"I know," I replied, my voice tight. "She's never hungry. It's a battle just to get her to eat a few bites."

Simon slowed his pace, turning to face me. "And you? How are you holding up?"

I shrugged. "Fine. Just getting on with it." My voice sounded hollow, even to me. "We didn't tell her about the scan results. She thinks it was her decision to stop the chemo, but the truth is, the doctor said it was pointless anyway."

"And the baby?"

I shrugged. "To be honest, I haven't had a chance to think about it. But thankfully, I've stopped feeling as sick. Looking after Mum and Dad is a full-time job."

Simon sighed, running a hand through his hair. "I'm so sorry, Geri. I'll stay as long as you need me to—I mean it."

I managed a small smile. "I know you will. But you don't need to put your life on hold. We'll probably need you more later when things get worse."

"Anytime you need me," he said earnestly.

As we reached the pub, James came out of the side door, his hands shoved into his coat pockets.

"Oh, hi, James."

"Geraldine. Simon."

Simon did a double-take, recognition dawning on his face. "Bloody hell—it's James Dunn!" He reached out, and they exchanged an elaborate handshake before bumping shoulders like old friends.

"Got anything yet, James?" I asked.

James shook his head grimly. "Nothing. Everyone who fits the build has an alibi. I hate going to the police without something solid, but we might not have a choice."

Simon's expression turned puzzled, so I quickly explained. "James and I are trying to prove Carl is innocent of the rapes, but we're not getting far. You saw how unreasonable Vinny can be."

Simon scoffed. "Did I ever."

"Total prick," James muttered.

We said our goodbyes, and as James walked off, Simon turned to me with a mischievous grin. "He fancies you."

I rolled my eyes, laughing. "You couldn't be more wrong."

"Trust me, it's obvious," he teased.

"Whatever," I said, mimicking his tone.

He pulled me into a playful headlock, rubbing his knuckles into my scalp. For the first time in weeks, I felt a spark of genuine happiness. With Simon here, it was as though the crushing weight of responsibility had eased, even if only slightly.

***

THE WEEKEND SLIPPED THROUGH my fingers far too quickly. Simon stayed until early Monday morning, promising to return on Friday. While I couldn't imagine Kevin being thrilled about Simon's frequent absences, I selfishly relished the comfort of having him here. We'd even shared a bed again like we used to. It was easy to forget the pain of our past when we were laughing and talking into the early hours, the details of our complicated history tucked away in the background.

After Simon left, Mum watched me with her knowing eyes as I tidied up the breakfast table. "You think there may be some hope for you two?" she asked casually, though her tone suggested she'd been pondering it all weekend.

"You know there's not, Mum," I replied, shaking my head as I wiped the counter.

"I know nothing of the sort," she countered with a mischievous glint in her eye. "He could be bisexual."

"Mum!" I laughed in disbelief. "I'm shocked you even know that word!"

She smirked, clearly proud of herself. "I'm not as green as I'm cabbage-looking, Geri. I've been about a bit, you know."

"I know, but—"

"So, is he? Bisexual?" she pressed, her curiosity unabashed.

"No, Mum," I said firmly. "He's gay."

She pursed her lips thoughtfully. "Still loves you, though."

"And I still love him," I admitted, my voice softer. "But not like that anymore."

She nodded, her expression unreadable, but before she could press further, a sharp knock at the lounge window caught my attention.

I went to the door and found Auntie Beryl standing on the step, her coat wrapped tightly around her. Her familiar smile softened the lingering ache from Simon's departure.

"Hi, Auntie Beryl. Come in. Mum's downstairs again today."

"That's good news," she said warmly as she stepped inside, patting my arm. "Is she up to a visitor?"

"You're not a visitor," I laughed, closing the door behind her. "You're practically family."

"Ah, that's nice, lovey," she said, her cheeks pink with pleasure.

"Fancy a cuppa?" I asked, heading toward the kitchen.

A few minutes later, I brought a tray of tea into the lounge, leaving them to chat while I escaped upstairs to tackle the beds. Changing Mum's sheets and tidying her room was always easier when she wasn't around to micromanage. I worked quickly, grateful for the rare stretch of solitude.

When I came back downstairs, Mum was fast asleep on the sofa, her frail chest rising and falling in a steady rhythm. Auntie Beryl glanced up from her teacup and smiled.

"You should've shouted me, Auntie Beryl."

"That's okay. She hasn't been asleep long."

"Have you heard anything from Carl?" I asked, sitting down across from her.

"Not a peep," she said, shaking her head sadly.

"You know James and I went to see him last week?"

"Yeah. I meant to ask how it went."

"He's not guilty, you know," I said firmly, watching her face closely.

She sighed and set her cup down on the saucer with a faint clink. "I want to believe that, Geri. He's my only sister's son, and it'd break her heart if she were here now."

"He's being set up," I said, leaning forward.

Beryl's brow furrowed. "Who by? Who'd want to set him up, and who had the chance to plant those clothes?"

"I don't know," I admitted. "But I do know it wasn't Carl."

She studied me for a moment, her sharp eyes probing. "How can you be so sure, lovey?"

I hesitated, my resolve firm even as my voice wavered. "I just am."

Beryl sighed again, her expression softening. "I hope you're right, Geri. I really do."

Chapter Thirty-Six

Geri

CHRISTMAS MORNING DAWNED BRIGHT and cold, the frost glinting on the walls and hedgerows as if nature had decorated in solidarity.

Inside, the house hummed with activity, warmth radiating from the kitchen and chatter filling the air. Even Mum, who'd spent much of Christmas Eve in bed, was determined to be part of the day, her resolve shining as brightly as the decorations strung along the mantelpiece.

Beryl had arrived at the crack of dawn, bustling in with her usual energy, offering to handle the lion's share of the cooking. She was clearly trying to stop herself from worrying about how Carl was spending his day stuck on remand in a prison cell. She didn't want to talk about it, and I respected her wishes. But, her being here left me free to focus on Mum which I was grateful for.

Dad had gone into Carlisle to fetch Nana, leaving the house to settle into a comfortable rhythm of preparation and anticipation.

"Right, missus—let's get you spruced up," I said to Mum. "I'll even do your makeup if you like."

She gave me a weary smile from her spot on the sofa, wrapped in her robe. "That would be lovely, thanks, love. But I don't think I'll manage much dancing today," she added, a touch of dry humour laced in her words.

I guided her upstairs to her room, where the salmon-coloured silk dress she'd chosen for the occasion hung waiting, its tags still attached. Once she slipped it on, it was clear it was meant to hug curves she no longer had.

"Hmm," I said, frowning as I adjusted the fabric. "What do you think about adding a belt?"

She nodded, and we cinched a cream-coloured belt around her waist, giving the dress some shape. I added a new silk scarf to her head and applied a touch of makeup—just enough to bring a glow to her cheeks. By the time we finished, she almost looked like her old self.

When Dad returned with Nana, I watched as his eyes filled with tears at the sight of Mum. He quickly blinked them away, his lips twitching into a smile as he stepped aside for Nana to enter.

"Grace—oh, thank goodness you're here," Nana declared dramatically. "This strange man forced me into his car!"

Mum laughed, the sound so natural it made my heart ache. "That's Max, Mum. Don't you recognise him?"

Nana blinked, her gaze darting between Mum and Dad. "Max?"

Dad nodded, producing a kazoo from his pocket and blowing into it with a comical toot.

We all burst out laughing, and I excused myself to the kitchen to check on Beryl, who seemed to be cooking enough food to feed the whole village.

At exactly 1 pm, James arrived, his arms laden with gifts.

"James! You didn't have to," I exclaimed, taking in the festive bags and parcels.

"I wanted to," he said simply. "Thank you for inviting me. Spending Christmas alone would've been miserable."

He'd bought chocolates and biscuits for everyone, including Beryl and Nana as well as beautifully wrapped gifts for me, Mum and Dad.

Mum's gift, a special microfiber pillow, brought a smile to her face. "It's perfect," she said softly, placing it under her head and pretending to fall asleep.

Dad was equally delighted with the solar-powered crank radio for his shed. "Brilliant," he said, grinning.

Then James handed me a tiny parcel wrapped in gold paper. My heart thudded as I opened it to find a fine gold chain with an emerald teardrop pendant.

"James..." My voice faltered. "You shouldn't have done this."

"Do you like it?" he asked, his voice low.

"Like it? I love it. But it's too much."

"No, it's not," he said, unclasping the chain and stepping behind me to fasten it around my neck. The warmth of his fingers brushed against my skin, and I realised everyone was watching. Mum's eyes glistened, a knowing smile playing on her lips.

"Right," I said, clearing my throat. "What are you drinking?"

James disappeared to fetch wine and beer from his car, returning with a box of chocolates and some homemade biscuits as a contribution to the day. Beryl, thrilled by his offerings, handed him a peeler and roped him into helping with the potatoes.

As their laughter echoed from the kitchen, I slipped upstairs to splash cold water on my face. The sadness of the occasion felt like a shadow pressing down on me, and for a moment, it became too much.

When I opened the bathroom door, I nearly collided with Dad, who was wiping his eyes with a crumpled tissue.

"Dad?" I whispered.

He shook his head, pulling me into a tight hug. The tears I'd been holding back spilled over, and we clung to each other, both of us breaking in the quiet sanctuary of the hallway.

When we finally pulled apart, I managed a wobbly smile. "I'd better fix my makeup."

"Good idea," he said with a weak grin.

I touched his arm. "What are we going to do, Dad?"

He sighed, his shoulders slumping. "I don't know, lass. I really don't. But we'll get through it. We have to. We have each other."

I nodded, hugging him one more time before stepping into the bathroom. As I stared at my tear-streaked face in the mirror, I realised he was right. We had each other, and for now, that would have to be enough.

I fixed my makeup quickly and headed downstairs to set the dining table. Mum had always been the queen of Christmas decorations, her flair for creating beautiful tables unmatched. I didn't have her eye for detail, but I did my best, arranging candles, holly sprigs, and her favourite silver place settings with care. By the time I finished, I felt a small spark of pride—it wasn't perfect, but it wasn't bad either.

Back in the lounge, Nana and Dad were laughing at some dated comedy show on the television, the sound of their shared amusement filling the room. Mum, curled up at the end of the sofa with her new pillow, was snoozing lightly, her breathing steady and calm.

By the time Auntie Beryl and James began serving dinner, it was exactly 3 pm—Mum's requested time to eat. Dad roused her gently and escorted her to the bathroom to freshen up, leaving me to oversee the final touches. The aroma of roast turkey and all the trimmings filled the house, wrapping us in an almost magical warmth.

Once we were all seated around the table, Dad surprised us by saying a short prayer of thanks. Not typically religious, the gesture carried extra weight, and we all murmured an "Amen" before reaching for the crackers.

"What do you call a bee with a quiet hum?" Dad asked, reading from his cracker joke with a theatrical flourish.

"I don't know—what do you call a bee with a quiet hum?" we chorused.

"A mumble bee!" Dad erupted into laughter, but it was Nana's confusion that made us howl when she made him say it again a little slower.

"I get that." She nodded earnestly, which only made us laugh harder.

"Okay, my turn," James announced. "Why did the hen cross the road?"

We groaned in unison before humouring him. "Why did the hen cross the road?"

"To prove she wasn't chicken," James said, wincing as he delivered the punchline.

"A hen is a chicken," Nana declared, shaking her head in disapproval, setting us all off again.

Even Mum joined in, offering her own: "Why is a foot a good Christmas present?"

"Why is a foot a good Christmas present?" we asked, already giggling.

"Because it's a stocking filler." Mum smirked, placing her green paper crown on her head with mock regality.

For the first time in years, we all wore silly paper hats without protest, reading each joke aloud with exaggerated enthusiasm. It felt good to laugh together.

"Okay, everyone—tuck in before it gets cold," Beryl urged, clapping her hands lightly.

The spread was magnificent: perfectly roasted turkey, stuffing, golden roast potatoes, creamy mashed potatoes, carrots, swede, parsnips, sprouts, peas, and rich gravy. Every dish was cooked to perfection, a testament to Beryl's skill in the kitchen.

Mum, however, barely touched her food. After a few bites, she slouched down in her chair.

"Are you alright, Mum?" I asked, my concern growing.

She nodded slowly, her eyes fluttering closed for a moment. "I'm wonderful, thanks, Geri," she said softly, putting her utensils down. Then, glancing at James, she asked, "Have you ever been married, James?"

James, caught mid-bite, coughed and quickly reached for his napkin. "Got close a couple of times," he admitted. "But it just wasn't meant to be."

"Why not? You're not gay, are you?"

"Mum!" I exclaimed, horrified.

"What? I'm just asking," she said innocently.

James laughed, his voice warm and easy. "No, Grace, I'm not gay. It just wasn't the right time or the right person."

"Do you think you'll ever get married?" she pressed, leaning forward slightly.

"I hope so—one day," James said, his tone sincere.

Mum smiled, the kind of smile that reached her tired eyes. "Sorry, everyone," she said after a moment, removing her paper hat and crumpling it into a ball. "I'm going to need a lie-down. Does anybody mind?"

"Of course not," we all replied at once, and Dad helped her upstairs, his hand steady on her back.

Once they were gone, Nana suddenly pushed her chair back with a loud scrape. "Where's John?" she demanded.

"John?" I asked, confused. "Oh—Grandad. He's not here, Nana."

"I want John!" she cried, her voice rising. "John!"

I stood quickly, placing a hand on her arm. "Nana, come on, finish your dinner."

She shook me off, her expression sharp. "I don't want dinner. I want to go home—John! John!"

"Dad will take you home when he gets back," I said, trying to soothe her.

James leaned in. "Where does she live?"

"A nursing home in Carlisle," I whispered.

"I don't mind taking her," he offered. "If you want to come along for the ride, that is."

I nodded gratefully. "Finish your dinner first." Turning to Nana, I said gently, "We'll take you home after dinner, Nana. Why don't you watch some TV while you wait? The Love Boat is on again."

Nana paused, considering this. "I like The Love Boat," she said, her agitation ebbing.

I exhaled in relief. "Come on, then," I said, leading her to the lounge.

When I returned to the table, Dad was back, his plate piled high once again.

"How's Mum?" I asked.

"Exhausted," he said, meeting my eyes briefly. "She was asleep before her head hit the pillow."

I nodded. "Nana was upset. She was calling for Grandad."

"I heard," he said with a sigh.

"James is taking her back after dinner."

"That's good of you, son," Dad said, glancing at James.

James smiled. "No worries."

Dad placed his knife and fork down, suddenly sad. "This didn't turn out to be such a good day after all, did it?"

Beryl patted Dad's hand. "It is what it is."

He managed a small smile and, as James cracked another joke about eating too much, I felt a flicker of gratitude amidst the chaos. No, it hadn't been perfect, but it had been real—and for now, that was enough.

Chapter Thirty-Seven

Geri

NANA DIDN'T PUT UP any resistance when we told her we were taking her back to the nursing home. In fact, she seemed almost eager, shuffling toward the front door with surprising speed, all thoughts of "strangers" apparently forgotten.

The drive was uneventful, the roads nearly empty on Christmas evening. With barely any traffic, we arrived at the nursing home in record time. As soon as we stepped through the security doors, Nana visibly relaxed, her tension ebbing away in the familiarity of the surroundings.

As the nurse came to escort her to her room, Nana turned to me, clutching my hand with a surprising strength. Her other hand pressed a crumpled five-pound note into my palm.

"Get yourself some sweeties, Geraldine," she said, her voice firm and insistent.

"No, Nana," I protested, gently trying to give it back, but she tutted impatiently and shoved it into my jacket pocket.

"Thanks, Nana." I leaned down to kiss her cheek, blinking rapidly to hold back the tears that threatened to spill. For just a moment, she'd been herself again—she'd known me. Even if it was a version of me from years ago.

"You okay?" James asked softly as we walked back to the car. His brow furrowed in concern, his mouth twisting in a sympathetic expression.

I nodded, though my voice wavered when I spoke. "She knew me then—just for a second. It's been years since she last recognised me, and I didn't want to let her go in." I sniffed, trying to steady myself. "Even if she did think I was still a little girl needing sweets."

James offered a faint smile. "That's got to be tough. I never even knew my grandparents. Both sets passed before I was born."

"That's terrible!" I said, my heart aching for him. As frustrating as my family could be, I couldn't imagine life without them. Poor James was so alone, except for his waste-of-space father, who barely acknowledged his existence.

James shrugged, opening the car door for me. "You don't miss what you've never had."

The ride back to the cottage was quiet, both of us lost in thought. When we pulled into the drive, I spotted Simon's car parked out front.

"Simon's here," I said.

James shifted in his seat. "I'll get going then."

"Don't be silly. You haven't had dessert yet—or played any of Dad's silly board games. No way are you escaping that."

James groaned, his face scrunching in mock horror. "Board games?"

"Dad insists—every year."

He hesitated. "Won't Simon mind if I stay?"

"Why would he?" I asked.

James shrugged, glancing out the window. "Oh, you know. Maybe he'll be jealous."

I laughed. "Trust me—he won't. And honestly, he'll probably enjoy the company. Now, come on."

Inside, Auntie Beryl was busy dishing up trifle, her masterpiece glistening with layers of sponge, fruit, custard, and cream.

"Who's for trifle?" she called.

"Me!" I said eagerly. "I love your trifle, Auntie Beryl."

Simon greeted me in the dining room with a kiss on the cheek and he shook James' hand, clapping him on the shoulder. I could see James relax, reassured by Simon's easy welcome.

It didn't last.

Simon's competitive streak flared during our marathon game of *Trivial Pursuit*. When James won the second round in a row—defeating Simon, the reigning family champion—the room erupted with laughter and light-hearted banter.

"Isn't it time you were leaving?" Simon asked, leaning back in his chair and theatrically checking his watch.

"Sorry to snatch the title away from you, but there's no need to be a sore loser," James teased, his grin wide.

Simon narrowed his eyes in mock outrage. "I thought you were a decent bloke. How wrong you can be."

"And I thought you'd be a gracious loser."

The rest of us groaned in unison.

"Low blow, James," I said, shaking my head.

Simon slapped the table. "I demand a rematch!"

"Not tonight," I said firmly, starting to pack up the game pieces. "It's already 11 o'clock, and that last game took hours."

"At a later date, then," Simon said, pointing a finger at James. "But don't forget."

"I accept your challenge," James said with a mock bow. Then he turned to Auntie Beryl. "Can I escort you home?"

"That's very kind of you, lovey." She smiled as he helped her into her coat.

Dad, Simon, and I stood at the gate, watching James walk Auntie Beryl to her door before heading across the green toward his hotel.

"Told you he fancies you," Simon said, nudging me with his elbow after Dad went inside.

I rolled my eyes. "You couldn't be more wrong, Simon."

"We'll see," he said, grinning.

I nudged him back. "Come on—let's get to bed."

Once we were in my room, I finally had a chance to fill him in on everything that had happened over the past week. The weight of the day began to lift as we talked, the familiar rhythm of our friendship grounding me in a way nothing else could.

***

BY MORNING, THE ATMOSPHERE in the house had changed. Mum had deteriorated so rapidly it was as if the person she'd been on Christmas Day—the one joking at the dinner table—was a memory from another time. She was weak, her breathing shallow, and every movement seemed like a monumental effort.

Dad, clearly shaken, called Doctor Jessop on his private number, who arrived within the hour despite it being Boxing Day. His presence, though reassuring, brought little comfort in terms of answers.

"She's lethargic and barely drinking," Dad explained, his voice tight. "Fluid's catching her throat—she's choking on it. What's going on?"

Doctor Jessop frowned as he examined Mum, his stethoscope moving methodically over her chest. "I can't say for certain," he admitted. "I think you should consider taking her back to the hospital for a thorough check-up."

Dad shook his head. "Not right now. We'll see how she is in a day or so."

But by Monday, things still hadn't improved. If anything, Mum seemed even more fragile. She wouldn't eat, barely sipped water, and spent most of the day drifting in and out of consciousness. Her face, once so animated even during her illness, was pale and hollow.

I couldn't take it anymore. I called the hospital and left a message for Doctor Price, or at the very least the duty oncologist, to call us back.

When Doctor Price called back, I put her on loudspeaker so Dad and I could both hear. "Doctor," I began, trying to keep my voice steady, "Mum's not herself. She's so weak, and she's choking on water. What's happening?"

Doctor Price's tone was calm but heavy with what she was about to say. "Unfortunately, it sounds as though Grace's tumour is growing back rapidly. This can happen with her type of tumour, I'm afraid. It's unpredictable. The best we can do now is focus on making her comfortable."

Dad cleared his throat, and I realised our hands were clasped tightly together. His grip was firm, but I could feel his fingers trembling against mine.

"We haven't had time to discuss this properly," Dad said, his voice low but steady. "But I'd prefer her to stay at home. If there's nothing more that can be done medically, I don't see why she can't be here with us."

There was a pause on the other end of the line before she replied. "If you're sure, Max. Caring for her at home won't be easy, but we can arrange resources to help you. Your GP and district nurses will assist, and if needed, Macmillan nurses can also support you. It's a team effort."

"She's been having terrible headaches," Dad said. "The painkillers you prescribed don't seem to be helping at all."

"We can increase her medication," the doctor said gently. "It will make her more drowsy, I'm afraid, but it will keep her comfortable and pain-free—and that's the priority now."

"How long do you think we have, Doctor?" I asked, my voice barely above a whisper. I knew Dad wanted to ask but couldn't quite bring himself to say the words.

The silence that followed was deafening. I felt Dad's gasp as he squeezed my hand tighter, both of us holding our breath.

"It's hard to say," she eventually replied, her voice soft with sympathy. "But considering how quickly the tumour seems to be progressing, I don't think you have very much longer. I'm so sorry."

The finality of her words hit like a tidal wave. Dad nodded slowly, his eyes brimming with tears he refused to let fall.

"Thank you, Doctor," he said quietly, his voice raw.

When the call ended, we sat in silence. My chest ached with the unspoken grief hanging between us.

"We'll take care of her," Dad said finally, his voice breaking. "Whatever it takes, we'll make sure she's comfortable, in her own home, with her loved ones surrounding her—it's the least we can do."

I nodded, unable to find words that wouldn't shatter under the enormity of what we were facing. Instead, I tightened my grip on his hand and leaned my head against his shoulder. Together, we would carry this burden—even if it felt impossible.

Chapter Thirty-Eight

Geri

BY THE TIME DAD emerged from his room, I had begun descending the stairs, heart pounding in sync with the muted hum of voices outside. The doorbell had just rung, and Auntie Beryl was smoothing down her black skirt before opening it.

Halfway down the stairs, I caught sight of a man in a sombre black uniform, his polished shoes glinting in the pale morning light. Beryl gasped softly, stepping back as though the air had been knocked out of her.

"They're here, lovey," she said, looking up at me.

I nodded, surprised by how steady my voice sounded. "We'll be right there."

From my vantage point, I could see the funeral director walk back to his car parked at the curb, the sound of the crowd on the village green growing louder in the background. My stomach turned as I realised how many people had gathered. I wasn't ready for this. I couldn't do this. I reached the bottom of the stairs and froze.

Then I felt Dad's hand on my shoulder. I jumped, startled. I hadn't even noticed him come down behind me.

"Let's do this, lass," he said softly.

I turned to him, gripping his hand tightly. His watery green eyes met mine, full of pain but unwavering. His lips trembled as he tried to give me a reassuring nod.

Together, we walked out the door.

The sight of the entire village, dressed in black, turning to face us as we emerged was surreal. It felt like stepping into a dream—a nightmare where everyone knew your grief, yet no one could take it from you.

A red car parked a few doors down caught my eye, and I saw Mum's sister, Auntie Sylvia, and her husband, Nigel, climbing out. The brief flicker of recognition was quickly dampened by the weight of why they were here. I raised my hand in a half-hearted wave before looking away.

Simon stepped forward, linking my free hand through his arm. He led us toward the waiting funeral cars, his presence steady and comforting. My stomach churned as I noticed Kevin standing just behind him. Simon had mentioned he might come but seeing him still sent a jolt through me. Surprisingly, I didn't feel anger or resentment—just a dull acceptance. He was here for Simon, and I didn't mind.

The ride to the crematorium in Kirkby Mayor passed in a blur, the silence inside the car heavy with unspoken thoughts. The service itself was a haze of hymns, prayers, and the sound of muted sobs around us. I held it together until the curtains began to close around Mum's casket. Then the dam broke. I couldn't stop the tears, my shoulders shaking as Simon hugged me, whispering quiet reassurances I barely heard.

Afterwards, we were ushered outside, where a sea of familiar and unfamiliar faces waited to offer their condolences. Dad stood stoically, nodding and smiling at the throngs of people approaching him. Many were strangers to me, and I couldn't help but wonder how they'd known Mum.

Simon excused himself to greet Kevin, leaving me by Dad's side. I scanned the crowd and felt my stomach flip as I saw Vinny heading toward me.

"Hi, Geri," he said, his tone uncharacteristically soft. "I just wanted to say how sorry I am. She was a lovely woman."

"Thanks, Vinny," I said, my voice barely above a whisper. "It's good of you to come."

"I don't attend every funeral in the village, but this one shocked me. It seemed so sudden."

"It was," I admitted, blinking rapidly to keep more tears at bay.

Vinny hesitated. "I know I'm probably not your favourite person right now, but if you need anything..." He shrugged awkwardly.

"I'll bear that in mind. Thanks. Are you coming back to the house for a cuppa?"

"I will, but I've got something to do first. Is it okay if I come along later?"

Before I could answer, James appeared beside me.

"Geri," he said, leaning down to kiss the top of my head.

"Thanks for coming, James," I said, nodding at Vinny as he backed away.

"I couldn't miss it. Your mum was a great lady."

"She was," I agreed, my throat tightening.

"If you need to talk, you know where to find me," James offered, his voice full of warmth.

"Thanks." I glanced up at him, my gaze inadvertently catching the patch of chest hair visible at the collar of his shirt. What was wrong with me? Checking out James at my mother's funeral—God help me.

"I see Simon's here. Are you going back to Manchester with him now?" James asked.

"No," I said firmly. "We're not together anymore. I told you that."

"Oh, I just thought..."

"You thought wrong," I said, cutting him off.

Before James could respond, a commotion nearby drew my attention. Dad had lunged forward just in time to catch Auntie Beryl as she stumbled, her face pale and stricken.

"Sorry, James," I said, gripping his hand briefly before hurrying over.

"I'll see you back at the house," he called after me. "And Geri—maybe we could grab a bite to eat one night?"

I hesitated, turning back. "I'd like that, James."

He smiled, his expression soft and hopeful, and for a moment, I felt a spark of something light amidst the heaviness.

But then Beryl pulled me into her arms, her familiar scent of white musk and Polo mints engulfing me. The memories hit me like a wave, and the tears I'd been holding back spilled freely.

I thought of that awful day—the blood-curdling scream as Beryl had painted Mum's nails, only to realise she'd slipped away. It had been so quick, so sudden, and even though we'd known it was coming, none of us were prepared.

"That was a lovely speech Simon made, lovey," Beryl said softly, releasing me.

"He's been amazing," I admitted, glancing over at him. "I don't know how I'd have coped without him."

"You'd have managed just fine," Vinny interjected sharply.

Ignoring him, I turned to Dad. "Are you ready to go?"

He nodded, and together, we made our way home, preparing for one final gathering to say goodbye to Mum. It wasn't perfect, but it was all we could do to honour her memory.

***

GETTING OUT OF THE car with Dad, Beryl, Simon, and a reluctant Kevin, I felt a surge of relief as I saw the familiar outline of the house. My feet were throbbing, and the normally comfy shoes I'd chosen that morning now felt like instruments of torture. The deep indentations they had left on my swollen feet were a testament to how long the day had been.

I heard the rumble of car engines pulling up behind us as other mourners arrived, and I knew I didn't have long before the house would be filled with well-wishers. The thought of more small talk and endless condolences made me want to turn around and hide.

Once inside, I rushed up to my room, slipped off my shoes and changed into a pair of soft slippers. After quickly reapplying my lipstick in the bathroom, I forced myself back downstairs to play the dutiful hostess.

The next two hours crawled by, a blur of polite smiles, tearful embraces, and bittersweet stories about Mum. Guests mingled throughout each room, filling the house with a low hum of conversation. Dad, surrounded by old friends and neighbours, seemed to draw strength from their company. Watching him laugh at someone's fond memory of Mum eased my heart slightly, but only slightly.

In the kitchen, Simon and I tackled the last of the dirty plates and glasses. I was grateful for the distraction.

"It wasn't too bad, as wakes go," Simon said, rinsing a glass under the tap.

"No, it wasn't," I agreed, though my voice lacked conviction. Truthfully, I felt completely wrung out, the ache of exhaustion and grief clawing at my insides.

The absence of Mum was like a gaping hole in the house. It felt wrong to see people in the lounge without her bustling around, fussing over guests, or tidying up in the kitchen. The vibrant energy she brought to our home seemed to have been stripped away, leaving behind a hollow, lifeless shell. Even the bright colours of her carefully chosen decor seemed muted.

I hated the thought of facing life without her. Every moment seemed heavier, filled with her absence. I caught myself doing the little things she'd insisted on, like hanging coats in the hall cupboard or putting away dishes straight after washing them, as if she might walk in at any moment to inspect my efforts. It was silly, but it brought me a small measure of comfort.

Kevin had left earlier to avoid rush-hour traffic. I'd assumed Simon would leave with him, but he'd decided to stay until Sunday. I wasn't sure how I felt about it. On the one hand, his presence was a distraction; on the other, I dreaded the moment I'd have to think about him leaving, too.

"Geri, you will promise to make a doctor's appointment next week about the baby, won't you?" Simon asked, breaking the silence. He'd finished the last of the dishes and was now perched on the kitchen counter, something Mum would have scolded him for.

"I will," I snapped, irritation bubbling to the surface.

"Sorry for hassling you," Simon said gently. "I'm just worried about you both."

"The baby is fine. I'm fine," I said, more sharply than I intended. "I just need some rest and to get back to some kind of normal—if that's even possible."

Movement in the hallway caught my eye. I turned just in time to see Vinny storming out the front door and up the path, leaving it swinging wide open behind him.

"Oh, hell," I muttered, my stomach sinking. "That's all I need now. The whole village will be gossiping."

"Don't be silly, Geri," Simon said, hopping down from the counter. "No one will care, and they'll find out eventually anyway."

"It's easy for you to say," I retorted, crossing my arms. "You're going home on Sunday. You won't have to deal with the whispers and sly looks. You know what this place is like."

Simon sighed, leaning against the counter. "What are they going to say, really? We're married. We're in this together—for the baby, at least. No one needs to know anything else."

"And what about Vinny?" I asked, my voice trembling. "He won't keep his mouth shut, Simon. You know what he's like."

"If it makes you feel better, I'll be coming up regularly to spend time with you—if that's okay."

"Of course it's okay," I said, my voice softening. "I just wish you didn't have to go at all. I don't know how I'll cope without you."

"You'll cope," Simon said firmly, stepping closer and placing his hands gently on my shoulders. "You're stronger than you think. And besides, you've got your dad."

I nodded, even though I wasn't sure I believed him. For now, it was enough to hold on to the small hope that I wouldn't have to face everything alone.

Chapter Thirty-Nine

Geri

MONDAY CAME AROUND FAR too quickly, dragging me back into reality. The house felt emptier than ever after Simon's departure the night before. Saying goodbye to him had been emotional, leaving me with a hollow ache in my chest.

With Simon there, I'd felt a degree of protection, a buffer against the worst of the grief. Without him, I felt exposed and vulnerable. He promised to return soon, but I knew Kevin's patience had its limits, and Simon couldn't stay forever.

James had also called in on Saturday, his visit bittersweet. He announced he was returning to Nottingham, reasoning that the absence of new attacks only bolstered the case against Carl. We had no other evidence to support our claims and so his police mates didn't want to make any claims against Vinny. Even Beryl seemed resigned to the idea that Carl might be guilty. How would we possibly convince anybody else?

On Monday morning, I made the call I'd been dreading. Katie, the receptionist at Doctor Jessop's surgery, was cheerful as ever, slotting me in for an appointment that afternoon at 2 pm. At least it gave me something to focus on, and an excuse to call Simon later, not that I needed one.

Dad stayed in bed until nearly lunchtime, something unheard of for him. Normally up at the crack of dawn, his extended rest was both a relief and a concern. I knocked on his door a couple of times, but he didn't respond.

When he finally shuffled into the kitchen, he looked a shadow of himself—unshaven, still in yesterday's clothing, and with the remnants of last night's dinner staining his top.

"There's tea in the pot," I said gently, rubbing his shoulder as he sat down at the small table.

"Thanks, lass," he muttered, his voice gruff.

"Can I make you something to eat?" I opened the fridge, scanning the sparse shelves.

"No, I'm right. I'll have a slice of toast later."

"I'll pick up something for tea while I'm out," I said, closing the fridge. "I've got an appointment with Doctor Jessop this afternoon."

Dad's head snapped around, his eyes wide with worry.

"I'm fine," I reassured him. "Just a check-up—you know, with the baby and everything."

He let out a shaky breath, relief washing over his face. "Thank God for that. I couldn't bear it if you got sick too."

"I'm fine, Dad," I said, taking his hand in mine. It felt frail, almost birdlike. "Do you want me to ask Beryl to come and sit with you while I'm out?"

"No, lass, that's not necessary. I'll be right."

"As long as you're sure."

It struck me again how our roles had reversed. I was the caretaker now—the one worrying if he was eating enough or sleeping properly.

***

At the surgery, Doctor Jessop confirmed what I already knew. My baby was due in just under six months. He spun his old-fashioned cardboard wheel and paused before announcing the date: June 16th.

My stomach flipped.

"Is there a problem?" he asked, lifting his head and peering at me over his glasses.

"Oh, no," I said quickly. "It's just... that's my mum's birthday."

He smiled kindly. "What a wonderful way to remember her," he said. "Of course, it's only an estimate. The hospital will arrange a scan to confirm things. You should hear from them soon."

I thanked him and left the surgery feeling a strange mix of emotions. The idea of my baby arriving on Mum's birthday felt both poignant and overwhelming.

Instead of heading straight home, I wandered up the high street, stopping at the butcher's for a couple of pork steaks. I wasn't a fan, but Dad loved them, and he needed cheering up.

I found myself lingering in the high street, drawn to the shop windows and the faint sense of normalcy they offered. Out here, surrounded by other people going about their lives, I could almost pretend everything was fine.

As I made my way back to the car park, a familiar police car pulled up beside me.

"Hi, Geri," Vinny called out, leaning across the passenger seat. "Can I give you a lift?"

"No, thanks, Vinny. My car's just over there." I nodded toward my little silver Nissan parked behind the stone wall.

"It's just... I wanted to have a quick chat. It's important. Maybe we could go for a short drive?"

I hesitated, unease prickling at the back of my neck. I didn't want to go anywhere with Vinny, but his tone intrigued me.

"Is this about Carl?" I asked.

Vinny didn't answer. He opened the passenger door instead.

Reluctantly, I climbed in, nodding politely at Doctor Jessop as he exited the surgery. I set my handbag and the butcher's bag in the footwell, fastening my seatbelt as Vinny swung the car into a U-turn and headed out of town.

"Where are we going?" I asked, puzzled as we passed the turnoff for Cumberside.

"To a favourite coffee shop of mine. They do amazing cream teas," he said, glancing at me with a grin.

My stomach growled audibly at the mention of food, and I felt my cheeks flush.

Vinny laughed. "I heard that."

I tried to laugh it off, but the tension in the car remained palpable. The road stretched ahead, flanked by dense woodland and towering oaks. It had been years since I'd been this way, but the landscape was as timeless as ever.

I glanced at Vinny, my unease growing. Whatever he had to say, it had better be worth the detour.

***

THE DRIVE FELT ENDLESS, but just as I was beginning to think we'd never get there before nightfall, Vinny pulled into a small, picturesque village called Camberley. I'd only ever driven through it before, and even then, always at speed. Now, I could finally appreciate how utterly charming it was. The streets were lined with quaint stone cottages, their windows aglow with warm light, and the air carried the faint scent of woodsmoke and damp earth.

Vinny parked outside a little coffee shop with a stone facade and ivy creeping up its walls. He got out and jogged around to my side to open the door.

"Thank you," I said, stepping out.

Inside, the atmosphere was just as charming—low lighting, mismatched wooden furniture, and the aroma of fresh coffee and baked goods. A small round table by the window caught my eye, and I made my way to it while Vinny followed.

Behind the counter, a dark-haired waitress appeared, looking slightly frazzled but cheerful.

"Oh, hello," she said, fastening an apron around her waist. "Be there in a tick!"

As we settled in, Vinny broke the silence. "How's your dad holding up?"

"Better than I thought he would," I admitted. "But he's like a lost little boy. It breaks my heart to see him like this."

Vinny nodded, his expression thoughtful. "I hear Beryl's been around a lot?"

"Yeah. She's devastated too. Mum was her best friend. They're both helping each other in a way, though."

"Good," Vinny said, leaning back in his chair.

I raised an eyebrow. "No offence, but I didn't peg you as the care-in-the-community type."

"Hey!" he protested, his brows knitting together. "I'm the local bobby. Of course, I care."

"Sorry," I said, grinning despite myself.

The waitress approached our table with the energy of a whirlwind, slightly out of place in the laid-back surroundings.

"Sorry for the wait," she said, breathless. "We don't normally see anyone this time of day, so I thought I'd dismantle the coffee machine for a clean. That'll teach me!" She laughed.

"No problem," Vinny said, flashing her a grin that could knock anyone off their feet. "So long as you've got a couple of scones left."

"You're in luck—I've just two left," she replied, her cheeks pink.

"A pot of tea for two?" Vinny asked, glancing at me for confirmation.

I nodded.

"And two scones with the works, please," he said, his smile turning up a notch.

"I'll bring them right over." She disappeared behind the counter.

"So," I said, leaning forward, "have there been any more developments in the rape case?"

Vinny sighed, his face darkening slightly. "No. Nothing. But to be honest, Geraldine, I don't expect there to be."

My stomach twisted at his tone. "What are you saying?"

"I admire your loyalty, but Carl's guilty," he said bluntly. "I swear to you."

"What are you basing that on?" I demanded, my voice rising. "A few clothes in his wardrobe? Clothes that could've been planted?"

"And how do you think the real culprit," he said, raising his fingers in air quotes, "got into the house? Beryl was away. That leaves you as the only other person with access—and you didn't even have a key at the time. No sign of a break-in either. It's open and shut, Geri."

"I still don't believe it," I said firmly, shaking my head. "So, what did you drag me out here for if not to talk about Carl?"

"You're mad at me."

"I'm not mad at you."

"Then why are you talking to me with tight lips?"

I opened my mouth to retort, then realised my lips were indeed pressed together. I forced a smile. "Just tell me, Vinny."

Before he could answer, the waitress arrived, setting down two enormous scones accompanied by separate dishes of butter, jam, and cream.

"Wow, that looks amazing," I said, almost salivating.

The waitress smiled, nodding toward a framed certificate on the wall. "Award-winning scones," she said with pride.

Vinny chuckled as she disappeared again, returning moments later with a tray holding a teapot, cups, saucers, and a jug of milk.

The smell alone was enough to make me forget my irritation. I sliced my scone in half, layering it generously with butter, jam, and clotted cream before taking a huge bite.

Vinny laughed as I ended up with a cream moustache.

"Right," I said, wiping my mouth on a napkin. "What's so important that you had to kidnap me for a scone?"

"Eat first," he said, smirking.

When I finally finished, groaning from the sheer amount of food I'd consumed, I leaned back in my chair. "Okay, spill. The suspense is killing me."

Vinny pushed his plate away and crossed his legs, leaning back with a casual air.

"Are you and Simon an item again?" he asked suddenly.

I blinked at him, taken aback. "Excuse me?"

"Well, he's been staying over a lot. I assumed you'd got back together. But now he's gone again, and I'm not so sure."

I let out a short laugh. "We're just friends. That's all."

"Good," he said, giving a half-nod, though his tone made me uncomfortable.

Suddenly eager to leave, I placed my cup on the table and reached for my bag. "We should go. The waitress looks like she's ready to throw us out."

Vinny glanced over his shoulder and laughed. The waitress was hovering at the counter, folding and refolding a tea towel while watching us intently.

As Vinny paid, I excused myself and went to the ladies room, needing a moment to collect my thoughts. Vinny's questions, his tone, the drive—it all felt a little too much, and I wasn't sure what to make of it. Something about the whole afternoon felt off.

When I returned, Vinny stood by the car, his arms crossed over his chest.

"Well, thanks for that," I said, forcing a smile as I joined him. "I won't have to eat for a week."

He grinned, but it didn't quite reach his eyes. He opened the door for me once again.

"Thank you." I slid into the passenger seat, trying to shake the uneasy feeling creeping into my stomach.

We started down the narrow country lane, the trees casting long shadows across the road as the sun dipped lower. I glanced at Vinny. His hands gripped the steering wheel so tightly that his knuckles were white. Every few seconds, his eyes darted toward me, the glances becoming increasingly frequent.

"Spit it out," I said finally, breaking the tense silence.

He cleared his throat but kept his eyes on the road. "The reason I was asking where you stand with Simon ... well ... I overheard you last week. Talking about being, you know, pregnant."

I froze. My fingers hovered over the seatbelt clasp as my mind scrambled. "Okay," I said cautiously.

Vinny glanced at me briefly, his voice softer now. "I just wanted to say ... you can rely on me. I've never been one to shirk responsibility."

I blinked, utterly confused. "I have no idea what you're talking about."

"You don't have to play coy, Geraldine." He gave a nervous laugh. "Are you saying you're not pregnant?"

"No," I said slowly. "I'm not denying it."

"Exactly." His tone shifted, filled with an unsettling mix of pride and determination. "And you clearly want to keep it. I just thought I should put it out there—if you'll have me, I'd be thrilled to be a dad. It's always been a dream of mine."

My chest tightened. The car felt impossibly small, the air thin. "What are you talking about?"

He turned to look at me fully this time, his face earnest. "The baby, our baby. I've been thinking about it ever since—well, since the condom broke. I was terrified at first, but now that it's real ... I'm happy about it. Really happy."

I stared at him, words failing me. Then, suddenly, it all clicked. The realisation hit me so hard I almost laughed, but the sound died in my throat. "Vinny ... oh, my God, you've got this all wrong."

His brow furrowed. "What do you mean?"

I swallowed hard, trying to steady my voice. "Vinny, I'm sorry, but ... you're not the father. It's Simon's. I didn't realise but I was already pregnant before we ... you know."

His grip on the steering wheel loosened as his face twisted into something feral. "What?"

"Vinny, I—"

The words barely escaped my lips before the car swerved. His head snapped forward, but it was too late. The bend loomed ahead like a giant, jagged maw.

My screams filled my ears.

The car careened onto the shoulder, skidding violently before slamming into the berm. The impact threw us sideways, the tyres shrieking in protest before the car jolted to a stop.

My hands trembled as I unclipped my seatbelt and stumbled out of the car. My knees buckled beneath me, and I gripped the side of the vehicle to keep myself upright.

"What the hell was that about?" I shouted, my voice breaking. My whole body shook, but not just from the crash. Something deep in my gut told me this wasn't over.

Vinny slammed his fists on the car roof, his face red and twisted. "Fuck! Fuck! Fuck!" His voice echoed down the empty lane.

"Vinny, calm down!" I said, though my voice was thin and shaky. A sharp pain shot across my stomach, and I bent over, clutching my side until it passed.

"We've got a fucking puncture!" he shouted, pacing wildly. He wasn't just angry—he was unravelling.

"Do you have a spare?" I asked, trying to sound calm. But my voice betrayed me. I could hear the fear creeping in, the cracks forming in my composure.

"Of course, I have a fucking spare!" he spat. His eyes were wide, his jaw clenched. For the first time, he looked dangerous.

I moved to the back of the car, ignoring the pain in my abdomen. I needed to keep my hands busy, to stop my mind from spinning. I opened the boot and began pulling out the mess Vinny had stashed there. A pink towel, an empty watch box, and a pair of boots.

And then I froze.

My fingers hovered over the boots. They were huge, far larger than anything Vinny could wear. Size 11. I turned one over, my breath catching.

The tread on the sole had a distinctive word etched into it: CAT. My blood ran cold.

The rapist wore size 11.

Vinny appeared beside me, his face unreadable. I dropped the boot and stepped back, my pulse pounding in my ears.

"You shouldn't have done that," he said softly, his voice almost tender. But his eyes ... his eyes were full of something wild and unhinged. "You shouldn't have looked, Geraldine."

The world spun as the pieces clicked together, and suddenly, I knew I wasn't walking away from this night unscathed.

Chapter Forty

Geri

I COULDN'T SPEAK. MY mouth opened, but no sound came out. My trembling hands clutched the boot as though it were a shield, a ridiculous talisman to ward off the horror before me. My mind screamed to run, but my legs felt rooted to the icy ground.

"You just had to meddle, didn't you?" Vinny said, his tone conversational, almost amused.

"I ... I don't know what you mean." My voice was barely a whisper, and I hated how feeble it sounded.

His lip curled. "You're a terrible liar, Geraldine. I thought I could trust you. I was even willing to change for you."

"Change?" My voice rose, cracking. "You're a rapist—a fucking monster. You can't just change that!"

I took another step back, but Vinny followed, his strides measured and deliberate. His sneer deepened, turning his face into a grotesque mask.

"I locked Carl up, didn't I? Charged him to make it all go away. And now look at you. Forcing my hand. Again."

"It's not too late," I stammered. My heel hit the edge of the drainage ditch—a six-foot-deep trench yawning behind me. "You don't have to do this. If you stop now—"

Vinny barked out a laugh that sent a shiver down my spine. "Stop? Geraldine, have you any idea what happens to cops in prison? They'd eat me alive. No, no, I'm past the point of stopping. But you?" He grinned, his teeth glinting in the fading light. "You're just getting started."

Desperation surged. With a guttural scream, I hurled the boot at him, pouring every ounce of strength into the throw. It hit his shoulder and bounced harmlessly to the ground. Vinny didn't even flinch. He laughed, slow and low, the sound rippling through the stillness.

"I'm done playing," he said.

I turned and bolted.

The cold air sliced at my lungs, and the ache in my stomach grew sharper with every stride. I pushed the pain down, ignoring the searing burn in my legs and the icy branches clawing at my arms. I couldn't afford to stop. Not now. Not ever.

Behind me, Vinny's voice rang out, mockingly jovial. "Run, Geraldine! Make it fun for me!"

I didn't look back. I knew he wasn't far behind. I could feel him closing in, his presence like a shadow pressing against my back. My heart pounded so violently it felt like it might burst. The thudding echoed in my ears, drowning out every sound except the crunch of my bare feet on the frostbitten forest floor.

The darkness fell faster than I expected, wrapping the woods in an oppressive shroud. My breath came in ragged gasps, the cold biting at my throat. I knew I couldn't keep this up. The pain in my stomach wasn't just an ache anymore—it was sharp, relentless, and soaked with a terrible certainty.

I was losing the baby.

My foot snagged on a tree root, and I went sprawling. My knees hit the frozen ground, sending shockwaves of pain through my body. I bit down a scream, knowing it would only lead him straight to me. Pitiful whimpers escaped anyway, tears streaming down my cheeks as I dragged myself upright.

There—a hollow beneath a massive tree. The trunk split near the base, forming a natural alcove cloaked in a tangle of branches. I crawled inside, pressing my back against the bark, and hugged my knees to my chest. My whole body shook as I tried to quiet my breathing, but the gasps came too fast, too loud.

In the stillness, every sound became amplified—the rustle of leaves—the distant hoot of an owl—the creak of a branch bending under unseen weight.

And then—a twig snapped.

My heart seized. I clamped my hands over my mouth to stifle a sob, squeezing my eyes shut. Maybe it wasn't him. Maybe it was an animal. Maybe—

A hand clamped around my ankle, yanking me forward.

I screamed as I was dragged into the open, leaves and dirt clawing at my back. Vinny loomed over me, his grin savage. His face was streaked with sweat, his hair dishevelled, and his eyes glinted with something unholy.

"That was fun," he said, his voice calm. Too calm. "But I was starting to get bored."

"Vinny, please—" I choked on my words. "I'm sorry! I'll do whatever you want, just—"

He knelt over me, straddling my hips, and leaned in so close I could feel his breath on my face. "You don't get to make the rules, Geraldine. Not anymore."

"Please," I sobbed. "The baby—"

His expression darkened. "I don't give a flying fuck about your bastard baby." His hands shot to my waistband, yanking at my trousers.

I thrashed, screaming, kicking, but he was too strong. His weight pinned me to the ground, his grip like iron. My hand flailed across the forest floor, searching for something, anything, to fight back with.

My fingers closed around something heavy and cold.

I swung.

The rock connected with the side of Vinny's head, and he howled, his body lurching sideways. I scrambled backward, my trousers tangled around my ankles, and I swung again, catching him across the jaw.

"You bitch!" he roared, lunging for me. His hand clamped around my throat, squeezing. My vision blurred, black spots swimming before my eyes.

Summoning every ounce of strength I had left, I brought the rock down one last time. The crack echoed through the trees, followed by a guttural, choking sound as Vinny's grip loosened.

He collapsed beside me, groaning, clutching his bloodied face.

I didn't wait. I ripped off the trousers, kicked free, and bolted barefoot into the night, the forest swallowing me whole.

I didn't know where I was going. All I knew was that I had to keep running.

Running for my life.

I tried to get my bearings, scanning the shadowy expanse of trees for any hint of the road. I needed to find the car. My phone was my only lifeline, my only chance of getting out of here alive. But I was hopelessly disoriented. I'd never been good with directions at the best of times, and now, with a raving lunatic somewhere in the darkness, my odds were non-existent.

The pain in my stomach clawed at me relentlessly. The truth was impossible to ignore now. I was losing the baby.

The thought drove a spike of anguish through me, but I couldn't stop. Staggering through the forest, I leaned against the trunk of a hazel tree, gulping air and squinting into the dark. My eyes had adjusted, but the woods seemed endless, each tree blending into the next. I was going deeper and deeper, and I knew it. The road felt like a lifetime ago.

But I couldn't go back—not toward Vinny. That left only two choices: left or right.

It wasn't even a choice, really. A coin toss in a nightmare. I turned left and pressed on.

Each step felt heavier than the last. My thighs chafed where they rubbed together, and the frozen air gnawed at my bare legs. The ground, carpeted with damp, decaying leaves, offered little comfort to my bruised and bleeding feet. I could barely hear myself think over the sound of my teeth chattering.

There was no sign of Vinny. Maybe I'd killed him. Maybe that final blow with the rock had been enough. The thought should've comforted me, but it didn't. Even dead, he haunted me.

Just as I was about to give up and turn back, I saw it through a gap in the trees. The road.

I stumbled toward it, tears blurring my vision. The asphalt stretched ahead like a lifeline, empty and still. No cars. No headlights. Just silence. But I was back on the right road—I was sure of it.

Hugging my arms around myself, I started running toward the spot where we'd left the car. Each step sent sharp jolts of pain through my body, but I didn't care. The freezing air bit at my skin, and my breath came in uneven, misty plumes.

When the car came into view, I nearly collapsed with relief. The doors were still open, the interior lights blazing, the high-pitched chime of the driver's door ringing out into the night. The sound grated on my nerves, but I didn't care. All I could think about was my phone. My handbag. My way out.

I reached the car and leaned against the door, my legs trembling. My bag was right where I'd left it—in the passenger footwell. I grabbed it, my hands shaking as I tore it open. Lipsticks, receipts, mints, a crumpled tissue—they all spilled out onto the seat.

No phone.

My heart sank. I rifled through the empty pockets, the zippered compartments. It wasn't there.

"Looking for this?"

I froze. The sound of his voice stopped my heart. Slowly, I turned toward him.

Vinny stood a few feet away, barely recognisable. Blood streaked his face, caking his hair and dripping onto his shirt. His eyes, wild and glinting in the dim light, locked onto mine. Between his fingers, he held my phone, dangling it like bait.

"Vinny," I whispered. "Please—"

"Shut the fuck up!" he roared, his voice echoing through the stillness.

My knees buckled, and I clung to the car door for support. I couldn't tell if I was shaking from fear or the cold. Both, maybe. My body was betraying me, my energy draining fast.

I tried to move, to scramble into the car, but Vinny was too quick. His hand shot out, grabbing a fistful of my hair and yanking me backward. I hit the ground hard, the impact forcing the air from my lungs.

I couldn't breathe. Couldn't think. All I could do was crawl, dragging myself forward as he loomed over me, laughing like a maniac.

The tyre iron. I spotted it just beneath the car, within arm's reach but not close enough. I stretched out, my fingers grazing the cold metal, but Vinny yanked me back again.

"Vinny, please," I begged, my voice raw. "My baby. I need to go to the hospital."

"And why should I care about your bastard baby?" His tone was mocking, cruel. "You didn't care about me. You just laughed. Always laughing."

"I didn't laugh at you!" I cried, clutching at any memory that might reach him. "I liked you, Vinny! Don't you remember? When we were kids—after the school play—I helped you wash off the graffiti."

He paused, his grip loosening slightly. "Yeah," he said slowly. "But you probably helped write it in the first place."

"No! I didn't. I was your friend. I thought you were kind. Handsome. Remember? I told you how handsome you were."

His lips twitched, and for a brief moment, I saw something human in his face. His hand fell away, and he turned to his reflection in the car window, smoothing back his blood-matted hair.

"You really think so?" he asked, his voice almost bashful.

"Yes," I said, inching backward. "Everyone from school would be jealous of you now."

As he preened, I felt my fingers close around the tyre iron. My heart thundered in my chest as I slowly pulled it toward me, hiding it behind my back.

"Of course they're jealous," Vinny muttered, his reflection staring back at him with a distorted grin. "They always have been."

"Exactly," I said, keeping my voice calm despite the panic bubbling inside me. "But, Vinny, it's so cold. Maybe we should get in the car—"

His head snapped toward me, his eyes narrowing. "You think I'm stupid?" he snarled, stepping forward. "Get up. Now."

I didn't have a choice. I clutched the tyre iron against my side as I stood, my legs trembling.

"Walk," he ordered, shoving me toward the trees.

My mind raced. I needed a plan. I needed to act. As we reached the edge of the road, I remembered the drainage ditch.

I turned, positioning myself so the ditch was behind him. My grip on the tyre iron tightened.

"Vinny," I said, my voice trembling. "We don't have to do this. Please—"

"Shut up!" he barked, raising a hand.

I didn't wait. With every ounce of strength I had left, I swung the tyre iron. The sickening crunch of metal meeting bone echoed through the night.

Vinny's eyes widened in shock as he stumbled backward, his arms flailing. Time slowed as his foot slipped over the edge of the ditch, and he fell, dragging me down with him.

The impact was instant, jarring, and excruciating. Pain exploded in my leg, sharp and all-consuming. Vinny's body lay beneath me, unmoving.

I couldn't tell how long I lay there. When I came to, the world was silent. The phone was in Vinny's hand—my lifeline—was so close but still out of reach.

"Vinny?" I whispered. Nothing.

With trembling fingers, I reached for the phone. No signal.

Tears streamed down my face as I leaned back against the cold earth. I wasn't getting out of this. I was losing my baby. And soon, I'd lose myself too.

In the distance, an owl hooted again. I closed my eyes, surrendering to the darkness.

Chapter Forty-One

James

"So, you're moving on then?" Marco, the hotel manager, asked, leaning casually on the counter as the final receipt printed.

"Afraid so, mate," James replied, his voice flat. "Nothing much keeping me here now."

Marco handed him the slip of paper, his expression tinged with understanding. "Paid up 'til tomorrow morning at ten. If you need more time, just let me know."

James folded the receipt and slipped it into his pocket. "Will do, boss. Thanks for everything."

As he stepped toward the door, his phone buzzed in his pocket. He pulled it out, lifting a hand in farewell to Marco. "Hi, Geri," he said, answering without hesitation. "I was just about to call—"

But the voice on the other end wasn't Geraldine.

"James, it's Maxwell Eve. I'm sorry to bother you, but I'm worried something's happened to Geri."

James's stomach tightened. "I'm just across the road, Max. Give me two minutes."

He shoved the phone into his jacket pocket and pushed through the hotel's swing doors, bracing himself against the bitter wind that swept down the street. The icy air gnawed at his face as he made his way to Max's cottage.

Max stood at the front gate, his worry etched in the deep lines of his face. Beryl hovered in the doorway, her arms wrapped tightly around herself as if warding off more than the cold.

"What's going on?" James asked as he reached them. They all piled inside, the warmth of the cottage doing little to ease the tension.

"Geraldine hasn't come home," Max said, his voice breaking. "She had a doctor's appointment this afternoon—two o'clock in Kirkby Mayor. No one's seen her since."

James glanced at the clock on the mantel. Almost six.

"Flaming hell. Have you rung around? Checked with her friends?"

Max's expression darkened. "She doesn't have many friends. Carl's ... well, Carl's in no state to help. You and him, you're about all she's got left."

"What about Simon?" James pressed.

"He's on his way," Beryl said quietly. "Her mobile's going straight to voicemail. We're worried sick, James. It's not like her."

James nodded sharply, already heading for the door. "I'll look for her. Call me the moment you hear anything."

The cold seemed even sharper as he climbed into his car and drove toward Kirkby Mayor. He checked every street, every lane, his headlights slicing through the dark. When he reached the doctor's surgery, the building was pitch-black, but his heart leapt when his lights illuminated a silver Nissan parked in the doctor's car park.

Geri's car.

He pulled alongside and jumped out, his boots crunching on the gravel. Peering through the frosted windows, he spotted a cream lace scarf draped across the back seat—he'd seen her wear it before. A strange mix of relief and dread churned in his gut. The car was here, but she wasn't.

He thought of Doctor Jessop. The man had lived in the old blue-and-white house on the outskirts of town for as long as James could remember. If anyone might have seen Geri, it was him.

The house glowed with the warm light of a dozen lamps, and the muffled bark of a small dog greeted him as he knocked on the heavy wooden door. After a moment, the door creaked open, revealing a woman in a pink robe with curlers perched on her forehead.

"Oh!" she exclaimed, patting the curlers with one hand.

"I'm sorry to bother you," James said quickly, "but I need to speak to Doctor Jessop. It's important."

She hesitated, then nodded. "Just a moment." The door closed, and James waited, his breath visible in the freezing air.

When it reopened, Doctor Jessop stood there, his grey hair slightly dishevelled but his smile warm. "James. Heard you were back."

"Not for long, Doc. I'm sorry to bother you, but I need to know—did Geraldine Eve come to see you today?"

The doctor's smile faded. "You know I can't discuss patients."

"I'm not asking for details," James said quickly. "It's just ... she hasn't been seen since she left home. Her car's still parked at the surgery."

Jessop's brows furrowed as he adjusted his glasses. "I noticed the car when I left this evening but didn't think much of it. She did make her appointment—was on time and seemed fine when she left."

"Did she say where she was going?"

"No, but..." The doctor hesitated. "Now that you mention it, I think I saw her with Vinny Martin. I can't be certain, but I thought she got into his car."

James's stomach churned. "Thanks, Doc. I'll check it out."

Back in his car, James tried Vinny's number. It went straight to voicemail. "Vinny, it's James. I'm looking for Geraldine. I heard she might've been with you earlier. Call me."

Frustrated, he drove back into Kirkby Mayor and pulled up outside the police station. Inside, he found himself stuck behind an elderly man who was recounting an absurd complaint about his neighbour's music habits.

Finally, James reached the desk. "Is Tom Sullivan in?" he asked.

The sergeant nodded. "You're in luck. He just came on duty. Give me a minute."

James paced nervously, his foot tapping against the tiled floor. By the time Tom appeared, James's anxiety had reached a fever pitch.

"Jimmy!" Tom greeted him with a hearty handshake. "Didn't think I'd see you before you left."

"I'm here for help," James said. "Geraldine Eve is missing. Her car's at the doctor's surgery, but no one's seen her since this afternoon. Someone said they saw her with Vinny Martin."

Tom's smile vanished. "Vinny?"

James nodded. "Neither of them is answering their phones. I'm worried something's happened."

Tom frowned, considering this. "I'll try to reach him on the car radio. Let's see what we can find out."

James exhaled, hoping against hope that Vinny's voice wouldn't be the one to answer. Something deep in his gut told him Geraldine was in trouble—and that time was running out.

James glanced at his watch as Tom disappeared into a side room, the weight of dread growing heavier by the second. It had been almost an hour since he'd left Max, and the uneasy feeling gnawing at him had turned into full-blown panic. Every minute that passed felt like another nail in the coffin of hope.

Tom reappeared, his face grim. "No luck on his radio or his mobile, I'm afraid," he said. "But I did check our GPS system. Vinny's car has been stationary for almost two hours."

James's stomach twisted. "Where?"

"That's the strange part. It's on the old Camberley Road. You know it? There's nothing out there—just miles of woodland."

James didn't wait for Tom to finish. The words barely registered as he bolted from the station, his mind racing. Woodland. Darkness. Geraldine was out there, alone—or worse. He shoved the key into the ignition and sped off, the tyres squealing as he rounded the corner.

The Camberley Road stretched ahead of him like a black ribbon, lined by towering trees that loomed in the headlights. His hands tightened on the wheel as he prayed he wouldn't be too late.

When he finally spotted the car, his breath hitched. Even from a distance, he could tell something was wrong. Both front doors hung open, the boot gaping wide like a scream frozen in time. The car was eerily still, as if it had been abandoned in a rush.

He pulled up behind it, leaving his hazard lights flashing, and jumped out into the icy night. The cold bit at his face as he approached, his gut churning with dread.

"Geraldine?" His voice echoed into the emptiness. "Vinny?"

Silence. Only the rustle of the wind through the trees answered him. He moved closer, his eyes scanning the scene. The car was partially jacked up, the spare tyre awkwardly half-fitted. It looked as if someone had been interrupted mid-change.

"Geraldine?" he shouted again, his voice breaking.

Peering inside the car, he spotted her handbag on the passenger seat. The contents were strewn across the upholstery—lipstick, receipts, loose change. It didn't look like Geraldine had left it willingly. His eyes fell on a flashlight lying on the back seat. He grabbed it, flipping it on, and a beam of light pierced the darkness.

The silence felt oppressive as he swept the torch around the car and into the surrounding woods. "Geraldine!" he called, his voice raw.

Nothing. Just the creak of branches and the distant hoot of an owl

As he circled the car, blue and red lights bathed the road, and the sound of an approaching engine shattered the quiet. Relief mixed with fear as Tom and another uniformed officer stepped out of the police car.

"Something's wrong, Tom," James said, jogging toward them. His words tumbled out, frantic. "The car's wide open. Geri's handbag's here, but there's no sign of her or Vinny. Something's happened."

"Okay, sir, calm down," the other officer said in a steady Scottish accent. "Let us take a look."

Tom nodded, his expression serious as he approached the vehicle, shining his torch inside. "You said the spare tyre was being fitted?"

James pointed toward the jacked-up wheel. "It looks like they didn't finish. Something interrupted them."

While the officers examined the car, James's unease deepened. He couldn't stand still. Torch in hand, he wandered further down the roadside, scanning the shadows that seemed to stretch endlessly into the forest.

He almost missed it. The torch's beam caught the edge of a drainage ditch, the sharp glint of metal barely visible through the undergrowth. He took a step closer, then froze.

His breath caught in his throat as the light fell on something pale and still. His heart thundered in his chest, the sound deafening in his ears.

"Tom!" he shouted, his voice a mixture of panic and desperation. "Over here!"

The officers came running, their boots crunching against the gravel as James stood rooted to the spot, the torch trembling in his hand. He could barely breathe as Tom joined him and shone his own light down into the ditch.

Two bodies lay tangled in the narrow trench, limbs awkwardly splayed as if they'd fallen—or been thrown—there. One was unmistakably Geraldine. Her blood-smeared face was turned to the side, her eyes closed, her body limp. Beneath her was a larger figure, motionless and unidentifiable in the dim light.

James's stomach churned, bile rising in his throat. "Is she—?" He couldn't bring himself to finish the question.

Tom crouched at the edge, his voice steady but strained. "Stay back, James. Let us handle this."

But James couldn't stay back. He dropped to his knees, the icy ground biting through his jeans. "Geri!" he called, his voice trembling. "Can you hear me? It's James!"

For a moment, there was nothing but the rustling of leaves. Then, faintly, a sound—a soft groan, barely audible.

"She's alive!" James gasped, hope surging through him.

Tom leaned further in, his torch fixed on her face. "Geraldine," he said firmly. "Don't move. We're here to help."

James's heart broke at the sight of her fragile form, streaked with dirt and blood. Her breaths were shallow, her body unnaturally still.

"Tom, hurry!" James pleaded. "She needs help."

Tom turned to the other officer. "Call for backup and an ambulance. Now."

As the officer radioed for assistance, James's gaze locked on Geraldine's pale face. "Hold on, Geri," he whispered, his voice thick with emotion. "Just hold on."

Chapter Forty-Two

Geri

SOMEBODY WAS STROKING MY face and murmuring softly. The voice was calm and soothing, but it felt far away, like it was being filtered through layers of water. Bright lights pierced my eyelids, and there was noise—so much noise—sirens, voices, and the dull thrum of movement around me.

I felt weightless as if I were floating up toward the sky. My mind latched onto the thought that someone nearby must be in trouble, but it didn't feel like me. It couldn't be. Could it?

***

"WAKE UP, SWEETHEART. COME on, wake up."

The voice was closer now, the words soft and tender. Was it James? It felt like a dream, the kind you never want to leave because waking up would ruin it. His hand brushed through my hair, lingering on my cheek. I didn't dare open my eyes, afraid I'd shatter whatever magic this was. If I woke up now, we'd both be embarrassed.

"Geri," James whispered, his voice cracking. "Wake up, my love."

My love. My heart jolted. That couldn't be right. James never called me that.

I forced my heavy eyelids open. His face hovered inches from mine, his eyes closed as if in prayer. His stubble was rough, his hair dishevelled, and his expression was raw with emotion.

"James?" My voice came out as a hoarse whisper, barely audible.

His chocolate-brown eyes flew open, and a wave of relief washed over his face. "Oh, Geri. Thank God. I was so worried about you." Without hesitation, he leaned down and kissed my forehead. Then, as if he couldn't help himself, he pressed his lips to mine.

It was over too quickly, leaving my lips tingling and my mind racing. "My baby?" I croaked, my hands already folded protectively over my stomach.

"The doctor examined you," James said, his voice steady but tinged with emotion. "The seatbelt caused a lot of trauma to your abdomen. They said the next few days will be critical."

"You mean..." My breath caught. "I'm still pregnant?"

He nodded, tears filling his eyes. "You are."

I closed my eyes tightly, trying to hold back my own tears. Relief and fear warred within me, the emotions too overwhelming to process all at once.

***

WHEN I OPENED MY eyes again, the light in the room had shifted. I must have dozed off. The faint golden glow of late afternoon spilled through a partially raised roller blind.

For the first time, I took in my surroundings. Blue curtains hung around part of my bed, and a vase of ruby-red roses sat on the bedside cabinet. The rich colour was so striking against the sterile white walls that I couldn't stop staring at them.

James was slumped in an armchair next to the bed, his head tilted back and his mouth slightly open as he snored softly. Even in sleep, he looked good. Too good. My stomach did that strange flip it always did when I caught him looking at me.

But then reality hit like a freight train. Memories crashed over me—running through the forest, Vinny's hands on me, the terror when I thought I'd lost my baby. It all felt surreal, like scenes from a nightmare I couldn't wake up from. Yet here I was, alive. The baby was alive. But Vinny...

James stirred, rubbing his eyes as he sat up. "Are you okay?" he asked, his voice groggy but warm. "Can I get you anything?"

I shook my head, exhaustion weighing me down. "How did you find me?" I managed to whisper, my throat dry and scratchy.

He got to his feet, poured a glass of water from the bedside jug, and brought it to my lips. "Drink," he urged gently.

I sipped, but some of the water trickled down my face and into my ear. James smiled and wiped it away with his sleeve before placing the glass back on the cabinet.

"Your dad called me when you didn't come home," he explained. "Doctor Jessop said he saw you getting into Vinny's car. Between that and some help from Tom, I was able to track you down."

"Is Vinny..." I couldn't bring myself to finish the question.

James nodded, his expression unreadable. "He's dead."

A strange sense of relief washed over me, followed by guilt. I shouldn't feel relieved, should I? But I was. My baby and I were safe, and Vinny couldn't hurt anyone else ever again.

"Do you know?" My voice was barely audible. "He's the rapist."

James nodded slowly. "It took time to piece it all together, but yes. Everyone knows now."

"And Carl?"

"Tom's working on it. They'll clear his name soon, I promise."

I nodded, my head sinking back into the pillow. The conversation was draining me, but I had one more question. "My leg... is it broken?"

James's face softened. "Yeah. Pretty badly. They had to use a couple of pins to set it. You'll be off your feet for a while."

"Thank you," I whispered. "For finding me. I thought I was going to die."

James reached for my hand, holding it tightly. "I thought I was too late," he admitted, his voice breaking. "I can't tell you what it felt like seeing you in that drain. I thought I'd lost you."

Before I could respond, the door flew open, and Simon burst in like a whirlwind. "You're awake!" he cried, rushing to the bed and planting a kiss on my lips.

James stiffened. He stood abruptly, grabbing his jacket from the chair. "I'll leave you to it," he said, his voice tight. He bent down to kiss my forehead. "Let me know if you need anything. I'll check in later."

As he walked out, my heart ached with the sudden absence of his presence. I barely heard Simon's tirade about Vinny and the baby. My mind was still on James—his touch, his words, his kiss.

Simon's voice cut through my thoughts. "Geri, are you even listening? That bastard could've killed you and our baby!"

"Simon, calm down," I said, exasperated. "I'm fine. The baby's fine."

Kevin, who had been lingering awkwardly in the doorway, stepped forward. "Let her rest, Simon. She's been through hell."

"Thanks for the flowers," I said, desperate to change the subject.

"They're not from us," Simon said, frowning. His eyes fell on the vase. "Oh, look—there's a card."

He pulled out a small envelope tucked between the stems and raised an eyebrow. "Shall I?"

I nodded, my stomach tightening.

Simon read the card silently, his smirk fading. He read it again, then handed it to Kevin without a word.

"What does it say?" I demanded, but neither of them answered. The tension in the room thickened as I reached for the card myself, my heart pounding.

My mind was racing, darting between fragments of the past few days and the uncertainty of what lay ahead. Exhaustion weighed heavily on me, but sleep felt impossible. When Simon and Kevin finally left, I was relieved. In the end, I'd pretended to drift off just to make them leave. The room had been too crowded with their nervous energy, and all I wanted was quiet.

The nurse came in, her voice a soft balm with its lilting Irish accent. She wheeled in a phone stand and plugged it in beside the bed. "Your father's on the line," she said gently, pressing a few buttons before handing me the receiver.

"Hiya, Dad."

"Oh, Geri, I've been beside myself with worry," he said, his voice trembling slightly. "Are you alright, love?"

His familiar tone brought tears to my eyes, and I gripped the phone tighter. "I'm okay, Dad, but I was really scared. Thank goodness you called James." Just saying his name sent warmth rushing to my cheeks.

"He's a good lad, that one," Dad said, his voice thick with gratitude. "His mum would've been so proud of him. When I called, he was round the house in minutes."

"God only knows what would've happened if he hadn't found me," I said softly. "It's a miracle he did."

"Don't talk like that, my angel," Dad said, choking back a sob. "I couldn't bear losing you too."

The raw emotion in his voice hit me like a punch to the gut. He'd been so strong since Mum died, but now, for the first time, he soun ded... old. Fragile.

"Hey, Dad," I said quickly, trying to soothe him. "It's okay. You definitely won't be losing me, I promise."

"I just got off the phone with Beryl," he said, his tone brightening. "She said Carl will be home tomorrow."

"About bloody time!" I let out a relieved laugh.

"That's all down to you, lass. But listen, you sound tired, so I'll let you rest. I'll come see you first thing in the morning."

"Okay, Dad. I love you."

"I love you too, sweetheart."

When the call ended, the room fell silent again, but my thoughts roared back to life. Mostly the card. The words were seared into my mind, refusing to let me rest.

> *To My One True Love,*
> *I have no intention of losing you for a third time.*
> *James x*

I'd read it a dozen times, and each time it left me more confused. Simon had mentioned a long conversation with James while I was in surgery, but he refused to go into detail. Still, he'd been annoyingly smug, certain he'd been right about something all along.

I pulled the card out of the bedside drawer, reading it again as if the words might change or offer me some clarity.

The door opened, and James stepped in, looking sheepish. His hands were stuffed in his jacket pockets, his shoulders hunched like he was bracing for a storm.

"Hi, Geri." His voice was soft, almost hesitant. His gaze flicked to the card in my hands. "You read it, then?"

"Yes," I said, meeting his eyes. "And... I have to admit, I'm a bit confused."

He let out a nervous laugh and ran a hand through his hair. "Maybe I was out of order, especially after everything you've been through. But I needed you to know. Once and for all."

My heart hammered in my chest, and I clutched the card tighter. "Then explain, James. Because I'm really not sure what to think."

He took a deep breath, his brown eyes meeting mine with a raw vulnerability I'd never seen before. "The thing is, Geri... I've loved you since school. You never even noticed me back then. You only had eyes for Simon. But I noticed you. Every smile, every laugh. My dad told me I'd get over it, but I never did."

I stared at him, stunned. The confident, capable James I thought I knew was nowhere to be seen. He looked like a frightened boy, baring his soul. My heart clenched painfully.

"When I bumped into you in the village that day," he continued, "I'd just come back to town. I thought you'd be long gone, but there you were. And when you told me you and Simon were separated... I couldn't believe my luck. You agreed to go out with me, and it felt like all my dreams had come true."

He paused, his gaze dropping to his hands. "But after that night, you disappeared. You were with Carl, then Vinny. I thought I'd lost my chance. Again."

"You never lost it," I said softly, my voice trembling.

James blinked, looking up at me with a mixture of hope and disbelief. "When your dad called and said you were missing, I was terrified. I prayed, Geri. I swore that if I found you, I'd tell you how I felt. No more hiding."

He stood and walked to the door, as if bracing himself for rejection. "I'll leave you to process everything. I know this is a lot."

"James," I called as he reached for the handle. My voice was steady, even though my heart was racing. "You're just going to leave? You're not even going to let me respond?"

He turned back slowly, his face etched with uncertainty.

I patted the bed beside me. "Sit down."

James hesitated, then crossed the room and perched on the edge of the mattress. His proximity made my heart race even faster.

"I didn't realise," I said quietly. "Not back then. And not now. I thought..." I trailed off, struggling to find the right words. "You told me the love of your life married someone else."

"She did," he said simply. "You did."

The air seemed to leave the room.

"When I finally worked up the courage to ask you out again, Simon showed up," James continued. "I thought I'd lost my chance for good."

I reached out, placing my hand over his. "Simon and I are just friends. Best friends."

"I know. He told me as much this morning. He said I needed to tell you everything."

"I'm glad you did."

His eyes searched mine, hope flickering in their depths. "So... is there a chance?"

I smiled softly. "The thing is, James, I can't afford to make any more mistakes. I have the baby to think about now."

"I understand," he said, his shoulders slumping slightly.

"But," I added, squeezing his hand, "if you're willing to take things slow, I'd like to see where this goes."

His eyes lit up, and the smile that spread across his face was enough to melt every last shred of doubt. "Slow is fine with me," he said.

For the first time in what felt like forever, I felt a spark of hope. Maybe, just maybe, this was the start of something real.

Epilogue

THE SUN WAS HIGH in the sky, and the warm rays bathed the balcony in a golden glow. Birds flitted from tree to tree, their melodies a perfect soundtrack to the peaceful morning.

"Do you think French birds sound prettier?" I asked, stretching out on the sun lounger.

Simon, lying on a matching lounger at the other end of the balcony, laughed. "I think everything sounds nicer with a French accent."

"Me too." I grinned, letting the soft breeze brush over my face. "I love it here. I just feel a bit guilty that your mum and dad left as soon as we arrived."

"You know how they are, Geri. They've always been like that—detached, always on the move. I don't think they'll ever change."

"No, probably not. But you'd think they'd want to spend more time with their granddaughter."

Simon sighed and propped himself up on one elbow. "Their loss, Geri. Don't let it bother you. She's got all the love she needs right here."

I nodded, my heart swelling. He was right. Our daughter didn't need anyone who didn't show up for her. She had us, and that was enough.

"I should grab a shower. They'll be here soon," I said, getting to my feet.

Simon smirked. "Me too. Last one to the bathroom makes dinner!"

I took off, moving faster than I had all week, but Simon's long legs got him there first. He slipped inside and slid the bolt across with a triumphant laugh.

"Aw, come on, Simon! I take longer than you to get ready!"

"No way, my dear. I won fair and square!"

"Pig!" I shouted, pounding on the door, but his laughter only grew louder.

Shaking my head, I headed to the kitchen to start on the vegetables. But when I stepped inside, Kevin was already there, apron on, chopping knife in hand.

"You two will never grow up, will you?" he teased.

"It's not me, it's him," I replied, and we both burst out laughing at how ridiculous that sounded.

Kevin smiled, a soft fondness in his eyes. "Don't worry about this. I've got it all under control. Go pamper yourself—I know how much this evening means to you."

Grateful, I wrapped my arms around his neck and kissed his cheek. "You're a superstar, Kev. Thank you."

By the time I'd showered and dressed, my nerves were on edge. I paced the floor, smoothing my dress for the millionth time, barely able to contain my excitement. When I finally heard the crunch of tyres on the drive, I practically flew downstairs.

I flung open the door just as Dad was stepping out of the car. He looked fantastic, tanned and relaxed, but the moment his eyes landed on me, they softened with emotion. Before I could say anything, he climbed the steps in two quick strides and swept me into his arms.

"I've missed you, my angel," he murmured into my hair. "How've you been? Where is everyone? Where's my granddaughter?"

I laughed at his rapid-fire questions, feeling the warmth of his familiar presence. "One thing at a time, Dad! Come in, have a drink. We'll sort the bags later."

The passenger door slammed, and I turned to see Beryl bustling up the steps, her arms loaded with brightly wrapped gifts. A massive purple sombrero perched on her head, somehow managing to look both ridiculous and perfect on her.

"Geraldine, you look beautiful—and so slim!" she gushed, pulling me into a hug.

"You too! You're glowing." I eyed her golden tan. "You'll have to tell me all about the trip. I hope you took plenty of photos."

"Oh, hundreds! I'll bore you senseless with them later," she said, waving her hand dismissively but beaming with pride.

They'd been on a world cruise. Something Mum had always dreamt of doing but never got around to, so they took her ashes with them.

A farewell trip for three old friends.

"Did you manage to see Carl when you were in Australia?" I asked.

"Briefly. We went out for lunch one day, but he only had a couple of hours to spare. He was heading to Fiji on a yacht—something to do with his new job."

"Oh, nice. I'm so glad he's okay."

We walked through to the kitchen, where Simon and Kevin had worked their usual magic. The air was filled with the mouthwatering aroma of roasted vegetables and fresh-baked bread. The table was set, and glasses of champagne were already being poured.

Dad clapped Simon on the back. "Looks amazing, son. You've outdone yourself."

Once everyone had a glass in hand, Dad turned to me, his eyes twinkling with excitement. "Alright, Geri. I can't wait any longer. Where's my granddaughter?"

"She'll be here in just a minute," I smiled as I slipped out of the room.

When I returned, James was right behind me, cradling our little bundle of joy in his strong arms. Grace was fast asleep, her tiny face peeking out from a soft pink blanket.

"Dad," I said, my voice catching, "meet your granddaughter, Grace."

James handed her to Dad with the gentlest of care, and for the first time in my life, I saw my father rendered speechless. Tears filled his eyes as he looked down at her.

"Hello, Grace," he whispered, his voice thick with emotion. "I'm your grandad."

Beside him, Beryl was already dabbing at her eyes with a tissue.

I glanced around the room and felt my heart swell. There was so much love here—so much hope. Grace would never want for anything, not with this incredible family surrounding her.

Simon and Kevin stood together, their arms brushing, their faces glowing with happiness. Their love for Grace was evident in every glance. We weren't a traditional family, but we didn't need to be. What we had worked, and it was beautiful.

I met James's gaze from across the room. He raised his glass and smiled, his eyes filled with adoration.

"To family," he said, his voice steady and warm.

"To family," we all echoed, our voices harmonising with love and joy.

I smiled, knowing in my heart that this was the way it was meant to be.

The End

I hope you enjoyed reading Embellished Deception. If so, would you please consider posting a short review? Genuine feedback is the greatest thank you an author can receive.

About the Author

Netta Newbound is the best-selling author of over fifty true-crimes/thriller novels/novellas to date including the Adam Stanley Thriller Series and the Cold Case Files. Her debut psychological thriller, An Impossible Dilemma, shot up the charts in 2016 in both the UK and US reaching #1 in several thriller and horror categories. This rapid success gained Netta a name for herself in the thriller genre. The Watcher also reached the top 20 in the US Amazon charts.

Originally from Manchester, England, Netta has travelled extensively and has lived and worked in a variety of exciting places. She now lives in New Zealand with her husband. They have three grown up children and four grandchildren.

Also by Netta

You can find all of Netta's books at your local Amazon store

An Impossible Dilemma

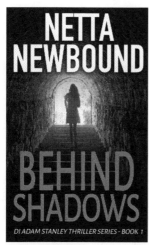

Behind Shadows

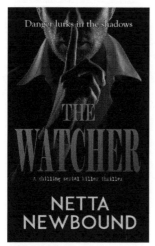

The Watcher

Made in United States
Troutdale, OR
04/03/2025

30311613R00178